PUBLISHER'S NOTE
This is a work of fiction. Names, characters, places, and incidents either are the product of the author's imagination or, are used fictitiously, and any resemblance in actual persons, living or dead, or locales in entirely coincidental.

Library of Congress Control Number: 2008923129
ISBN-13: 978-0-9815668-0-1

Printed in the United States of America
10 9 8 7 6 5 4 3 2 1

To order copies contact: (Enclose *Certified, *Cashier's Check, or Money order for $14.95 + $4.95 for shipping and handling. If two copies are more add an additional 2.00 for shipping/handling. *Bulk orders available at special rates.* Make *check or money order payable to: Karla D. Baker).

Mail to:
**The Write Message
PO Box 3071
Paterson, New Jersey 07509**

E-mail: karlabkr@yahoo.com
http://www.myspace.com/thewritemessage

Formatting: Karla D. Baker
Editor: Miriam Tager

DEDICATION

ANTHONY M. ROBINSON,
(1988—1995)
A precocious child, son, brother, and friend
who lived by example,
and died a mentor.

CRAIG T. ROBINSON JR.,
I look back and remember those rough times and I look
at you and see that you are becoming a man of
integrity, morals, and values. I am so proud of you and
your accomplishments of staying on track in a world
full of taint influences. I am so proud to be your mother
and to see the mold of *man* coming through.
Know that *you* are destined for greatness and don't let
anyone steal your *joy*.
Ma

CORELIA BAKER,
(1974—2005)
Lil' Sis, it seems like just yesterday when we were
having another sisterly moment over the phone. You
were talking about becoming a Registered Nurse, and I
was talking about writing a screenplay for
"Anonymous" and it becoming a movie like Terry
McMillan with Waiting to Exhale or How Stella Got
Her Groove Back. We knew, in our hearts, we knew
that we could do it. Oh, how our minds drifted into
fantasyland and we laughed ourselves sick. Why'd you
have to leave so soon? I'm still trying to get that one
break wishing you were here to cheer me on, "Go Sis!
Go Sis!"
Loving you always,
Sis

THE *L*AST

Feeble
My momma named me Feeble
'Cause I let my legs open wide
Invited him in for some pumpkin pie
And soda pop
We had no time to chitchat
No time for him to weasel out his last name
No damn time to stop the impulses
That raced
The thrusts, the moans
The hard-on of want raw, instead of well done
Momma said you could want all your heart desires
and come out
Empty handed.
What she knew?
She said, "I was a teen too. I had to wrap my scarf
around my head tight. And sure 'nough my momma
was right."
There was no light in my view so I did what I wanted
to do.
I nixed momma off with the wave of my hand
Where your man?

Feeble
Crumpled and discarded
As if a bad dream
Yet, I was a nightmare come true
As he tasted me, stroked me, and I deep-throated his
unspoken word
I was a nightmare as he was coming
No need to know the last
My mind wandered off
Thinking that the trees become brown paper bags
We must recycle Mother Earth,
Why was I not as significant as the trees?
I spread wider to oblige him, still deep in thought

Heard him whisper how good my juices were
Yes, we were two sexed driven beasts
Vocalizing nothing in the last
I still didn't know
But he whispered, "My last is A, B, C, D, E, F, G, H—"
This Negro was pulling my chain
Scrambling his words in my brain
His words weighed thin
Followed by his sly grin
As I drifted heard the trees bellowing in the wind
I sighed,
As his shade spotlighted me
I was alone
Still pondering the last.

Feeble
Stroking him like he was my last,
No need to know his last
For I was a nightmare come true
Over a million disintegrated
And a million more climbed into their resting place
To mourn for their feeble souls
And he came again, and again, and again,
Deaf ears closed like casket doors
As memories of our "family tree"
Mercy, she too didn't know his name
And another, and another, and another
There was where we bonded.
Stroking the same death
I was a nightmare come 'cause he already came
We were both on first name basis
AIDS
Not a bad dream
Not a nightmare
R-E-A-L-I-T-Y
Our blood ran thin
Memories faded
Pseudonym memoirs were written
Names became insignificant
And numbers became our last.

Anonymous

KARLA DENISE BAKER

ONE

STARTLED.

Body sodden in a cold night's sweat. I struggle to sit up; my body shudders as I rest my chin upon my cinnamon-colored knees, dazed. Forcefully I swallow, tasting the acidic residue that thinly coats the rear of my tongue. My face furrows. *He* deliberately haunts me, rewinding me back to that ill-fated day. Palpitations stir my weariness. My fragile heart beats irregularly as I lay my clammy left hand against my chest hoping to calm the clattering anxiety. I'm thinking. Thinking of how *he* relentlessly makes a fool of me.

My deep-set brown eyes coat with fury. Perspiration leaks from under my hairy armpits as I sit jittery for several minutes. Finally, I settle. My knock-knees crawl to the foot of the bed, as I lean over to open the wicker chest to pull out Ma'am's old chiffon fuchsia throw. My overlapping shoulders resemble Alec Wek's—the model. My feet pedal backwards to prop my back against the wicker weave headboard.

I kneel down, fighting away the furry dust balls from underneath, and pull out a pair of navy blue kickboxing shoes to exert some energy. I am fighting *him* recklessly. It shields me from the entrenched demon that competes in my head. I don't feel comfortable joining a class on the outside, so I have been training at home to turn my body into a defense machine. I feel powerful. My body's strong, fit, and disciplined. I workout for a half hour until the intensity causes my muscles to swell. The enormous pain circulates throughout my body, but I keep pushing and pushing myself. Preparing myself for the inevitable. Yes. I think *he's* still out there.

I stop my workout 'cause my stomach churns,

unsettled as bubbles formulate like Alka-Seltzer. Quickly I fast pace it to the bathroom. Diarrhea and regurgitation collide, forcing my body to react. *Why must I suffer?* Dehydration becomes an enemy so I stretch out my rigid arm to pull a small cup from the cup holder and ingest plenty of tap water from the bathroom sink. I slump over, arms tightly hugging the love handles on each side of my stomach in unbearable pain, and sit on the toilet. I yearn to shed an ugly cry, but only moisture forms in the corners of my eyes as I whisper, "I can't take it anymore." Coolness of the checker-board tile floor soothes my fiery feet. I wipe my delicate skin, flush the toilet, wash my hands, and find my way back to my bedroom to lie down. The contortion upon my face stresses misery. A teardrop finds its way down my skin, rolling slowly making a path for the next. Nostrils clog as I struggle to breathe freely. Every step I take I inhale bitterness. *God.* Time elapses quickly as I cover my body in the intertwining yarns of Ma'am's throw.

Still. I lay still in this one-bedroom apartment as my distressed mind drifts back to when my life drastically changed. It's mind-boggling. Uh-Huh. I wish that I can have some sort of clarity, a reason as to why. Yes. What did I do or say? Or, didn't do or say? My life's so full of mayhem.

I stand before my mirror harassing myself trying to make some sense of it, but nothing makes sense. I keep hearing *his* breathing. *His* breathing. I shut my eyes and in slow scenes I picture everything. I feel *his* hands on me. I smell *his* stench. I taste *his* saliva on my skin. I feel *his* nails cutting into me. *His* dick ripping and shredding my insides. I am dirty, nasty, and disgusting. I'm losing my way. No, I've lost my way. The pressure is hard and thick. Something triggers inside me. Questions become a nuisance as the evil twin in me, Avona, interrogates.

"You. It was YOU who provoked him!"

"How?"

"You have the nerve to ask! Chile, please, by

dressing too provocatively, silly."

"I don't dress provocatively."

"Yeah. Right! Honey, you sashayed with the sway of your voluptuous hips trying to lure men in. Let's keep it realllllll."

"NO! I didn't."

"Then you act as if you're not aware? Okay. Chile, I don't have time for denial. You used to strut your stuff, coming across all puffed-up and shit, with your expensive Christian Dior streaming in the air."

"SO!"

"So, you're a whore! Walking around with your big ass and your titties hanging half way out. Let's keep it real, okay. Honey, you walk around thinking that you are above all others, nose up in the air. Ms. High and Mighty. Walking around like your shit don't stink. It's nauseating. I'm surprised you are still alive to look yourself in the fuckin' face."

"What!"

"You heard what I said!"

"You act as though I said c'mon and get it. C'mon, take my stuff, Mister. No. No! I'm not going to allow you to put this mess on me. I didn't ask for this. No. He, He, He, came and TOOK IT!"

"Whine, whine, like a fuckin' baby as always. Ain't nobody tryna hear that whimper of yours. When you gonna understand that no one cares about you."

I come to. The voice is badgering me. I lower my head. Mentally, I have somehow been brainwashed into thinking that I did this to me, but I didn't, and yet every single day, I'm being punished for it.

I had refused a rape kit. I felt, taste, smelt, and lived it. His filth was all over my person. *What's a rape kit gonna prove?* Did I really think that *he* would have been caught? And then I thought about having to stand behind a glass partition to pick *him* out of a line up. It would've been a waste of my time because I never saw *his* face. The thought sickened me. My word should've been enough! The beating should've been enough! I wanted to forget. I wanted the pain to go away. I wanted to bury *him*. Seeing *him* would have stirred up more havoc in my life. I wanted it to go away. Just go away.

It's one-year earlier and I am at the doctor's office for a routine checkup when I notice two middle-aged women talking loud enough for me to overhear their whole conversation. One is lighter-skinned with beady eyes, an oblong nose, and puny lips with a small black mole right above her upper lip, penciled eyebrows, and she wears a God awful auburn wig. The other woman is darker with a medium build, plump cheeks, deep dented dimples, big eyes, a widespread nose, full lips, arched brows, and long strands of reddish-brown hair in tight curls. Anyway, they sit talking and the lighter-skinned woman asks with a stuttered lisp the darker-skinned woman how her son is doing in rehab. Apparently, he has a drug-addiction and is pretty hooked on heroin.

The darker-skinned woman turns slightly to address the question and says "Oh, he's doin' fine. Thanks for asking."

The lighter-skinned woman says, "HHe sstill in that DDetox program?"

"Yes."

"HHow's he ddoin'? I hear tthey have all types of mmens in those pprograms. You kknow ggay, ssstraight, and in bbetween. You kknow ain't no wwomens in there with tthem. They have those ttendencies. You kknow. Then tthey come hhome with all these ddiseases and ssuch. MMessing uup with that ccracky ssmack, hheroin, all that ssshit, and then bring it hhome. CCome out here ssshaking mmo' tthan us wwomens. Huh."

The darker-skinned woman stares straight ahead, remains silent, and with a slight annoyance in her tone says, "Well, without *that* program and the counselor who came to that program people wouldn't know a thing about all these diseases out here."

There is silence between them.

The darker-skinned woman turns herself back around facing her friend and says, "Let me tell you somethin', there was a counselor who went to that program once a week to talk to those mens and if he hadn't, my son would have never thought about the diseases out here. You see, without him caring, doin' his job, taking time out of his day, traveling to and from to speak to those gentlemen's who were trying to rebuild themselves a lot of them would be *dead!* That Counselor instilled somethin' in my son to take it upon himself to raise his hand when the questions arise about being tested for HIV/AIDS. No one on the outside was preaching to him. Hell, not even Pastor G. was preaching about it in Sunday service. It had to take my son messing up his damn life, destroying his body and mind to get him to realize that his lifestyle could very well kill him deader than a door knob. And he got tested!" She raises her hand mid-level in the air as if to say, "Don' mess with me when it comes to my chile."

The lighter-skinned woman bows her head in shame at running off at the mouth. Then she lifts it, glues her lips and releases them. "II'm sssorry. II...II...ddidn't...II...II wwasn't tthinkin'. May II ask wwhat was hhis test rresults?"

This catches my attention. I turn to look their way. The darker-skinned woman wrinkles her upper lip pressing it against the bottom one.

"Positive. His results came back positive." She swallows hard.

I stare into space after hearing the woman speak. I feel sorrow and I wonder why because I don't know her, the other woman, or her son. While I am at the doctor's office I decide to have them test me for HIV/AIDS. I know there is nothing wrong with me. Yes, I have had men in my life, but the men I deal with are clean, polished, and successful. I don't mingle or socialize with deadbeats, drug-addicts, or hoodlums. I have had relationships, not one night stands. About a week and a half later I get my results back from Dr. Fulmore.

It's a Tuesday, in July. The sun shines brightly. The day is slightly humid. I receive a call from Dr. Fulmore's office at my place of employment, Bruman & Prescott Law firm in lower Manhattan. His nurse, Violet, states that the good ole' doctor needs to speak with me face-to-face. Violet's voice doesn't sound out of the ordinary, so I assume things are good.

Dr. Fulmore sits in his chocolate leather chair. His fingers are interlocked in a balled fist, and are folded on his mahogany desk. He leans forward, eyes overlooking his lenses with a blank look on his face. He seems lost...distant. I greet him with a nod and sit down sinking into the soft rust leather chair. He gives me half a smile, which kinda makes his lips look like he once had a stroke. His eyes wander around the room. He extends his right hand up to his mouth and clears his throat a couple of times. I grow impatient, tapping my fingers on the arms of the chair, waiting. My eyes travel up to the off-white ceiling, and then lower to his camel colored walls with pictures of the anatomy. Slowly I move them across to his library of a thousand books, and then down to the mixed woven tweed wall-to-wall carpet of brown, beige, and rust, and then I end up at his mahogany desk.

"Avery," he pauses to scratch his throat. "Avery, I received...." He takes his gold-tone wire framed glasses off his face, pinches the inner corners of his eyes, and then places his glasses back on. He scratches his throat in between like he needs a lozenge. "...your blood work results came back." Dr. Fulmore stops speaking. There's deadness in his office, but I hear movement outside the door. He looks at me in a peculiar way that I will never forget. It's like he wants to spare my feelings and my life. I feel it. I see it in his crystal blue eyes. But I guess he realizes he can't, so he has to force the words out. His words spew out like blood from a slit wound.

"Avery, I regretfully have to advise you that you are HIV-positive." He slowly lowers his head as if I am a child who has been scolded by her mom.

I am stiff, silent, in disbelief. Then it transforms into anger. I want to walk outside of my body, leap over the desk, and strangle him until his eyes bulge out of their sockets. I am enraged and scared all at the same time. My eyes stretch wide in astonishment.

"What! Doc, there must be a mistake." In a crackling voice I say, "Dr. Fulmore, are you sure?" *God I plead for him to have made a mistake.*

"Yes." He dabs his taupe tanned forehead with a white handkerchief.

"How are you feeling, Avery?" he asks.

"I don't know how to feel, Doc. How am I supposed to feel?" I ask with a befuddled look on my face.

I shut my eyes tight. And in that moment of darkness I experience it again. I swallow the hard lump embedded in my throat. My skin is dank and cold. My eyes change to bloodshot red. They widen. *"HE DID THIS TO ME!"* My mind is full with rage. Figments of my imagination are kickboxing against *him*. I become numb, bewildered, and belligerent. I am like a volcano ready to erupt. Inside me combustive red-hot lava watercourses down the sides of my guts. I see bold letters highlighting "silence=death" in neon. I drop my face into the palms of my hands, and silently scream from within. Then stand, pace, and shout with my fists balled and my arms fighting the air, "the son-of-a bitch!" I massage my temples in a circular motion as tears swallow up my eyes. I sit back down astounded, hugging my skin, digging my fingernails into my upper arms cutting off my circulation. Dr. Fulmore is watching me with a teary eye. It's a preview of my HIV life unfolding.

I feel tainted blood running through my veins. Blunt forces stun me as I listen to Dr. Fulmore speak of a disease that kills the T-cells. Immune systems break down, while germs cling to invade. He explains "viral load" (how much HIV is in my bloodstream). The warmth of my blood runs cold and my faith evaporates. I'm HIV-positive. I am left speechless. I stare into space, until I realize that I am still sitting in Dr. Fulmore's office. I stand up, my body is sedated with pain, my feet are tingly and my toes crack with each step. I take baby steps to the door. I leave his office a changed woman. In my car I sob uncontrollably. I pound my hands against the steering wheel, wildly honking the horn. My hands tremble as I put the key into the ignition to travel a long, agonizing journey home.

♥ ♥ ♥

LYING ON MY bed I recall this Rape/HIV Counselor, Mrs. Margaret McCarter at Hopkins Hospital and Medical Center trying to convince me to get tested. I ignored her. The leggy Caucasian woman with green eyes, brunette hair, medium frame and bleached teeth stood before me. I remember it plain as day. She told me that there were many women who are sexually assaulted and don't report it. She lectured me on sexually transmitted diseases and the importance of using a rape test kit.

Then Mrs. McCarter asked me if I had ever had a sexually transmitted disease and at the time I had felt violated about her invading my privacy. I felt it was none of her damn business. What did all of that have to do with me being raped? Obviously her snooping didn't seem to faze her because she just kept on yapping in her screechy, annoying voice.

I didn't know what Mrs. McCarter was trying to imply, but I took offense. I felt like she was throwing darts at me. My five-foot-eleven-inch body was brutally, savagely beaten. My life was almost taken! Was she blind? Why was she lecturing me about sexually transmitted diseases? Why was she still up in my face? WHY?! Why wasn't she looking at me, instead of talking about shit that I didn't even care to hear about! I had such a dead stare, which finally grasped her attention. She shut the hell up and then tried a different approach to get through to me. She grabbed some pamphlets and walked back and handed them to me. She disregarded the expression on my face as she explained the many group meetings she had for people like me. She gave me her business card if I decided that I was ready to join her group, and she even gave me a 1-800 number for 24-hour assistance in case I needed to talk to someone. I blocked everything she said out of my mind. After I was discharged, I left the hospital and threw all her pertinent information into the garbage. I just wanted to go home. I had gone home to exfoliate my sullied body until my skin peeled off.

♥ ♥ ♥

DURING MY SECOND visit to Dr. Fulmore he kneels down in front of me as I sit in the rust chair, and touches my shoulder in an attempt to soothe and console me.

"Avery, you can still live a healthy life. In today's world HIV does not automatically mean death. For instance, Magic Johnson has been HIV-positive for years and has not contracted the AIDS virus. You have to discipline your mind, body, and soul to want to live. Your perception can help to manage and control the effects of the disease on your life." Dr. Fulmore rises to his feet and walks towards the window and gazes out.

He sits back down in his chocolate leather chair and makes eye contact with me. My eyes speak for me as I sit in deep thought. Magic Johnson's rich. Common sense should tell Dr. Fulmore that with money you can buy all the medications in the world to not become infected with full-blown AIDS. I'm not rich! I don't have his status. I can't just go to the pharmacy and rack up on pills to prevent me from having full-blown AIDS. I can only live right, take the medications advised, keep stress out of my life, watch my dietary intake, and believe in the Almighty Man upstairs. My life's a cycle of frustration, and I have to adjust. What if I didn't have medical coverage, then what? Where would that leave me? Seeking assistance from the state? I shrug my shoulders and gently caress my hands across my weary face.

I feel like I am living in the damn jungle where it's survival of the fittest. I am constantly inhaling and witnessing bodies and minds decomposing. I close my eyes hoping the imagery of young and old bodies dying will disappear forever. I am tired. I roll my eyes in slow motion under my eyelids they sit still.

I try to envision in my mind how folk's perception of me will change. I have become a recluse, dropping off the face of the earth. I don't know why it concerns me so, but I'm skeptical of how others will react. Often I picture people cringing as they extend terms of endearment as they slide on yellow rubber gloves up to their armpits before they reach out to hug me. They wear masks as to not inhale the virus and cross their two fingers like they're afraid of getting the cooties. They hope nothing becomes airborne. Phobias create the illusion of knowledge, leaving me in a desolate place of seclusion. I have come to the realization that I'm befriended solely by my shadow.

I sigh, close my eyes, and stare at the four walls trying to block out the shadow of myself still not whole.

T wo

IN THE WEE hours of the morning, a frantic sound disrupts my sleep. I hit the snooze button. Turning on my side I stare at a display that reads 4:00 a.m. My eyes droop desperately wanting to return to sleep, but I can't. I flip through TV channels with my remote hoping that if I watch a late night movie it will make my eyes heavy and suspend my consciousness.

Morning slowly creeps up on me as the sun rises with its orange-yellow glow. I struggle to get my groggy self up, lean my back against the headboard, and slowly maneuver the kinks out of my neck. I get out of bed and walk my ashy bare feet straight to the bathroom to wash my face and brush my teeth. After which, to get my blood circulating I do a twenty minute workout on my treadmill. The perspiration runs down my face. My white men's nightshirt is spotted with sweat. Adrenaline runs. My legs tingle, and my heart pumps. I huff a heavy sigh and feel physically drained.

I run a bath and soak for a half hour. I think of indulging on tiny pieces of mouth melting Godiva chocolate that I have hidden in the refrigerator, but it's too early. My fingers crinkle like raisins. As I stand streams of bath oil and scented water flow down my sheer legs. I step out of the bathtub, towel wrap my body, and sit on the black Mayfair toilet seat to caress my skin with a light fragrant oil of vanilla musk.

A loud rumbling comes from the inner lining of my stomach. After I get dress I walk into the kitchen, and reach for my meds from the top of the refrigerator. I pray every single day that my regimen will help keep things stagnant, protecting me from full-blown AIDS. I remain faithful to my routine.

The Granny apple green walls with embroider mint leaf floor covering uplifts me. I make some egg whites, turkey sausage, wheat toast, and pour a tall glass of apple juice. As I'm washing the dishes I notice the caller ID on my kitchen phone flashing. Dr. Fulmore's office must've called to remind me of my two o'clock appointment on Thursday.

What can I say about Dr. F.? He has a salt cut which gives him a distinguished look. He keeps himself well-groomed with his Caucasian skin that has a hint of color from his recent Caribbean cruise. Dr. Fulmore is my blessin' from God. I mean that. The man's thorough, yet concise. He truly cares about me and that kind of compassion isn't easy to find. He takes the time to understand how this disease leaves open wounds towards life.

I can't help but to think about how things used to be. Fulfillment consumed my life before. I often wish I could turn back the hands of time, to finish pursuing my life where I left off.

Flashbacks seem to distract me. I clean up the kitchen and go into my bedroom and pick up my journal, Sis, and start to document my past.

July 12th, 2008

Dear Sis,

Back in the day, Sis, I considered myself to be above average. I captivated men because I was fierce! I was polished and eloquent and carried myself like a sophisticated lady. When it came to me, men were like sweet mango on a hot summery day. Talk about delicious. I would hear them say as I walked by, "There goes Avery with her fine self." The sweetness that I displayed was sincere and many men were enticed, but none really were looking for a meaningful relationship. At least that was what my instincts told me. I don't think they took me seriously. And back then, I didn't want to be serious. I wanted to play with no strings attached. You know...no commitment. A lot of them were sexy as h. e. double l. Men would pass me in the streets of downtown Paterson. I saw them everywhere; in Bank of America on Main Street,

Simply "The" Best Barber Shop on E. 18th Street, Xclusive Beauty II and Red Cyber City on Broadway. While I stood in Record City buying a couple of gospel CDs or in front of Nu-Xpressions Gallery of Arts on lower Main Street, admiring the African artwork, men would turn their heads, wink their eyes, and wet their lips at me. Yeah, they lusted for a taste of me. And in New York it was like a field day of men, especially at Diamond Cuts Barber Shop on 8th Avenue (bet. 39th & 40th St.), and LEVELS on 125th Street (bet. Amsterdam and Morningside Ave), and Turning Heads on Lenox. Most were successful and others tried to make it seem like they were, trying that gift-of-gab but I had a sense of smell for success. But I wasn't a gold-digger. I supported myself. My main motive for dating only successful men was power. I was addicted to the power that they had. Hoping it would rub off on me. And it eventually did. Men were enthralled by me willing to drop their Hanes boxers and hand over their wallets. I never asked for anything because I was forced to be independent. From the top of my head down to the bottom of my French pedicure toes, I was a diamond. My persona exemplified strength and confidence, not arrogance. Most women were intimidated by this and drew their own conclusions. A well-educated woman who knew what she wanted and was not afraid to get it threatened their sense of security. Most women despised me because they perceived me to be anti-social. I didn't connect very well with the heffas, so I kept to myself. They would mumble under their breath, while calling out, "Hey gurl!" Women sure knew how to keep a lot of drama flowing and I was not used to biting my city tongue.

Folks had the tendency to call me conceited without getting to know me. I was very secure about myself. While all the insecure women huddled in a circle to keep each other warm, confidence exuded from my pores. Women hated me because their husbands or significant others used to look at me like eye-candy when I was in their presence. Obviously these men were being deprived at home and that only intensified the escalated looks as they grew hungrier. Nibbling on Vienna sausages and saltine crackers when they could have a full coarse meal of Jack Daniel's steak, mash potatoes, buttery corn on the cob, and some fluffy buttered rolls, complimented by a chilled bottle of Chardonnay was not competition. Dessert, of course, was me. I used to enter the bedroom in my six-inch red stilettos; all sleeked down in melted dark chocolate with nothing on but a G-string, a bowl of whipped cream and some dark juicy strawberries in my hands. After I was through, my man would be full to the brim with whipped cream outlining his mouth. That was Avery's style. Hello!

Therron Bolton, a.k.a Hypnotic (1990). Sis, close your eyes and imagine a tall, six-foot-one inch, white chocolate complexion and big olive-green eyes. Yes, Hypnotic had some black roots in him. He had a medium build with a flat washboard stomach. The man was nice! He knew how to treat a girly girl. He was spontaneous and over indulged me with gifts and sweets. He spent quality time with me and made me feel like Queen Sheba. I treated Hypnotic like he was the Long Ranger. Yes Sis, that's what I said, Long Ranger because his penis was long as hell! I was attentive and responsive to satisfying his every need. And he reciprocated the same in return. Our lovemaking consisted of rose petals covering the bed, champagne bubble Jacuzzi, warm caramel and much, much foreplay. He caressed me from my feet to the tip of my head. Ooh! I still get goose bumps every time I think about him. Sis, he was never forceful and every stroke was delivered with a gentleness that would make me want to climax multiple times. Hallelujah! Yes. Like the river runneth over. He was concerned about pleasing me and he did not care how long it took. We always used protection. Hypnotic never saw it any other way. His preference was LifeStyles Sheer Pleasure. And he was indeed a pleasure. He was the sweetest man I ever knew. Unfortunately, as soon as our relationship started to take off he received a job promotion at WNC2 as a Producer and had to relocate to California. Damn.

Sis, sundae comes to mind when I think about Bit-of-Honey. Lord, have mercy! I envisioned warm melted butterscotch with cool whip and a maraschino cherry on top. Honey! That was Heath J. Efferson (1991). Woo! He would stand before me gleaming, just glossed down with his tan-colored muscular frame all covered in lusciousness. He made my pulse rise and my toes curl. Shoot, they're curling now!

Bit-of-Honey was just that, with sweetness. His five-foot-eleven inch of man was adventurous, humorous, and a woman needs a man who can make her laugh. I loved men who were confident, but not arrogant. I didn't mind a man being well-groomed, actually that turned me on. Smelling like he's ready to be licked down. Bit-of-Honey definitely had what it took. He was an Entrepreneur, too, owning a chain of upscale Beauty salons. Any man focused on a dream and doing what it took to achieve that dream was very attractive to me. I loved a man with some fire in his belly. But everything that looked good wasn't always good for you. Sis, Bit-of-Honey and I were not a love connection so we went our separate ways. Life's too short to be wasting time with a man who couldn't see beyond himself.

I need to take a break so I put my journal down and go into the kitchen to make a quick organic almond butter and jelly sandwich. I start to smile about back in the day because those times were fun. I seemed more in control of my life, back then. I open the refrigerator reach for the Silk soymilk, sit down at the kitchen table and poured a glass. I stare into space, while nibbling on my sandwich. After I eat, I clean up my mess and I go back to my bedroom.

I pick up my journal and re-enter my journey back in the day.

Sis, I must tell you about a gentleman named Brian Adler, a.k.a LoJac (1991-1992). I had someone who made me feel so special, like a precision gem. LoJac pampered me, more so than Hypnotic. He would have given me the world if he had it and placed it at my feet. I've never encountered a man who was so generous in my entire life. I kept asking myself, why was LoJac willing to damn near give me the shirt off his back? Or give me his last dollar out of his pocket? I never really understood LoJac's ways and deep inside, I always thought he was putting up a good front. You know, putting on airs. Let me tell you something, I was wrong. Dead wrong. I thought being around him for a great length of time would eventually bring out his true colors. The man was legit. He was genuinely generous, but a little too clingy for me. He wanted to be with me all the time, like when I went shopping, to the beauty salon, the Laundromat, the car wash, the dentist, or even to the damn library. That was a little too much for me. He seemed so unsure of himself. I had to question why he was so insecure. The man was drop-dead gorgeous. I mean, Brad Pitt, gorgeous. He could have had anyone he wanted. LoJac knew how to treat a lady, like a lady. He had that spiritual touch about him. He made me feel wanted. He seemed afraid to let me out of his sight, for whatever reason. We dated for a year and I thought that I could handle things, but his clinginess overwhelmed me.

LoJac was six-foot-three inches with a milky-white complexion, polished, clean cut. He wore business suits because he worked as a Finance Analyst. I never saw him looking bad, not even early in the morning. He was high maintenance, though.

During our year of dating we had sex three times a week. That was enough for him. LoJac was definitely different from any other man that I'd ever dated. He was not hard up for sex. He was more focused on the depth of one's soul. His spirituality was his essence of love.

I must admit every time we made love, we did not always use protection. But then we talked about our irresponsibility. We were too comfortable with each other. I truly believed that LoJac wanted a family with me. The man was very expressive about how deep his feelings were for me. But he never uttered the word, "love". Come to think of it, neither did I. That word seemed so powerful and controlling to me. I was afraid to open myself up, to let my guard down, and allow any man to touch the core. Love seemed deep, emotionally draining and I didn't want to be attached to a feeling that seemed so unfamiliar to me. Nevertheless, I remained in the relationship with him.

I experienced a big scare that changed everything. We were very connected and LoJac made me feel safe. Gradually I felt my feelings growing for him and then I got scared and faked like my period was late. I guess I felt if he thought that I was possibly pregnant that he would break-up with me. I got panicky; became a sharpshooter with my mouth, and seemed very, very nervous. I gave a hell of a performance. I'll admit STDs; HIV/AIDS were never on my billboard. I remember telling LoJac that I was late and he seemed cool and collected. He wasn't worried at all. I guess he really wanted a family with me after all, but I didn't share his vision. So we took different paths to find happiness. I actually cried when we split up because I felt somewhat lost—within myself. But I was content with being alone.

I lay my journal down on the nightstand and stretch my body out to take a catnap. My eyes stare wide at the ceiling and I can't help thinking about my best friend Johnnie Rivera, a.k.a Johnnie-come-Lately. I crack a smile, raise my slightly tired body from my goose down pillows and pick up my journal to find a passage on Johnnie.

Hey Sis,

My best friend Johnnie popped into my head. Every time I think about him I chuckle. He's Latino.

Johnnie was very interesting. We were working at Bruman & Prescott Law firm in lower Manhattan when we met. I was a Paralegal and he worked on the same floor as an Executive Accountant. Back in 1999, we had a company Christmas dinner party coming up and the day before he asked me if I would accompany him. He seemed well mannered, such a gentleman, I could not refuse. We went and started to have a lovely time, until this fine gentleman distracted me. I was looking and so was Johnnie. I was a tad bit disturbed by that, mainly because Johnnie didn't even blink. His eyes were glued to the man. I thought he might whisper to me what color underwear the man had on. I tried to let it slide, but he kept looking out of the corner of his eye. I was heated inside. That's when I questioned if Johnnie was bisexual. Time definitely would tell. By the end of that night, we both realized that we were not going to make a love connection and decided to be friends. We've been ever since.

I remember one day the second week in March of 2000, we were at this Chinese restaurant in West Paterson, New Jersey, and Johnnie confessed that he was gay. I knew way before that conversation. There was something about him where I literally felt we were like girlfriends. He seemed a bit surprised because I had never said anything to him about it. To me, it didn't matter. I thought then he was living in denial, afraid to come out of the closet. I understood why because some folks would look down upon someone living that lifestyle instead of getting to know the person. It didn't bother me. Johnnie was the best "girlfriend" I ever had. We've been through a lot together. Things that make you really appreciate that person. We were like adhesive, strongly connected. He consoled me many nights when I was distressed. He cared for me numerous times when I was sick. Now, that most definitely was a true "girl" friend.

Johnnie left the company and went back to school to get his license in Cosmetology. I always told him to follow his dream. With both of our busy schedules and his weekends occupied, we didn't have much time to keep in touch. He later started working for this upscale salon in Upper Manhattan called *Beautiful, a very polished salon where people with boo coo money would go. Yes. Celebrities. Johnnie was doing pretty well for himself.*

I am going to give him a call. *I miss him.* I pick up the phone, and call his home number, and a woman answers, which indicates that I have the wrong number. *Johnnie must have moved or changed his number.* I search the drawer of my desk for my red book to see if I still have his cell phone number. Then I pick up the phone and call his cellular. My hands are shaking a little. I think I am nervous to hear his voice. Johnnie's voicemail picks up and I leave a brief message with my phone number. *He is probably going to scream once he hears my voice. I can't wait 'til he calls me!* I sit down and return to my journal.

Sis, Johnnie has that even honey-tone, smooth and flawless baby bottom skin. He has thick eyebrows, a well-groomed goatee with connected side burns. Nice looking. His voice would go from high to low depending on the conversation. He's hilariously funny. His fashions extraordinaire expressed, "Hate it", "Love it", and "Boo, don't do it ever, ever again." Ooh, I used to almost choke on spit from laughing so hard. He kept my stomach hurting. Boy, I used to love that. Those days were fun.

Ring...ring.

I reach over and answer the phone, and as I lift the receiver I glance at the caller ID. *Oh...my...God, it's Johnnie!*

Excitement runs through my body. Johnnie and I talk briefly. "Short and sweet" that's his motto. The man has not changed a bit. We hang up and I grin from ear to ear.

Johnnie gives me his new address in Harlem, and wants me to stop by tomorrow. Tomorrow's Wednesday. I'm biting my upper lip because that's somewhat of a tiny issue for me. My hands shake, as I pace the floor. I'm flustered. I don't look like I used to look. I've lost some weight, not a lot, but enough for him to notice. Bottom line, I don't feel attractive.

Ma'am used to always say, "When you look good; you tend to feel even better." Strangely enough, I've changed because back then I was overly confident about myself, but after this ordeal that confidence has slowly lessened. My being seems to have vanished into a shell of hibernation.

T HREE

THE VELVETY BLACK sky unveils a cobalt blue spread of brightness as my eyes open around 11:00 in the morning. Sunlight filters through my bamboo Venetian blinds as my entire body pimples with anticipation to see my best friend. I get up, make my bed, pull out some undergarments from the dresser, grab an outfit and lay it on the bed. I go into the living room and then backtrack to the bedroom indecisive about what to wear. I decide on something a bit more comfortable: khaki Capri's, beige tank top, two-tone mule shoes, and my straw hat. I open the window and stick my head out thinking that I might catch a cool summery breeze only to be greeted by a gush of humidity. I spread my arms and face with some SPF5, put on my shades, and head to Harlem.

Sitting in my black Ford Five Hundred for a brief moment, I glance around Laurel Street in Paterson, New Jersey, and then put the key in the ignition and drive down West Broadway, towards Route 80 East. Traffic is minimal until I reach the George Washington Bridge. The congestion of people cutting each other off trying to get through the tolls irritates me. It takes a while before I drive through with my E-ZPass. Slowly maneuvering my way into the right lane of lower Henry Hudson I exit at 125th Street. I take in the scenery of the crowded streets. I pass the Apollo to see who will be appearing. I see many street vendors selling their goods: jewelry, CDs, DVDs, books, hats, white oversized Ts, Shea Butter, fragrance of Pussy-willow body oil cascading in the breeze, Black soap, and an assortment of belts in every color. My spirits rise, feeling refreshed to see others walking on the town. Johnnie lives in a Brownstone at 121st and Lenox. His building stares me in the face as I pass it to find a parking space. The vibe of the streets makes me feel alive. I inhale honey roasted peanuts, cashews, and chicken and beef shish kebab. They smolder in the air. The voices of different ethnicities sound like Reggae music to my ears. I'm thrilled, but nervous. My palms are a little damp, eagerly wanting to see Johnnie. When I reach his building, I stand still for a moment looking myself over and gently ring his doorbell.

I hear footsteps approaching the door and then the door opens. Johnnie stands before me in his tall frame with a huge smile on his face. I'm so happy to see him that I immediately give him a brotherly, hug patting his black T.

"Hey Girl, Come on in here and have a sit down. What's up? How you been, girl?" Johnnie sits down on the olive green loveseat with his right leg overlapping his left, and looks me dead in the face.

"Johnnie, I've been fine." I sit on his butter-cream leather sofa. My legs are pinned together.

"How's life been treating you, Johnnie?"

He laughs and then says, "Love, you know me, I've been livin'." Leaning back he places his feet on the cherry wood end table, and stares at me with his mouth hanging open. "Oh... no...you...didn't. No, you didn't cut your hair. Girl, I can't believe you went natural and short. Not the woman who had to have the straight look like Cher. Girl, stop playin'. Damn, it's been a while since I've seen you."

Johnnie walks over to me and examines my hair with his touchy-feely self. He massages my scalp and pokes fun. I laugh.

"Yes, it has been a while since we've seen each other, Johnnie." *There's something different about him.* My eyes are glued to him, as he walks towards the living room window and stares out. His thin framed back faces me.

"Love, you still working for Bruman & Prescott Law firm?"

I bite my bottom lip and then reply, "No..., I'm currently working for a small law firm in Paterson. It's close to home. I work as a consultant." I lower my head briefly because I feel like a low-down liar. I want to change the subject so I say, "Johnnie, how long have you been living in Harlem?" I walk near the living room window and stand side-by-side Johnnie as we both stare out at the traffic.

"Love, I moved here sometime in November of last year." His eyes pierce mine and then he walks back towards the loveseat and sits on its arm. His eyes are heating my back as I remain by the window and stare out.

"Why did you move from Paterson, Johnnie?" I ask as I sit backs down on the sofa to get comfortable. An eerie feeling comes over me and I can't help myself, but discreetly stare at Johnnie. I massage my fingers because they tingle.

"I just needed a change of scenery." And then he asks me if I would like anything to drink. He gets up and walks down a narrow corridor towards the kitchen to get us some beverages.

A nauseating feeling comes over me. I rub my stomach and try not to focus on the pain by admiring Johnnie's apartment. It's beyond words. He's doing very well for himself and his apartment displays his success. Everything complements each other. The art pieces tell meaningful stories. Johnnie's admiration for figurines: Annie Lee's "Loving Arms," Daddy's "First Love," Sarah's Attic, Inc. The Classics "Tillie Clown," are all gorgeously arranged in a glass and cherry wood armoire. African masks hang on his earth tone walls and bring warmth to his apartment. For some reason I'm extremely nervous and my hands are sweaty, so I rub them against my Capri's leaving streaks of wetness. As Johnnie walks back into the living room I eyeball him holding two glasses in his hands. He places them on the authentic African elephant coasters and sits down on the loveseat. I reach for a glass and sip the lemonade-ice tea.

Johnnie doesn't look like himself at all. He's lanky in his vintage jeans and his skin is blotchy and somewhat drawn, detailing the structure of his cheekbones. His eyes are extremely large and he's wearing his hair long and straight. It's a dead giveaway. It's becoming, but not his style. His cough is a rattling phlegm sound. He picks up a plastic cup that is next to the bronze lamp and coughs, bringing up some nasty stuff, which he then spits into the cup. I turn my head feeling nauseated because it sounds gross.

"Johnnie, are you okay?" My forehead crumples and the wrinkles soften.

"Girl, I am fine." His eyes wander around the room and he scratches his throat again. I am not a bit convinced. Johnnie doesn't look fine. He puts his feet back up on the end table and grabs his remote to turn on the CD player.

We talk and listen to music for hours. Time speeds by and it's now 8:00. I tell him that I should be getting ready to go so I stand up, and stretch my arms out to embrace him with a hug. Johnnie literally falls into my arms. He clings to me and I can plainly feel his bones. They are sharp to the touch and my eyes become watery. His body smells of a combination of Polo Black cologne and sickness. With everything in me I try my best to keep my composure, but when I look in his pinkish eyes he breaks down in tears. I notice that he has several large lesions on the side of his neck where his hair is covered, and close-up I see powder foundation lightly covering his face. I have never witnessed Johnnie crying before. This is a profound moment. I continue to hold him until he gives me a signal to let go.

Tears flow down my face as I ask Johnnie if he wants to talk. The ticking of the wall mounted clock breaks the silence. And a look of distress appears on his face. He swallows a couple of times and then looks me in my eyes.

"Love, I have *AIDS*."

I catch myself from fainting by shutting my eyes tightly. My heart damn near stops. Uncertain of what I have heard I open my eyes and the look on Johnnie's face confirms it. I exhale an invisible ring as if I just smoked a cigarette while mumbling under my breath, *Lord Jesus. Girl, get it together.* Suddenly, that's exactly what I did. Whatever inner strength I have takes charge of the situation. I sit down and hold Johnnie. I want to protect him from the world. We are both tearful.

Softly I say, "Johnnie, I'm here for you." I gently massage his back with compassion.

It annoys me that he didn't tell me at first but I keep my calm. "Johnnie, why didn't you call me?"

"Love, I didn't call because everyone who knows that I have AIDS has shunned me. I thought you might have done the same thing. I don't think I would have been able to cope if you had turned your back on me, so I didn't subject myself to the humiliation of finding out." Johnnie's eyes are red and flooded. He stares at the floor as his tears ease down dripping onto the oriental throw rug.

Damn. Is this how it is going to be for me?

I debate over telling Johnnie about my situation knowing that it's not the appropriate time. But I question, when it will be.

"Johnnie, does your family know?" I ask while wrapping my arm around him touching his pointy elbow.

"Yes, they know."

"Are they supportive?"

I move closer to him on the loveseat and inhale his body scent.

"Girl, they have practically disowned me. No phone calls, visits, no nothing. They are some selfish bastards." He raises his head and then lowers it again, his hair hiding his face.

"You know, Johnnie, I remember all the times when they called you when they needed something!" My eyes cut sharp, but my voice remains soft spoken.

"Yeah, Girl, I remember. I bent over backwards to help them out." He shakes his head, rolls his eyes, and twists his lips in disgust. "Love, it's like a smack in the face. I had to stop working at the salon because my boss, Mr. Angelic, found out before I could tell him. It wasn't like I was trying to keep it from him. I was just waiting for the appropriate time. I guess I waited too long and someone beat me to the punch. He confronted me and I just couldn't lie to him. The man was too good to me. He requested that I take a paid leave of absence until I found other means of supporting myself. The man felt pity for me. He said that I was one of his best stylists. Girl, he wanted to take me places, move me up the ladder, but he feared once his clients found out it may affect his business. I understood, and left peacefully. He sent me the fruit basket on the dining room table."

"Johnnie, what is it that I can do for you now?" I gently lift his chin and stare into his painful eyes.

He remains silent.

"Johnnie, please talk to me?"

"Love, you know life is funny. There are so many different paths that I could have gone down. I thought I made the right choice. How naïve could I have been to think that I had found love with the man I've been dating for eleven years. Eleven years of giving my heart and soul to him. Eleven years of bowing down to him and kissing his selfish ass to show him that I was different from the rest. I lost a part of me in those eleven years because the last three years were hell. Pure hell! I felt empty inside even though he was here physically, but mentally he was always somewhere else. I could feel it in my spirit and my heart ached. He never wanted to talk about what was happening between us. Deep down I knew that whatever problems we were having we could work them out together. I was willing because I loved him enough, but obviously he wasn't feeling the same way. I was insignificant in his eyes. He had to have known that he had the virus. How can someone who once loved you do something like that so easily? He deceived me with false promises, touching me in a way that no one ever could. We made passionate love and then he left me in the coldest of night with no explanation, why do I have to die alone?"

Fountains of tears overflow from Johnnie's eyes and a wail of pain echoes through the house.

I pat Johnnie on his back and say, "Shhh. Shhh. Johnnie, I don't know. Based on what you've said the only thing you've done was give him your heart."

The lump in my throat is inflamed and as I swallow I feel the pain that I hear in Johnnie's cry. I pause and wipe the tears from my eyes. Johnnie makes me feel like breaking down and balling. But I'm trying to get myself together and it isn't easy. I look into his eyes and I see his heart crying for nurturing, like an infant. *God help him!*

Johnnie recovers, and wipes his sapped eyes. "Love, it was so ironic that we went to that company Christmas dinner party because my lover had walked out on me a week before, and then a month later we reconciled." Johnnie's eyes widen and he takes a long, deep, breath. I stop breathing for a second.

I literally hold my breath, numb. I drift back to that night. *I worked for Bruman & Prescott prestigious law firm and I handed in my resignation a month in advance because I was ready to pursue other things. I didn't know that my whole world would be turned upside down. I had lost control of me. I was so distraught that I couldn't even branch out and challenge my destiny. All I could think about was if anyone knew. Paranoia got the best of me and I surrendered. I gave up everything because of fear. And now Johnnie's telling me that he has AIDS. He could have been infected back then. Wow! That's too scary.*

I speak from my heart. "Johnnie, God has a tendency to bring people in your life for a reason. Everything means something. Maybe that's why you and I are friends 'til this very day." I tap him on his back and express that I really should be going. He walks me to the door and we exchange a hug. I tell him to call me either tonight or tomorrow.

In my car I sit pokerfaced staring at the road as

the traffic light turns to yellow, red, and then green. I am very emotional on the way home. I picture in my mind a reflection of what will become of me if I don't take care of myself. I promise from that day forward that I will do everything Dr. Fulmore advises. *I don't want full-blown AIDS. I don't wanna die.*

My blood's simmering thinking of Johnnie's lover possibly knowing he had the virus, and still doing nothing to take precautious for himself or Johnnie. It flares my frustrations as to how he could plant his dirt, and leave with no explanation. I grow furious so I try to divert my thoughts by turning on the radio.

I arrive home at 11:00 mentally drained and fatigued. I slowly enter the kitchen and walk towards the refrigerator. I pull out some lettuce, tomatoes, cucumbers, red onions, fresh mango, strawberries, and Perdue's boneless chicken to make a grilled chicken salad with a splash of Wish-Bone Red Wine Vinaigrette. I pour a tall glass of ice tea to wash it down. Sitting at the kitchen table my mind travels back to Johnnie. I wipe the greasy film off of my forehead with a napkin and take a few minutes to rewind my day.

It has been a day that I wish I could change for the better. Unfortunately, I know that it can't be done and it hurts me deeply. I get up, leaving my plate on the table, and walk into the bathroom. While undressing to take a shower I visualize how I would look thinner. The thought enters and exits my mind because the imagery is not pretty. I step into the shower as the water drenches my pores. I shut my eyes and see Johnnie; I see his face, thin frame, and his eyes that tell a story of loneliness and sorrow.

The water flows down my mountain of hips, buttocks, and streams off my feet, replenishing my body with a baptism of faith. I tune into my surroundings, listening to the siren from the police car and fire truck. I hear laughter and talking from folks on the street. Little Marisa from next door is crying as her mother, Sonya, sings her a lullaby in Spanish. All the sounds compound into a world full of music and realism. I lean my head back and let the water saturate as I reach for the bottle of shampoo.

After taking my shower my body struggles to enter my bedroom. I can't shake the feelings from within. I turn on the AC and plop on the bed with my arms extending towards the back of my head, my elbows pointed, shielding myself from harm. I buckle my knees into a fetal position, feeling distorted by Johnnie having AIDS. I can't function with normalcy. Cries muffle staining my pillow. *WHY, WHY!* My head throbs; eyes slouch as I move my forefinger in a circular motion trying to ease the intense pain. I feel like vomiting; ejecting all the poison out of my system and starting anew. But I can't and neither can Johnnie. Johnnie makes a valid point when he says that life has many paths. There are so many decisions as to which road to go down in life. But what if there's no option? Who suffers? I mirror the answer everyday.

Ring-ring, ring-ring,

"Hello."

"Hey, girl, it's me. I just called to make sure you made it home okay."

"Yes, Johnnie, I've been here for a while just relaxing." I wipe my eyes with my vibrating hand and try to crack a smile so he won't detect that I am crying.

"Well, Luv, I'm about to take it down a notch and get myself some zzzzzzz's, so I can be refreshed for tomorrow."

"Yeah, Johnnie so am I. I will call you tomorrow. Good night."

"Good night, Love."

After I hang up I know I can't go to bed. My tense body can't relax so I grab my journal off the nightstand to alleviate some pressure. My head throbs. Eyes ache. The migraine compresses so quickly that I want to cry. The pain seems unbearable. I gently glide the pen against the paper and try to articulate my troubles.

FOUR

I AWAKE CHILLED to the bones from leaving the air conditioner on all night. I get out of bed, turn off the AC, and open the windows to give the room some warmth. Ten o'clock moves leisurely as I stretch my body, standing tiptoe on the balls of my feet. I glide my feet across the hardwood floor into the bathroom of cool tile. I inhale the whisper of honey that comes through the gap of the window. There is also a potent fragrance of freshly cut grass making my nose itch as someone in the neighborhood has recently mowed their lawn. I sit on the toilet and stare at my reflection. I analyze myself in the full-length mirror, neck, breasts, arms, and stomach. I get undressed still staring at my twin wondering if a man saw me nude if he would find me attractive. I shake my head, drop my face, not certain if it even matters because what lies underneath will push him away from me within a second's time.

The phone rings.

I pull a towel from its rack and wrap it around my body and walk hastily towards the phone.

"Hello."

"Hey girl, it's me."

"Hi, Johnnie."

"Did I wake you, Love?"

"No, I'm about to take a shower. What's up?"

"Love, I feel like getting out for a bit. Would you like to join me?"

"Well, I haven't made any plans for the day, so that's fine with me."

"Great! Let's hook up around four-ish?"

"Okay. I'll see you then, Johnnie."

After we hang up I cut my eyes up to the ceiling and smirk, "You sly Fox. I knows whachu tryna do. Uh-Huh. You're using Johnnie to get to me. Yep. Lord.

You're slick. But I ain't mad at yah."

After my shower I make a big breakfast, wondering what Johnnie has planned for the day. Knowing him it's something spontaneous. He has this thing about doing whatever he wants at any given moment and as long as I've known him that has not changed. His enthusiasm jumps out and clings to me contagiously. And his spirit reminds me of gold, it's genuine. He's just one of kind. I admire him because he doesn't restrict himself from anything and he's not one to try to impress folks. He's himself.

Three o'clock rolls around rather quickly. I stumble over my feet contemplating what to wear. I put on my baby blue T-shirt with a long jean skirt and open toe sandals. Looking down at my feet, I realize I need a pedicure. I search the closet, and tucked in the back is the strap of my baby blue Coach bag. I grab it along with my Joss Stone CD while hurrying so as not to be late. Johnnie has no patience. And when he starts preaching, he just doesn't know when to stop until I have to bring that evil twin of rudeness out and say, *"Shut up, would you, ppppppppplllllleeeeaaaasssseeee!"*

I open the door to my building and a glow of brightness nearly blinds me. It's a scorcher. In the car I turn up the AC full blast, and crack the driver's side window letting the vents blow warm air that eventually turns to coolness against my glossy face. After I drive through the tollbooth, I call Johnnie from my cell phone and let him know that I'm getting close to his neck of the woods. Soon I see him standing on his stairway, dressed in some vintage jeans, a soft pink tunic shirt, and a pair of flip-flops. His thin fingers are running through his fine hair. Johnnie waves once he sees me pulling up and then he trots down the stairs with a men's satchel resting on his hip and a huge smile painted on his face.

"That's right; I have taught you well about being prompt. All right now!" Vainness exudes from Johnnie's face.

He swears he's my Papi.

"Where do you want to go, Johnnie?" I ask. I turn and subtly look him over.

Johnnie puts on his seatbelt, adjusts his seat to lean back, puts on his shades, and applies some Carol's Daughter almond lip butter.

"Love, let's go to Greenwich Village and chill out."

"Okay." I crack the sunroof window and flip on the radio.

We park and walk to Old to New. Johnnie yells out, "Juney... JuneBug. Where yah hidin'?" Juney, a cool biracial brother, with thick dreadlocks dangling down his back, comes from the backroom in his slouchy Rocawear jeans, oversized T, and Jordan sneakers.

"Yo' Johnnie, how have you been, bro'!" He walks towards Johnnie and they pat each other on the back. I am surprised that Juney doesn't question if everything is all right with Johnnie. Johnnie doesn't look like himself and Juney has known him for years. Way before I knew him. Possibly he's so overjoyed to see him that he doesn't even notice.

"Juney, I've been fine, honey." Johnnie says, winking.

"Long time no see, Johnnie. Where have you been hiding?" Juney asks as he kneels down and grabs some garments out of a cardboard box. He puts them on hangers, and places them on a steel rack.

"Honey, I've been home chillin' like a couch potato." Johnnie says mimicking his arms like JJ in *Good Times*.

I laugh.

Juney turns his attention towards me and asks, "Avery, how have you been?"

"Oh, I'm fine, Juney, just fine." My eyes wander because I have just told a bold faced lie.

"How 'bout you, Juney? How's business?"

"Avery, business is booming. What brings you two here today? Looking for anything in particular?"

Johnnie glances around the store and smugly

says, "No Babe, you of all people should know me by now. Juney, sweetie, you are losing your touch." A couple of seconds later Johnnie's voice rises, "This is what I'm talkin' 'bout. Ah yeah!"

"What, Johnnie?" I curiously ask.

Johnnie raises a pair of back in the day jeans from the women's section. It's an old pair of Jordache jeans that he insists I come and take a look at. I walk over to him and listen to him babble on and on.

"Sugar, these vintage jeans are it! Look at the detail in the stitching and the color of the thread. Now, that is hot!"

"Johnnie, those are women jeans." I say looking at him weirdly.

"I know Love. We are on a shopping spree for you." Johnnie bursts out in laughter.

"Stop playing, Johnnie."

"Yes girl, I need something to keep me busy and when you come to my house and look so plain Jane. Live a little, don't be afraid of a little color. After I am through with you, hon, you are going to killll it!" Johnnie exaggerates his neck, snaps his fingers, and places his pinky in his mouth, and makes a puckering sound.

My face lights up so full of joy. Johnnie really lifts my spirits.

After being at Old to New for nearly two hours we finally leave with me carrying two full bags of clothes. Johnnie looks a little flushed in his face so I suggest that we stop and grab something to eat. I am treating so he has the choice of any restaurant. We go to Katz's Delicatessen on East Houston Street. This deli has the best Rueben and Pastrami sandwiches.

After our meals we decide to go to Nuyorican Poets Café on East Third Street. The Hostess, Mahogany Browne hits the mike to open the show. About a half hour into the show, Johnnie excuses himself for a moment and then returns with a cunning look on his face. *He's up to something. A* few minutes later Mahogany Browne has introduced the next poet.

"For all of you I have a special treat. The next poet is a gentleman from the audience who has a way with words, enough to convince me to let him get on stage. He's a first timer enjoying the ambiance. Well, he has something on his mind that he wants to share. Let's give it up for Future."

Everyone claps as I turn around looking for *"Future"* and then all of sudden, low and behold, Johnnie stands up and walks on stage. *Huh? What's he gonna do?* I sit glued to my seat. He stands with confidence. *Damn.*

"What's up? Whhhhhhaaaaatttttsssss's UUUUUUUPPPPPPPP! I just wanna take a moment of your time, if you don't mind. I'm not prepared so bear with me. This is kinda an impulse thang. But I appreciate you hearing me out." Johnnie clears his throat and begins.

Farewell, my Love

I say to you, farewell
For all you've given me
In times of need
Good and bad

You've never left my side
Through all the tears I've cried
Smiles I've spread
Laughs I've raised
You've given me
Rain or shine
Peace of mind
To carry on with my days of praise to God Almighty
You've given me friends of different shades
To calm my nerves in times of dismay

Who've crave my presence
And question my resemblance
Of an old soul who mimics someone they've known
before

Although you know I'm uniquely me

Son, brother, friend
All combined in thee
I say to you, farewell

With bright sight
Inhale of sweet hot roasted peanuts in the air
Of light breezes running through my hair

Of sound

Car honking, dogs barking, children cries
Music—country, reggae, r & b, soul
All influential
In moods of happiness and sorrow
In times of break-up with loved ones
Reconciliation of old flames
Reliving past experiences
That brightens up future days
And shows relevance
In all kinds of ways
To teach and leave as remembrance
Of what used to be
And rides away in waves that roar
No more pain
As waters calm
Spirits dance on waves
That touches ocean sands
As women and men
Women and women
Men and men
Hold hands

Expressing their preference
Not undressing with deception
Pleasing all and not themselves
I say to you, farewell

For all of your blessings

That has exploited me
To be—who I am
Who you've chosen me to be
I am a gay man
Whole heartedly

Living a life of wretched pain

Inside these veins run amuck
AIDS
A gift my lover gave
Within a red box
Inscription on his note card read
"Best of luck."

As he left the scene
I thought it was a dream
But it is my reality

So I say to you, farewell

Before my day finally comes
When body turns to dust
A new day is reborn
I would then become
A memory
For all who choose to grieve,
Hopefully some of you will remember me
A gay man with a dream
Who fulfilled with will
A final parting with soul
Not all grow to be old
Within this world today
So everyday must be a day
To blow out candle wishes
Leaving behind words of faith
To strengthen and pave ways,
For those who have no guide
No one to mimic or idolize
This I leave behind.

I say to you, farewell, my love

My love
My life.

Johnnie walks offstage to silence. And then, out of the blue, a roar comes from the crowd. A standing ovation of palms clapping sound like drums beating. Everyone applauds at his honesty and bravery. Johnnie's, piercing eyes, and persona has riveted everyone. It blows me away. Looking around I see that women's mascara has ran. Men connect with their eyebrows raise high and then low. Everyone seems to feel Johnnie's powerful words. Johnnie has touched the core of all that sit here. I can say that it will be a moment in which, I will never forget. I open my arms to embrace him. And we both break down in tears amongst all these strangers.

Since it's still kind of early Johnnie and I drive to Central Park to unwind. I park the car, pop open the trunk and reach for my plaid blanket. We stretch the blanket out on the ground, lie down, and gaze at the blue water sky.

Johnnie looks at me without humor and says, "Love, if you could have anything in this world at this very moment, what would it be? Don't take a moment to think about it because you already know. Just say it, no matter how stupid it may sound." He rests his head on his folded arms.

I remain silent absorbing Johnnie's question. I don't feel the need to sugarcoat my words so I speak with honesty and from the heart.

"Johnnie, I want a partner, lover, and friend. Walking hand and hand, kissing in public, you know. A man who knows me inside and out where words need not be spoken, and it is all in the look. The look that says we are in *love*. I never thought that I would say this, but I'm ready to explore life a little more. I've been hiding within myself, scared to venture out. It's funny because I used to be so content with being alone, but I realize with your help that life should not be lived day in and day out in the house with Sis."

Johnnie looks perplexed. "Who's Sis?"

A ruby cloud smothers my face as I laugh to shade my embarrassment.

"Sis...she's my journal. I interact with her so much that I actually believe she is my sister." I lower my head and hide my face in the palms of my hands and chuckle.

"SisterLuv, you need to get a life," he says as he moves closer rubbing my back.

"Johnnie, all jokes aside, I've been inspired by you because you are spontaneous. I mean, you live your life expressing that you are happy to be alive. You don't let things discourage you or stop you from doing what you wanna do. You're positive and confident and outspoken about your beliefs. I wanna learn, grow, and connect with the outside world. I've really learned a lot from you today and it has opened doors that I never knew existed within me. I just want you to know that I appreciate you and I would never take our friendship for granted. I love you."

I sit up on my knees teary-eyed, which turns into me sobbing into my palms. Johnnie gets on his knees and holds me by my waist, ever so gently, and I put my head on his shoulders and cry. I feel the air from him breathing on my ear.

"Avery, I love you, too."

I pause. Johnnie has never called me by my first name. I weep because at this moment Johnnie says that he loves me, and it fills me so full of hope. I mean, I feel it in my stomach, back, and at the core of me. It has seeped through my thin skin. His voice remains soft and he sniffs my fragrance, inhaling me as if he is bottling my scent. I relinquish all of the feelings of fear from my being, and embrace Johnnie. I can feel his energy flow into me. My body electrifies with high intensity and then a slight cramp creeps up on me. My eyes squint, nose crumples, and I remain still in his arms until it subsides. A feeling of security comes over me in the arms of love. I'm loved by a man who has never traveled my internal walls. I'm loved wholesomely.

We sit in the park for about an hour and the evening air has a slight chill that makes Johnnie break out with fine little bumps on his arm. This alerts us that it is time to head home. We walk to my car and a nauseating feeling lines my stomach making me want to vomit, but I don't.

Once we arrive at Johnnie's apartment I ask to use his bathroom and rush right in. *Damn, I just made it in time before everything I ate ended up on the bathroom floor. I hope he didn't hear me.* I feel dizzy like I need to lie down. I hear India Arie playing. *Johnnie loves himself some India.* He is in his living room singing. The brother's singing his heart out. *I never knew he could sing.* All these years there is so much that I don't know. After getting myself together, I meet him in the living room. He is singing to the mirror with a brush in his hand as a microphone. I smirk.

"Johnnie, what would I do without you?" He smiles and opens his arms and I walk right into *love* and rest my head on his chest as we slow dance. A part of me doesn't want to leave, but I know I should be heading home. Johnnie walks me to my car. I tell him that I will call once I get home. He waves, good night as I pull off. I turn on the CD player and listen to Lyfe Jennings cruising 125th Street. It takes me about forty minutes to get home because there is an accident on Broadway across the street from the Integrity Masonic Temple in Paterson. I have had a long, but good day. I think about Johnnie getting up in front of a bunch of strangers and expressing himself. I still can't believe that he did that. Sometimes it makes me wonder about what could've been between us. What am I thinking? God doesn't make mistakes; Johnnie and I are meant to be best friends.

The night air has a delicate breeze that's comforting. But as soon as I arrive home and step one foot in my apartment the sweltering heat hits me smack dab in the face. It's miserable, muggy heat that's difficult to sleep in, even with a fan on. I roll up the windows and pull down the screens and sit down on the edge of the bed. It's not quiet outside, but I image that it is in my mind. I go to the window and watch the mosquitoes swarm the telephone pole. The night's ambiance attracts some couples to stroll the streets enjoying each other's company. The faint humid air kisses my velvet skin and I drift off. *A pair of strong masculine hands caresses my skin.* I close my eyes actually feeling it as my mouth gapes open and there is nothing but teeth. I'm floating for real, but once my brown eyes open disappointment laughs in my face. I sit alone. *How pitiful!* It's obvious that I'm yearning for companionship. I sidetrack myself by preparing to take a quick shower, and then have a cup of Celestial Seasonings peppermint herbal tea, and a good book to read.

Within the last few days with Johnnie I've spiritually grown. I remind myself to give Johnnie a call letting him know that I made it home. I pick up the phone in the kitchen. Johnnie's phone rings twice and then his voicemail picks up.

"You have reached Johnnie. Stop playin' and leave a brief message at the tone."

"Johnnie, it's me, just calling to let you know that I made it in. Give me a call. Love yah, Bye."

I wonder where he stepped off to. Maybe he's in the shower. In the bathroom I turn the nozzle to the shower when the phone rings. I quickly run to answer it.

"Hello."

"What's up, girl?"

"Where were you when I called, Johnnie?"

"I went to take the garbage out and got stopped by my next-door neighbor. She's a sweet elderly woman who's always concerned about me. It feels good to have someone ask how I'm doing. Love, why are you breathing so hard? What were you doing? Are you alone?" He chuckles.

"Johnnie, stop playing you know that I'm alone."

"Honey, I don't know anything. You could've gotten a booty call, and picked up your piece on the way home. What's his name? Do I know him?"

"Oh, you got jokes. Ha, ha, ha, Johnnie."

"Girlfriend, someone has to keep the comedy alive. So, Love, what were you doing?"

"I was just about to take a shower."

"Well, take your shower and we can talk tomorrow. Okay?"

"Sure Johnnie. I'll call you after my appt-."

"What, Love?"

"Johnnie, I said I will call you tomorrow late afternoon."

"Good night, Love."

"Good night, Johnnie."

Damn. I almost slipped up and told him that I have a doctor's appointment. Good thing I spoke softly. I will tell him in due time, just not right now because everything's good. And plus, it's no big deal because Dr. Fulmore just wants to speak with me. He's mostly checking on me out of concern. This HIV thing it's still relatively fresh. I head back in the bathroom to take my shower.

Later I put on my champagne silk nightshirt and walk into the kitchen to place my silver kettle on the stove to simmer for a nice hot cup of peppermint tea. I crawl into bed and snuggle with one of Bernice L. McFadden's books, "The Warmest December." But I can't keep my mind from drifting so I put the book on the nightstand, and just stare into space. I come to when I hear the kettle whistling. So I go into the kitchen for my cup of tea. For some reason, I have Johnnie's poem on my mind. I keep picturing him reciting it with such feeling. Johnnie's deep. With my tea I go back into the bedroom to watch TV.

I am getting drowsy so I turn off all the lights to make it pitch black. I lie in my bed wondering how

Johnnie's doing. I sense that he's putting on airs for me. And it disturbs me a bit because I don't want him to be afraid around me. *He should know that I'm his best friend through good and bad.* I can't seem to erase him from my mind not even for a few moments. Maybe if I just lie here eventually I will fall asleep. I feel a supple breeze against my feet from the window. The flicker of the streetlight makes a shadow on the wall. Finally, my mind goes blank and I double up the goose down pillows and shut my eyes. But I have not fallen asleep. My mind is still traveling long distances. Eventually, I shut my eyes again, and doze off.

A sharp pain in my chest wakes me. I seem to have the sniffles also. I don't feel like I have a cold or anything. Maybe it's from being out in the night air? I get up, shut the window and put the fan on low. I cannot afford to be coming down with a cold. I snuggle back into bed covering myself with the throw, as a light wind caresses me from the fan. My eyes become heavy and I fall back asleep.

The sound of a cat meowing in an alley breaks up my sleep. It's 6:30 a.m. I'm sweating profusely from being under the throw, so I remove it from my damp skin. The light wind circulating from the fan makes me shiver and then sneeze. After I sneeze triple times I lean forward and reach for the tissue box that sits on the nightstand. I walk towards the bathroom. I have stomach cramps. I'm hot and then cold, happy then sad. I'm overwhelmed. In the bathroom I turn on the bathtub faucet and pour two capfuls of alcohol in the water like Ma'am used to do when I was a child. I ease my body into the eucalyptus for a half hour. After my bath I glide some Shea Butter to moisten my skin and then stretch my arms overlapping my nudeness with a fresh nightshirt and panties. I crave a hot cup of apple cider so I go into the kitchen and pour some Red Jacket Orchards apple juice into a mug and put it in the microwave for a few minutes. I sit at the kitchen table sipping as thoughts run through my mind. My muscles limp slightly, my eyelids shut slowly as I lean back yawning with exhaustion. I can hear my bed calling me. "Avery, Avery." So I raise my tired self up and head back to the bedroom with my eyes half shut, bumping into the bedroom door and chipping the nail on my big toe. I climb into bed and drift into a dream.

Where am I? I can hear the sound of rippling water. Smell the scent of salt. I can't see because I'm blindfolded. I have been accosted and taken somewhere deserted. There is a man who speaks fluent French in my ears. I've been kidnapped. A ransom note has been forwarded to my residence but I have no kin. There's a reward for my capture of one million dollars. I am well known in the public eye. The FBI is frantically searching for me. We hear a helicopter above our heads. My blindfold is taken off. There before me stands a debonair man, and I am on a deserted island. There's a fire burning to keep us warm. We are spotted on the island. There's a boat coming forth, which washes ashore. We are surrounded. Three men walk up to us and ask us how we got there? Is anymore with us? Another man shows us a picture of a woman missing for a month. He gives her name and I looked him in his eyes and say, "I kno nothn about tha ecause we hav no techno here. I kno nothn." I use an unfamiliar language. He looks me over peculiarly again and says, "But...But...You resemble her. It is amazing. You could be her twin." I shrug my shoulders. I don't want to give up my world of paradise. I have finally found a man who has gone out of his way to capture me. To keep me. No. I don't want to go back to a lonely life. He wants me and I want to be wanted by this dashing man.

Five

MY ALARM CLOCK startles me as it flashes the time. It's 9:12 a.m. I have slept like a baby. I quickly snatch some tissues out of the box on the nightstand as I feel a sneeze coming. And just as I bring the tissue to my mouth a thunderous sneeze comes out. I feel a sharp pain in my chest, like I have heartburn, so I remain still for a few minutes. I gently rub my chest until the pain eases.

Today is Thursday, and I will be seeing Dr. Fulmore today.

God, I hope that I am not seriously getting sick.

I kneel down beside my bed, interlock my fingers and pray.

"Lord, I pray that You continue to lay Your hands upon me, healing with faith to believe that all the pain shall pass. I open my heart to You. Amen."

In the living room I slip in a CD of Vicki Winans. Her song, "Shake Yourself Loose," sends chills through me. Being HIV-positive can be so unpredictable, one minute I am up and about and the next minute I am weak and on my back. Over the months I've learned to examine the slightest little symptom and give it importance instead of denying its existence. These are the times I wish I had my parents. And as I think back, there have been so many opportunities for me to reach out to others, but I seem to always delay my callings. Mostly because of my own issues and of course the fear of being rejected comes into play. Johnnie knows that feeling all too well. I don't want to ever encounter such a feeling of vulnerability. Knowing that my skin is not thick I'm afraid it will literally chew me up in a half second's time.

Entering the kitchen, I feel a little nauseous, but

force myself to eat a light breakfast. After eating, I rest until 12:30, and then start to get ready for my doctor's appointment.

Ring-ring, Ring-ring, ring.

"Hello."

"Yeah, girl, it's me," says Johnnie.

"Hey, Baby."

"Love, do you have any plans for today?"

"Around what time today because I have something to do around 3:00."

"Well, call me after you're done with your plans. Maybe we can have dinner later this evening."

"Sounds like a plan. I'll call you."

"Alright, girl, talks to you later."

"Goodbye."

"Not goodbye. Talks to you later, Love. You know that I hate that word, good-bye."

Johnnie sucks his teeth.

"Sorry, talks to you later, Johnnie."

Johnnie's so set in his ways, but the man has some serious inner strength. I sit on the sofa, curl up like a snail and fall back asleep.

I awake from the intercom buzzing. Feeling lethargic, I glide my lead feet across the hardwood floor to press the intercom button and say, hello, but no one answers. I go into the bathroom and run a bath. I run my fingers through my hair, and realize that my ends need to be trimmed. It has been months since my hair has been done. As I submerge my left foot in the water, a stinging sensation hits my skin like a bolt of lightening. My reflexes act quickly. I lift my foot out of the tub until the temperature is reduced to lukewarm. I lean all the way back and rest my head on the cottony bath pillow. The fragrance takes me away, and I coast off wishing I could be in a different place and time. I crave intimacy like I once had back in the day. This life I'm living has left me alone. I don't have a man in my life. Reality sets in. I'm a lonely woman living with HIV.

Later I put on my fleece dress and wear flip-flops that expose my non-polished toes. Usually when I go for my doctor visits, Dr. Fulmore will sit down with me for fifteen minutes and talk. The man has a great sense of humor, which makes it a lot easier for me to follow through and go to all my appointments. It's very important to me to have a doctor that's assertive, but who can also demonstrate compassion. Before I walk out the door I give myself a once over glance giving my final approval. I have become too self-conscious.

Traffic's bumper-to-bumper due to an accident on the cross streets of Main and Grand. As I get closer I don't see what all the fuss is about because both cars have pulled over to the side of the road. *People can be so nosy.* I arrive at Dr. Fulmore's office on time, sign in, and sit down reaching for a magazine. The central air is a bit chilly, so I put on my fleece jacket. I sit near the front desk and talk to the nurse, Violet. We talk about our favorite movies, music, and our make-believe movie star husbands. Of course my choices are between Nicholas Cage, John Travolta, Matt Dillon, Simon Baker, Edward Norton, Ryan Gosling, and Ethan Hawke.

A few minutes later the medical assistant, Praise, calls my name and I go inside. She asks me to stand on the scale and then tells me to wait in room number three for Dr. Fulmore. Nervousness takes charge and I try to ease it by sitting in the chair next to the examination table. My mouth's getting dry and I need a ginger ale to calm the queasiness in my stomach. I hear Dr. Fulmore's voice in the next room with another patient. He's in a pretty lively mood. Five minutes later he enters the room.

"Hello, Avery."

Dr. Fulmore smiles and positions his glasses.

"Hello, Dr. Fulmore." I lift my head and crack a false smile.

"How have you been doing, Avery?"

"Oh, Doc, I've been doing fine."

"How have you been feeling? Any changes that I need to know about? Feeling fatigue, loss of appetite, any dizziness, insomnia, or weight loss?" He skims through my chart while asking me a multitude of questions.

"Well, I've been sneezing lately and I am not really able to sleep well at night. I also have night sweats. I have been under some stress, so that may be why I can't sleep well. I have nausea, but my main concern is a sharp pain in my chest when I sneezed this morning. The pain didn't last long, but the fact that it happened is a big concern." I look directly at Dr. Fulmore as he writes my symptoms down on the chart.

"Okay, I'll check things out and we shall see what is what. Avery, I want you to come sit on the examination table for me. Breathe in and out."

There's silence in the room.

"Is there anything else going on that I should know about?"

"No, Dr. Fulmore."

"You feel like you have a slight temperature. Take some Tylenol before bed tonight. Looking at your chart it looks like you have lost three pounds. When you don't have a really big appetite drink a can of Ensure Plus just to help maintain your weight."

"Okay, Doc."

"I want you to go and get an x-ray done today for your chest. Violet will give you the directions to the Image Center. She can call to confirm a time before you leave. Other than that, you look well. I see that you are taking good care of yourself. I am very happy to see that you are sticking to your course of therapy." Dr. Fulmore puts the chart underneath his arm and closes the door behind him.

After he leaves the room I take a hollow breath and look up at the ceiling and thank the Lord, again. I meet with Violet to make the appointment and to get directions to the Image Center. She writes down the address and confirms the time.

When I arrive at the Image Center in Hackensack, I sign in and sit by the window waiting to be called. A chill flushes through me so I snuggle in my fleece jacket and sit back. Not even twenty minutes have passed, but I'm anxious to get out of here. After a half hour of imprinting my buttocks into the soft multi-colored woven chair, I want to leave. My eyes roll with impatience. Finally, a strong feminine voice calls out, "Avery Love."

A nameless Caucasian woman, with a petite frame, cat like eyes, thin lips, pointy nose and dirty blonde hair with thinning streaks of highlights directs me to a corner room where coldness crowds around. My nipples harden. She dangles a gown with two fingers pinching it and extending her arm to hand the faded blue gown to me. Then she turns and walks out of the room. *Pleasantness does not become her!* She reminds me of a drill sergeant. I undress and a few seconds later there's a knock at the door and before I can answer she barges right in. *How rude!* The nameless woman asks me a few questions with her eyes glued to the chart and makes no eye contact with me. It really annoys me. Then it's as if a dark covering surrounds me. An uncomfortable feeling layers my skin. *She knows.* Why else would she treat me so badly? Suspicion clutters my thoughts. The nameless woman speaks with a dry, stale, humorless tone. And I know that there is no way I can crack her solid as a rock shell. She appalls me. Inside I bleed due to the blunt force of her cruelness. She takes my x-ray and then she turns away. She speaks very quickly letting me know that my doctor will contact me with the results and then she walks out of the room. I lower my head, close my eyes, and then get dressed.

I decide to stop at the nearest supermarket to pick up some groceries before going home. I'm feeling a bit nervous, but in a moment the feeling diminishes.

At home, I put my groceries away, kick off my shoes and sit on the sofa. I'm exhausted. My entire body wilts. I notice the caller ID blinking, but I don't rush to the phone to see who has called. I don't want to move. I am in a vegetated state and I think my body needs a moment to shut down. I snuggle into the soft leather and close my eyes and fall asleep.

When I wake up I feel groggy and it makes me feel weird like I have drunk a case of beer or taken some strong medication.

Finally I get up and walk over to the answering machine to check my messages. I bypass the first message and listen to the second, which is from Dr. Fulmore's office. I shiver slightly as I hear his voice.

"Hello Avery, I wanted to let you know that I received your results back from the Imaging Center. Based on your history I know that you exercise quite frequently. At first I thought it might have been Angina, which is a discomfort in the chest when some part of the heart doesn't get enough blood. It would feel like pressure or squeezing with the sharp pain. But you stated it only lasted a few seconds. Normally, with Angina it would last longer than a few seconds. What I am going to suggest is that you lessen your physical activity just to see if the sharp pain ceases. If it happens to reoccur, please call me and make an appointment. Other than that everything looks good. I called in a prescription to your pharmacy for a refill of your medication, so you can go there to pick it up. God Bless."

I really don't like when he leaves me messages because I feel like I'm about to hyperventilate. Everything becomes a blur. My biggest fear is that one day Dr. F. will call with some devastating news, and my world will shatter into tiny fragments. I know I don't have the endurance to handle that as of yet.

Its 7:30 so I still have time to get to the pharmacy and pick up my prescription. My body feels clammy and cold so I enter the walk-in closet and get a sweater before leaving. Quickly I pick up a CD, not paying attention to which one.

When I get to my car, I slip in the CD, and all of a sudden I hear India Arie. Instantly, I think of Johnnie and remember that I never did call him back.

Once I arrive at Mr. Clyde's Pharmacy I notice a few people walking through, but it's not much traffic. The evening's tranquil. A tingle of coolness runs through my body, as the old folks would say, "A spirit just walked through me." Mr. Clyde's heavy door makes me work hard to open it. I keep telling him that I am not trying out for the bodybuilder's competition. He just cackles like I just told a joke off of Def Comedy Jam. And then I just stand there with this dumbfounded look upon my face waiting for him to compose himself.

"Avery, I know that is not you walking in here!" Mr. Clyde says, as his face lights up. He adjusts his glasses on his nose.

"Yes, Mr. Clyde, it's me."

Mr. Nathanial Clyde, a fairly elderly man, is aging well into his early sixties. His crown of gray gives off a shimmer. He has butterscotch-colored firm skin, eyes with puffy bags and darkness underneath. He walks with a limp from having an injury back in his youthful days. His bifocal glasses extend off of his nose as he constantly looks over the lenses. I often wonder why he does that, but he must have his reasons. He has a southern tone, born and raised in Raleigh, North Carolina. His wife and three daughters came to New Jersey for a change of pace. After he finished his schooling, he opened up the pharmacy and has been in business for over twenty years. His old fashion hospitality is a pleasantry to embrace. He's always greeting folks with a smile. He says, as long as I keep walking through his door, he never has to worry about me. He has a grandparent's disposition, and he's always concerned about folks. He says I remind him of his oldest daughter. He has taken a strong likeness to me. Unfortunately, his daughter died three years ago from breast cancer. He always says that she was strong willed and stubborn as a mule. I remember the first time he told me her story and he had this glazed look in his eyes like he missed her so much. Yeah, Mr. Clyde, he's good people.

While Mr. Clyde fills my prescription I feel him looking me over. He tries not to do it noticeably, but I catch him every time. He knows when I've lost or gained weight, and every time I'm about to leave the store he hands me a case of strawberry Ensure Plus. He knows it's my favorite flavor. I gladly take it, no need to be unappreciative because at least someone shows concern.

"Well, Avery your prescription is ready. Um, one is on back order. Do you have enough to last or have you already run out?" Mr. Clyde looks over the counter for my response.

"No, Mr. Clyde, I have enough to last until it comes in. It usually takes a couple of days, right?"

"I'll call you as soon as it comes in."

"Okay."

He waves his hand for me to come closer towards the counter and then he hands me a bag with my medication in it.

"Thank you, Mr. Clyde, and you have a good evening." I say as I walk to the door.

I can hear Mr. Clyde fumbling for something. And then I start counting, one, two, three...

"Oh! Avery, I almost forgot," he calls out behind me.

I smirk because I know it is a case of strawberry Ensure.

"Here you go. I almost forgot to give you this," he says, holding the case in his hands.

"Thank you, Mr. Clyde."

"Take care." He palms my right shoulder and smiles showing the gold cap in his tooth.

"I will, Mr. Clyde."

I pop open my trunk and place the case of Ensure in the corner. I get in the car and head for home. While driving home a bloodcurdling feeling comes over me. India's song "Ready for Love" is playing and it seems so emotional. I listen to the words all the time, but this time they are piercing and her voice turns into Johnnie's. I can literally hear him singing with such feeling. Tears form and I hurry home so I can call him back. My stomach's upset. It's like I have just drank a pint of spoiled milk. I have a headache and my body's clammy even more than before.

As I enter my apartment, I hear the phone ringing. I can't seem to get to the phone in time, so the voicemail picks up. Finally, after putting the case of Ensure in the cabinet in the kitchen, I have the opportunity to listen to Johnnie's message. I call him back but an unfamiliar male voice answers.

"Hello."

"Hello, may I speak to Johnnie." I look at the phone baffled.

"Sure, hold on while I get him." The man says.

"Hello."

"Hey, Johnnie."

"Girl, what's up?"

"Not a thing. Sorry that I'm getting back to you so late."

"Oh, girl, that's fine."

"Are you okay, Johnnie?"

"I'm fine. Just entertaining a long time friend. I get tired of being here alone sometimes just listening to the cars pass by. You feel me?"

"Yeah, I feel you, Johnnie. Well, don't let me keep you from your company. I'll talk to you tomorrow."

"Sure."

"You have a good night, Love."

"Good night, Johnnie."

I'm relieved. Johnnie sounds okay. Maybe I'm just wary from my own issues. I will probably feel more in control if I could just tell him the truth. My conscience says yes, but the words just won't find their way out. I feel bad, but what else can I do? I have so much going on within me and it's difficult at times to cope. The man has company over because he gets tired of being alone. I can't blame him. I feel trapped and I have no outlet, other than writing in my damn journal. I feel the inner me boiling. Tears release from my eyes because I'm frustrated at having no one to console me in my time of need. I have to pull myself together alone.

Shit! It ain't easy! Hot bubble baths can only do so much to soothe my nerves! Listening to music can only do so much by allowing me to escape into another zone! And sipping on hot cider and herbal tea can only do so much to warm my insides allowing me to get some sleep! Everything seems to be done with me in this empty apartment alone. *I can't take it anymore! I want my old life back! And where's the bastard who did this to me? How am I supposed to live?* I can't be intimate with anyone because I am afraid, afraid to feel love and loss.

I take bottomless breaths to relax because I have gotten myself worked up over something that I can't change. My frustrations are building and I'm getting damn tired of wiping away saltwater from my eyes. I miss having someone to hold me. I miss the kisses and handholding. Fantasizing about it doesn't do anything but make it harder to accept. Sure, I can have a relationship, but it will never be the same as before. Precautions always have to be top priority. Who wants a relationship if everything has to be somewhat dictated? Who wants to date someone HIV-positive? I sit back, stroking my chin trying to think of anyone I've previously dated who would be willing to follow these guidelines. Unfortunately, no one comes to mind.

I walk over to the CD player and slip in Mary J. Blige. Every time I hear her sing I think about how even she found a special man who helped her cope with the reality of being an alcoholic and a drug user.

"Sing it Mary!" See this is what pisses me off because even Mary eventually found her soul mate! Maybe I am not getting out enough, but where do you go to meet people? I am not the clubbing, bar, or house party type. My idea of a night out is dinner, a comedy show or a poetry reading. I hear they have poetry readings at Hue-man in Harlem. *Maybe I should start going?* I bet Johnnie would love to go with me. I don't have any other friends, but Johnnie. Interaction with women never amounts to much, mainly because they always tend to stir up drama—a major turn-off for me.

Maybe I'm not the approachable type? I haven't really felt anything for another person until now. Johnnie brings that out of me and that green-eyed monster is exposed because I feel jealous of someone else being there for him. I can't be cloned, so why shouldn't someone else be there. He always had friends around him at least, up until he took ill. Then his friends dwindled off and he was left with only the true friends. Maybe I'm not jealous of his friend? Maybe I'm envious of Johnnie? I can't be like him. If anything should ever happen to him then I'm left alone trying to weather the storm of survival. Inner strength is not something I can turn on and off when I need it. I was not born with it. But then again, I've made it this far so I must have it in me. I guess a person really doesn't know if they have it or not until something happens and they do what they have to do.

My inner voice says to call Johnnie, but I already spoke with him once tonight. I wouldn't feel right calling him again. He may think something's wrong with me or think that I'm purposely trying to ruin his night. I'll wait until tomorrow.

In the bedroom I grab my journal to vent my frustrations.

Dear Sis,

I'm feelin' blue. I can't find it within to tell Johnnie the truth. I just can't do it. He is my family. What am I supposed to do? How am I supposed to start the conversation off? How? I know that I will be totally lost without him should anything happen to him. It would be like starvation because I feed off of him. I love him that much.

I'll talk to you later, Sis.

I lay down on the bed. An hour later my sleep is broken by a tear rolling off the side of my nose, curving and falling off of my cheek and onto the pillow. A part of me feels empty, with nothing left within to express my emotions. My instincts are speaking loudly and I want to close my ears so I can't listen, but my arms cannot drown out the sound. Johnnie comes to mind again and I quickly reach for the phone. Sweat trickles from down my forehead as my body tightens.

Ring-ring, ring-ring, ring-ring.

"You have reached Johnnie. Stop playin' and leave a brief message at the tone."

"Hey Johnnie, it's Love, I know it's early, but you were in my thoughts so I decided to give you a call. You're probably still asleep. Give me a call once you get this message. Love yah."

Johnnie's probably in a deep sleep depending on what time he went to bed last night. I'm sure he'll call once he gets up. I can't go back to sleep so I make breakfast. As I prepare my scrambled eggs I glance at the wall clock and realize that it's 7:30. Johnnie's going to think that I have lost my mind calling him so early. After I eat I mope around waiting for the phone to ring. I watch TV, read a magazine, and paint my toenails cherry apple red.

Twelve-thirty approaches and Johnnie still hasn't called me back. *Maybe he stepped out with his friend last night and ended up staying at his house?* He always checks his messages. *He'll call.* I feel so stupid. There I was talking on the phone with Johnnie's friend and didn't even bother to ask his name. *Idiot.* But Johnnie seemed so excited to have company over so there was no need for me to put in my two cents. I sit on the sofa, motioning my hands against my face and slowly letting them glide down. My neck feels tense. I turn to the left and then to the right to loosen the kinks. I lean over to grab a blanket and then position myself so that my neck won't stiffen. I monitor the clock with precision, tuning everything else out, but the ticking of it. I am chilly so I wrap the bottom half of the blanket around my feet. Distractions keep me weary. Deep in my gut I feel something's wrong. The inner sack of my stomach feels like it's going to erupt with puke. I want to call again, but it might make him think that I'm a stalker. So I wait until 1:30, and then I call. I feel the tension building. My temples, forehead, and around my eyes are stressed. I get up to make a hot cup of cider, hoping to relax. My mind travels back to Nuyorican where Johnnie stood on stage reciting his poem. The look in his eyes poured out love. Sipping sparingly, the phone rings and I rush to answer, but I'm discouraged by it being a wrong number. I return back to my imprint on the sofa, sip my cider down to the last drop and then place the mug on a coaster on the end table. My eyes slowly shut into a world of darkness.

I later wake up with saliva drooling from the right corner of my mouth. I stretch my arms out to loosen the stiffness. Slowly, I walk towards the window and gaze out at the sky. I turn to look at the phone to see if there are any messages. It's 11:20 and there is no message. *It's not like Johnnie not to return a call from me.* Puddles of tears stagnate in my eyes. I hang my head down hoping all is well. Trying to preoccupy myself, I turn on the radio, but every song that I hear makes me think about Johnnie even more. I feel myself tumbling. Looking outside of myself I see myself slowly falling like a glass fumbling in mid air and then smashing into smithereens. I don't want to panic, but anxiously I pick up the phone and speed dial Johnnie's number.

Ring-ring, ring-ring, ring-ring,

"You have reached Johnnie. Stop playin' and leave a brief message at the tone."

"Hello, Johnnie, its Love. I'm calling again. Give me a call okay?"

I'm at a loss. I bite my hangnail until it bleeds. I don't know anyone that knows Johnnie other than Mr. Clyde. His family doesn't keep in touch with him. *Damn!* I don't think he has heard from his ex and I don't even know who that person may be. My blood boils. I'm stroking my chin racking my brain trying to recollect if Johnnie may have mentioned anything to me to help me find him. A name would certainly help. *SHIT!* His neighbor, but what is the person's name? *Concentrate! Concentrate!* I can't recall if he ever said a name. Rage circulates within me as I dash towards the door, snatch my keys off the hook, and rush down the stairway. I pull open the lobby door, jump into my car and drive like a bat out of hell to Harlem. Traffic's hectic and everyone seems to be in a rush. My fingers tap on the steering wheel, and I yell in road rage for folks to move out of my way.

When I get to Johnnie's place, I double-park and leave my emergency lights flashing. I fling the car door open, and ring Johnnie's bell. Only seconds pass in between each ring but there's still no answer. The apartment lights are off. Hysterically, I ring everyone's bell in the building until someone finally answers. A young Caucasian man with a cane comes to the door. He has a brace on his right leg. I introduce myself and apologize for disturbing him. He tells me that he knows Johnnie from passing in the hallways.

"Do you remember the last time you saw him?"

He says, "I recall seeing him yesterday with a gentleman as they got into a black BMW." Tears form in the corners of my eyes.

"Ma'am, are you all right?"

I lift my head up as high as I can. "Yes," I say in a whisper. "Thank you, sir. Sorry to have disturbed you." My sluggish body glides back to my car. I'm sick inside, not certain if I can make it back to Paterson. Something's wrong. *God give me a sign, a clue, something?* I can feel it, just as I can feel the light breeze against my skin. Something's so very wrong.

On my way back home I hit traffic and I grow impatient. Once I arrive home I grab the New York phonebook and start to call all the hospitals in Johnnie's neighborhood. No one has a Johnnie Rivera registered. It's a good sign, but my gut instincts do not let up. I persuade myself that everything's fine, but I feel the opposite. My heart hurts. I am weak with the thought of my friend possibly being alone, hurt, or worse. Yes, his neighbor says he saw Johnnie leave with his friend, but who's to say that his friend did not drop him off somewhere. Who's to say? Only three know of his whereabouts, Johnnie, his friend, and God.

S_{IX}

THERE'S NO ECHO, screech, thump, or squeak; my apartment's completely quiet. It's like someone's in mourning. I sit thinking about the last time I heard from Johnnie, which was on July 20th. It's Monday, August 2nd, and the phone still has not rung. I have called him so many times that I can't leave any more messages because his answering machine is full. I have no clue as to where he could be and I'm petrified that something has happened to him. My eyes are swollen and are unable to open. There's a small crease in between so I can see where I'm going. I'm trying to give him the benefit of the doubt hoping that he will either call or just stop by unexpectedly. You never know with Johnnie. I'm contemplating whether to call the police and report him missing. It seems like I have no other alternative.

I yell out, "Johnnie, wherever you are know that I love you!" I pick up the phone and simultaneously the buzzer goes off. A rush zooms through my bloodstream as I walk towards the intercom.

"Hello."

"Ms. Avery Love, please?" The man asks.

"Yes, this is she. How do you know my name? Who are you?"

"I'm a lawyer representing Johnnie Rivera. My name is Byren Clausen." The man says in a soft tone.

"How can I help you, Mr. Clausen?" I ask as my eyes water.

"Ms. Love, I have something to deliver to you from Mr. Rivera."

"Please, come up."

After I buzz Mr. Clausen in I stand in front of the door with my knees buckling. Seconds later, there stands a Caucasian man with salt-n-pepper tapered hair. He has a well-groomed mustache, thin-framed glasses which enhance his bluer, than blue eyes. Facially, he has thin wrinkles around the creases of his eyes and mouth. He looks to be in his late forties or going into his early fifties. He has on an expensive suit. Mr. Clausen greets me with a smile.

"Ms. Love?"

Haltingly I say, "Yes."

I invite him in.

"Mr. Clausen, would you like anything to drink?" My eyes roam the apartment.

"No, thank you, Ms. Love."

I move the blanket and pillow off the sofa and invite him to have a seat. He sits down and places his briefcase on the end table and opens it. I sit down on the sofa with my legs crossed stiff as a rock. Fidgeting, I fold my arms, and then my hands as if I am back in preschool, afraid to look Mr. Clausen in his eyes. So I blankly look at the window and listen.

"Ms. Love, I know this may be a bit of a surprise having me come to your home. Johnnie advised me to do it this way. I apologize for any inconvenience this may cause." Mr. Clausen's eyes cut to the side as if he feels uncomfortable.

"Mr. Clausen, is...Um, is Johnnie okay?"

"Ms. Love. Mr. Rivera has died. He had pneumonia."

He touches my hand and then shuts his eyes for what seems like a quick second.

I go ballistic, jumping to my feet, running rampantly around my apartment, completely lost. I fall, get up, fall again, scream, cry, and scream again. My body tightens, teeth grinding, gritting, rainstorms pouring down like hail balls, and then dropping to my feet. I hold my chest that has tightened, hugging my skin, pulling my skin, pinching my skin, digging my nails into my skin, biting my lips, tightening my lips, pulling my hair almost from its root and shouting! "BLOODY MURDER!" The news echoes. It's earth shattering to my mind, body, and soul.

There are wails of screams. "NO...NO...NO!

NO...NOT JOHNNIE, NOT MY JOHNNIE! Please tell me there has been a mistake, please tell me it isn't so... Please. NO, NO, NO! WHY, WHY, WHY! LORD. WHY HIM?!   NO,   NO,   NO! JJJJJOOOOHHHHHNNNNIIIIEEEE!"

Mr. Clausen sits in silence. He listens to me mourn my loss. The look on his face shows empathy. I try to restrain my open wounds by lifting myself off the floor and dragging my feet back towards the sofa, sitting down as I hug myself tightly hearing him out. I murmur Johnnie's name. Tears run down my drained face.

"Ms. Love, you have my deepest condolences. Johnnie considered you to be his family. He loved you very deeply and talked quite frequently of you."

Mr. Clausen looks into my eyes and does not blink. Tears roll down as I wipe my stained face with the back of my hand. I smear it with the tail end of my shirt. My nerves are frazzled. Words release from my mouth in a stutter.

"MMr. CClausen, wwhen aand wwhere ddid hhe ddie bbecause II ccalled aall tthe hhospitals iin hhis aarea?"

"Johnnie died Thursday, July 29th, at around 10:40 p.m. in the company of Mr. Javis Cline, a friend of his. He died at Mr. Cline's residence in Philadelphia."

"OOh, sso tthat wwas wwhy tthe hhospitals hhad nno rrecord oof hhim." I raise my feet onto the sofa and clench my knees.

"Yes, he gave Mr. Cline a follow-up on what needed to be done and who to contact. He's requesting to be cremated and advised Mr. Cline which funeral home to notify because he had already made pre-arrangements upon his death. Mr. Cline called me yesterday and I decided instead of sending you a letter I would come in person because Johnnie was also a close friend of mine."

"TThank YYou, MMr. CClausen. II rreally aappreciate yyou ttaking tthe ttime oout ffor mme."

I try to smile, but it hurts.

"You're very welcome. All the information for the memorial service is enclosed in this envelope. There is something else I have to give you." He reaches into his briefcase and pulls out a folder with two envelopes.

"Ms. Love, one envelope contains a letter personally written by Mr. Rivera and the other envelope advises that you are his primary beneficiary." He hands me the two envelopes.

I bat my eyes.

"II'm JJohnnie's pprimary bbeneficiary?"

"Yes, he chose you Ms. Love, to be his primary beneficiary," he says nodding his head in confirmation.

I sigh in disbelief.

"BBut...BBut...MMr. CClausen, JJohnnie hhad AAIDS. Nno iinsurance ccompany wwould ccover hhim." I say, still flustered.

"Yes, you are absolutely correct, no insurance company would provide coverage if he tried to get coverage after becoming infected. But Mr. Rivera, had coverage prior to becoming infected." Mr. Clausen touches his chin with his right hand and nods.

"OOhh."

"Mr. Rivera started a policy back when he was eighteen and continued to allow it to grow. He had big dreams and felt that whoever received this money should be able to fulfill their dreams. This is his way of saying thank you for being there."

"WWhat about his ffamily, Mr. CClausen?"

Mr. Clausen talks around my question.

"Johnnie considered you to be his only family." He closes his briefcase. "Well, Ms. Love, I have other engagements I must meet. Unfortunately I wish our meeting was under more pleasant circumstances, please take care." He stands with his briefcase in hand.

"Thank You, Mr. Clausen." I stand, pull my shirt tail down, take a deep breath, and walk him to the door. We shake hands and he leaves.

Closing the door feels like closing the door on

my life. Johnnie is a big part of it. I feel sick inside. I walk intently to the bathroom looking into the mirror with beet red eyes. Wiping away tears, I lower my head, turning on the faucet, leaning over as my face nearly kisses the sink. I rinse my face with cold water drifting as the water splashes onto the floor wetting my bare feet. I exit the bathroom consciously leaving the water running. I hear it running but I don't have the energy to go and turn it off. My eyes slightly blur and I have to use my hands to pat the sides of the narrow wall down the hallway leading to my bedroom. My body's shaky. I fall onto the bed releasing screams of anguish.

"Why? Johnnie. He's all I had. All I needed. Why! My motivation. My reason for surviving. Lord, what am I supposed to do? What? I miss you Johnnie. Come back! Come back and I will care for you. Please come back! Don't leave me alone! I can't live without you. Jesus, help me! Please? I have no reason to live. There is no one left. Please, Lord? Why does it hurt so much? I can't cope with not having you with me, Johnnie. I should have been with you. If God called you to go home at least you would have been in my arms while I held you."

My fingers stand erect at the ceiling and my face wrinkles, my eyes droop, and my lips tighten, as I try to hold back the storm of tears. My eyes darken.

I yell out, "You never gave me the opportunity to console you, Johnnie! Why? The one thing I could've done." I stand and throw my arms up in the air resentful. I am cussing and fussing at him as if he was right there in the room with me. "You...you... took our friendship and stomped the hell out of it and gave it to someone else. Like, I didn't have any goddamn feelings. Like, I was some stranger in your life. Why?" I bow my head.

"Johnnie, I've failed you as a friend."

I sit down and hold my head between my thighs, running my fingers through my thick hair. Solid as a rock I stay in that position for what seems like twenty minutes. Faintly, I hear music coming from the living room. I stand, still unstable, and walk out of the bedroom. The closer to the living room I get, the clearer the music becomes. I hear India Arie, but I know that I have not turned the CD player on. *Maybe it's the radio*, I think. As I walk towards the CD player I can clearly see that the CD is playing. I am afraid. Is it possible? Can it really be Johnnie? *Is it you?* The flickering of the living room lamp startles me. My eyes widen with skepticism. I fall to the floor, and cower in the corner near the door as tears fall from my beet red eyes. Tears continue to fall as my fingertips affix my skin, wiping the snot from underneath my nose before it touches my lips. Suddenly, a woody scent lingers in the closed quarters and warmth surrounds me. Goosebumps scatter upon my arms. Dry lips crack and sting in each crease from the moisture of my saliva. I bite my nails. *Is it you, Johnnie?* A strong presence emerges. I feel hot air being blown in my face. My eyes water as I steady the room. This forceful energy draws me in. Unfamiliarity takes me under its spell. I am no longer afraid, more like at peace. My head hangs low in dismay. *Why is this happening?* I know that there's a reason for everything, but why now? Life is just starting to be fulfilling.

My stomach growls from hunger and my head's pounding in agony. I lift my body up off the floor and walk over and sit on the sofa peeping at the two envelopes that lay on the end table. Finally, I pick up the one from Johnnie. My hands are sweaty, ripping the seams as I slowly pull the letter out. I can't help but to start crying and I haven't even started reading, yet. I unfold it carefully and position myself on the sofa.

July 29th, 2008 10:22p.m.

Hey Beautiful,

Wipe away those tears, Love.
I'm sure you are in distress at this very moment. I wish that I could be there to console all the pain away, but

unfortunately I can't. I don't want you to stress about me because I'm free. Free from pain and suffering, free from abandonment from my family and friends. Free from discrimination of those whom do not know me by my first name. It was hell living in a world of confusion and corrupt small-minded people. This world is ruthless. I am the same person I was before I became ill. And those who truly know me know that I would never do anything to jeopardize their well-being. It is not in my character. Please don't consume yourself with things that you cannot change. I am always there for you in spirit. Trust me when I say I know exactly how it feels to be alone, and feeling trapped within concealment. Life is for the taking, exploring, learning, teaching, and living.

Love, live your life with fulfillment. I know that we haven't had much time to discuss what you are going through in your life. I just want you to know that I already know life hasn't been very kind to you. You've been carrying a burden on your shoulders for too long and now I must help release that burden. You're probably wondering what I'm talking about. Well, I know that you were raped. You're probably wondering how I found out. Well, that's not important. The important thing is that you are okay. I could see something different in you when you came to visit me. But I did not feel the need to lecture you or make you discuss it with me. It is difficult enough trying to accept it, let alone having someone else preach to you. That is definitely not my style. Many days and nights I felt like I wanted to pick up the phone and call you, but something deep inside of me said, "Give her some time to allow this to absorb." Oh, it is a hefty load to carry, I'm sure. Fear sets in, emptiness, feeling hollowed as if nothing matters anymore. Living with AIDS is no different. There were many days when I felt like taking my own life, but God assured me that I would be missing out on a lot of things. I questioned. Yes, I questioned God asking, what kind of life is this? Having to take multiple medications on a daily basis, disinfecting everything I touched because I felt insecure, afraid to use public bathrooms because of my own issues. I had panic attacks because I felt alienated by the world for judging me because I have AIDS and because I'm gay. I enjoyed the company of a man who made me laugh, cry, and made love to me passionately. Punish me because I am only human. I did nothing wrong! I played by the book and later I got burned because I fell in love. I wasn't a whore who just slept around for kicks. We shared a life together, which I thought was based on faithfulness and again in life sometimes we are blind by love. I am a victim of that. I have lived a life of honesty and integrity and I can die with dignity. Dignity!

Listen, sweetie, you have to be strong and find your calling in this life. If you surrender your body it will weaken and you will deteriorate to nothing in a moment's time. Oh, I remember when I first saw you standing there looking polished from head-to-toe. I said, "Now, that is a woman with style, class, and sophistication all rolled up in one. Fierce!" You are beautiful inside and out. It is time to explore as you stated when we were at the park that night, explore and find true love. Love is waiting for you to step out and venture forth. Venture at your own pace. I know that it is easier said than done, but it is possible. There is true love in this world. Life can still be fulfilling as long as you take care of yourself. Stay away from negativity and remain positive, no matter what. Don't burden yourself with drama of men who are not willing to give you 110% because you are worth all the riches in the world. In times of drama, honey, dismiss and keep on steppin'.

I'll continuously look out for you and when you need to talk I'll be listening. Please, know that I am okay. Do me a favor and promise me that you will do your best to be happy. I have a surprise for you! I'm sure there is something that you've always wanted to do, go, or just wanted for yourself. I want you to finally have it. I know that you quit your job and I'm sure it is a burden trying to make ends meet so this is my way of saying, thank you. Thank you for being here for me. Thank you for listening, talking, crying, and holding me. Thank you for understanding and standing strong with me. Don't allow

that horrific experience to stifle you. Control your life until you stop living, you deserve more than that. You owe it to yourself to fight for happiness. Love, you're going to have to thicken your skin and go for yours. Confidence is the key. You used to be the queen of "confidence" back in the day. Thinking about it makes me laugh. I hope I was able to bring a smile to your face. Keep smiling, living, and searching for your destiny. It waits for your entrance. I thank God everyday for bringing us together as one. In my heart we will always be as one.
I love you,
Johnnie

I can't stop sniffling, tears roll so quickly down my face and onto the letter. I reach for the other envelope and tear it open. I pull out a check in the amount of one hundred thousand dollars. I shiver like a leaf, feeling as though I am about to go into convulsions. Internally I'm bleeding because the pain is so devastating. I let out a scream that could have made the whole building shake like an earthquake. *Oh, my God! Johnnie! Johnnie!* My fingers interweave in the kinks of my hair. Depression thinly layers my psyche making me feel like I need a dose of Prozac to calm down, but the need only instigates and I pulsate with rage. Tossing throw pillows, breaking the center glass of the bi-level coffee table with a sculpture, breaking the Mikasa crystal by throwing it at the decorative mirror. I knock down the wooden vases with silky long stemmed tulips and smash two lavender ceramic table lamps on the floor. They splatter into big and tiny fragments. I fling a picture of Johnnie against the shelf doors of my CD holder cracking the glass. *What am I doing! God help me, please? Help me, please?* I fall to my knees and lay my wounded body on the floor and weep.

Never in a million years could I have ever thought of receiving this amount of money. Johnnie thought of *me* on his deathbed. In his last moments, he took time to write *me* a letter. I tighten my lips and press my right hand against my chest, feeling the throbbing beats of my heart that squash against the cavity of my chest.

The tears become less as I think about how grateful I am to have had a best friend who loved me so much. But I still wish I had the opportunity of properly saying, "See you later." I wanted to be able to hold him, comfort him as he shut his eyes to go to sleep, never awakening again. Johnnie was so considerate of my feelings, knowing my secret and never divulging a word of it. Thinking about it now makes me feel guilty about lying to my best friend. The worst part of it is that he knew all along, at least part of it. It makes me realize how fear can make things so complex. But Johnnie took the burden off of me so that I could move forward. Johnnie definitely was one of a kind. More like an angel in disguise.

Seven

GONE ASTRAY, with no desire, will, or fuel left in this pathetic body to face the music of gloom. I dread the rendition of "see you later," as if it were a Broadway play. I wish it was a dream that I could somehow awaken from with Johnnie standing before me. Oh, how I long to hear his voice, touch his hand, listen to him sing, or smell his body scent. Losing him feels like a piece of my soul has parted down a stream. It's difficult to absorb—to move forward. And I honestly don't know where to start, but I owe it to myself and Johnnie to at least give it a try. God, I miss him so much.

Going to his memorial service I fear will only exhibit my anguish for all to view. Johnnie won't have a viewing because he requested to be cremated. After which, he wants his ashes to be sprinkled out of a helicopter over New York City. *Only Johnnie would request something so extraordinary.* He is the only one capable of building my nerve up to actually walk inside that funeral home. I start scratching, trying to fake myself out like I just broke out in hives. It's not working. Then I look at my skin and caress it as if I am stroking Johnnie's face. *Damn.* I hold my head down, sulking knowing that I have no other option. I have to go. Go and express with my deepest condolences and say, "See you later," with respect. I can't very well let Johnnie down a third time.

Bitterness chisels a deep incision in my mouth. Infuriation smolders my thoughts of Johnnie's family because he could've been in Harlem instead of dying in Philly. But no, no one wanted to open up their arms and welcome him in. They all showed him their backs. Thick mucus slings at his mom. I feel no guilt. She gave birth to him and regardless of his life preference—he was still her son. *How dare she?* How in the hell can a mother abandon her flesh and blood because he's not living up to her standards? She always said that he was living a life of sin. "God made women and men for a reason and he went against all that was moral." Yep. That's what she used to say to him. I never knew that love has a nametag on it. Who's to say whom you'll fall in love with? She was way out of line. But I never confronted her. It's not my place and plus Johnnie had no problem speaking his mind.

Empathy engrosses my person and I can only plead from within that everyone who attends will express their sympathy and take their dramatic, nosy, phony, chit chattering, whispering asses home. And I will scream if anyone asks the stupidest question about if his lover is present. I will scream bloody murder with bulging eyes and my middle finger pointing towards the door. But hopefully I won't have to go there. I hope those who come to pay their respects will act in a civilized manner.

I mope around all morning, smelling the sourness from under my armpits and between my legs. My mouth has a tart taste and my face has dry pieces of dead skin dangling. Contrary to my usual morning regimen, I don't want to move to even wash my own stank ass. Even my insides are redolent of death. I'm trying to waste time before I have to accept the unacceptable. I don't feel that I have the strength to do it. But I have no choice.

It's now 9:30 a.m. and I still haven't moved. I know that I need to get up. I lift one leg out of bed and then the other, finally standing somewhat unbalanced, feeling sick to my stomach because I haven't eaten since early yesterday. The smell of food repulses my nostrils. I walk into the kitchen, untwisting the potato bread and grabbing a slice. I pull small pieces at a time while standing, pausing in between as each bite takes me a few minutes to swallow. I have to force it down with a small glass of Perrier sparkling water. It seems like an eternity getting that one slice of bread down. I'm indecisive of what to wear as I walk back into the bedroom. Skimming through my closet I search for the proper attire and then choose my black pantsuit and purse to match. Searching through my Ashley red oak dresser I reach for my undergarments. I kneel down to look underneath my bed for my black heels, I head for the bathroom, entering, and turning the nozzle of the shower and allowing the water to spout out and fill the bathroom with steam. I pull off my layers of sourness and throw them in the dirty hamper as if I am Michael Jordan shooting hoops. The mirror is so fogged up that I don't even want to take a look at myself. I put my feet into the shower and watch little beads of water scatter upon them. I lather, the tiny soap bubbles foam into white cotton balls all bunched together. I stand under the showerhead and let the water line my back. My body is so tense. Exhaustion consumes me like I have just ran a marathon. I'm filled with so much grief. I don't want to say, "See you later," to Johnnie. I selfishly want him here with me laughing, talking, hugging me, and loving me as he did so generously. My emotions take over and I feel as if I am going to lose it, but I suppress my feelings. I won't know what to do, how to feel, or what to say once I get there. An uneventful moment recaptures scarred wounds, a reminder of when I had to bury my parents. I become disgusted, turn off the water, step out of the shower and towel dry. I haul my feet into the bedroom and get dressed.

I look myself over twice before I walk towards the door, and grab my keys off the key hook. Opening the door to the building the world seems to have changed into an unknown world. Everything is different at this very moment.

Once I arrive at Heaven's Gatte Funeral Home on Market Street, I see that the parking lot is full to capacity. I take several deep breaths before opening my car door. The surroundings are desolate with only the clicking of my shoes to be heard. I pause. Then I walk slow as running molasses to the front entrance door, gripping my fingers around the door handle. My feet are like cement, I can't move. Finally, I do. Scents of peppermint, rosemary, lavender, and fresh pine splash all in my face. Flowers accentuate the lobby. I track the rug, pacing, before I enter the closed doors. I finally say, "Avery, this is it," and open the door. Slowly, I lift my head to see many faces, but none of which are familiar. I sit in the back row looking over; still not seeing a familiar face. A program is on the floor near my feet, quite apparently I am in the wrong room about to express my "see you later," to a total stranger. Quietly, I rise and start to pace again. Johnnie's in the room farther down the corridor. The corridor is so long and the walls seem to be closing in on me. Hyperventilation is stirring up inside, but I manage to restrain myself. Pulling the door open and stepping one foot at a time I lift my head and open my eyes, viewing only a young man in the first row. I exhale and walk towards a book with bold print, dated, August 3, 2008. There's only one signature, Javis Cline. *He was with Johnnie when he died.* I sign my name underneath his and sit down quietly. My blood's starting to stew because his family is not present. His so-called friends are not present. There's a sterling silver urn on top of a polished maplewood table. An 8x10 picture sits with tall, long stemmed, red roses on each side. Johnnie has a smile that brightens up the room. Buried deep within me I feel shame for his parents, siblings, so-called friends, and his lover who abandoned him. Staring into space, tears fall like quarter-sized raindrops. In my mind I'm furious. *Those selfish, good-for-nothing... They couldn't even find it within themselves to at least come and pay their last respects.* I want to punch something, but I keep my composure. I move closer to the front row and sit right across from Mr. Cline. He glances over. I smile and nod to say hello. I'm prudently looking over at him trying to get a better view. He looks to be in his mid-thirties, with evenly tanned Caucasian skin. His brunette hair has a glazed shine with an enhanced dapper mustache. He has a goatee, and he's very well dressed as his shoes shine complementing his charcoal gray suit. He looks as if he has a membership at the nail salon because his hands look very well groomed. His eighteen-karat gold watch sparkles with diamonds as it rests on his wrist. I can't detect the color of his eyes and it bothers me. Looking in his eyes can tell me if he's sincere or not. I want confirmation. I need it for myself. Knowing that Johnnie was in good hands could uplift some of the burden off of my shoulders and heart.

I turn to look towards the door hoping that it will swing open and a flock of folks will enter. Unfortunately, that never happens. A few minutes' later Mr. Cline stands and walks toward the table. He unbuttons his three-button suit jacket, and begins to speak with an Italian accent.

"We are gathered here in memory of our dear friend Johnnie. All of us will miss him dearly."

Javis holds his head high and speaks as if the room is full of folks.

The room is packed like jammed sardines with folks shoving for elbowroom. Little children running around while their moms and dads are fussing for them to sit down and be quiet. There are three elderly women crying, as they'd dab their eyes with their hankies. The men sat still listening while friends held back their tears, smiling to shade their pain. While the teenagers talk amongst themselves, whispering and giggling. Close cousins unable to stomach the pain scream loudly as they are escorted out. There are many tearful eyes, swollen with redness. Johnnie's mom straps her body to the table, palming the urn, crying hysterically for her baby dying before her and then falling to the floor, as his brothers and sisters all huddle around her trying to lift her up and carry her broken soul out. She faints and they all sob in mourning. It's surreal, but real as I envision the way it should be to soothe the emptiness in the room.

"My name is Javis Cline and I met Johnnie through a mutual friend. We connected right away because he was genuine and full of life. I can honestly say that he was one of a kind." Javis smiles.

"The night that Johnnie died he told me that he felt blessed and that he appreciated me being there. One tear slowly rolled down the side of Johnnie's face and he smiled. His face glowed and he whispered softly, 'I'm ready to go home, Javis.' I couldn't believe it was happening. I held his warm hands and they slowly turned cold. He closed his eyes as if he was falling asleep and he smiled this incredible smile that lit up the room."

Javis tightens his lips trying to hold back his tears. He wipes his eyes.

My chin begins to shake and waterfalls form in my eyes. I search for a tissue in my purse, dabbing the corners before they fell.

"Johnnie Rivera will truly be missed. I'll miss him. He was like a brother to me."

Javis's voice stammers.

It cuts through me like a sharp knife. I moan and groan in my seat wanting to regurgitate all the pain inside. Yowls echo from the pit of my stomach and I quickly place my hands to my mouth. My body stiffens as Javis continues to express his deepest sorrows. He becomes emotional, wiping the tears with the back of his hand. *His eyes are brown.* He has a look of trustworthiness and it makes me feel more at ease. Johnnie's definitely in good hands. Javis sits down as the music begins to play from the overhead speakers. It's Johnnie's favorite song, "Purify Me" by India Arie. An enormous amount of despair overcomes me and I wail with grief, rocking back and forth in my seat. The hands of a man reaches out to me and we stand and hold each other tight. The man is stroking my hair gently. I bury my head in his chest and smell Polo Black. He reminds me of Johnnie. The man's mint breath welcomes me as he whispers in my ear, "let it all out." His voice soothes me as he gently massages my back. I look up and realize that the man is Javis. I hold him tight as if I am holding Johnnie. Deeply looking into his eyes I feel warmth and empathy. He hands me his silk handkerchief and we both sit in a moment of silence. My sniffles echo. Javis reaches for my hand and interlocks his fingers with mine. *This is something Johnnie would have done.* I close my eyes seeing Johnnie's face, seeing his smile, and hearing his voice as if he's right here.

I love you, Johnnie.

Javis and I sit for a few more minutes and then he stands and walks towards the table, picks up the urn, and turns to give me the look that it's time. Time to go and make Johnnie's request a reality. I slowly rise to my feet. We walk out of the back door of the funeral home and Javis says that he will drive his car to the location near Teterboro Airport in Teterboro, New Jersey. We're both silent, just the music is playing. When we arrive at the destination we hear a helicopter, but cannot see it. Within minutes it's visible as it circulates the dust in our faces. Our arms rise shielding our eyes and our hair blows in the wind. The helicopter lands and Javis opens the door. I step in first and greet the pilot. I reach for the urn while Javis gets in and shuts the door. *Johnnie's in my hands.* I am scheming, wanting to keep him, but I know that I can't. Johnnie never specified where he wants to be, so Javis and I decide Central Park. I have sentimental reasons as to why but Javis just goes along with it. Finally reaching our destination, Javis opens the door, says a few words, as do I and then turns the urn upside down. Johnnie's ashes dance on air, freely. Johnnie's free from all the pain he endured. Free from being judged for his lifestyle. Free from having AIDS. He's a child of God that was never neglected or abandoned. He's loved unconditionally. I understand more than I could ever imagine. Johnnie's free. Javis turns and looks at me. His eyes express comprehension and we connect for that moment. My mind drifts. I can see Johnnie reciting his poem. I see the look on his face when strangers listened attentively to his words, some in relevance and others touched by his profoundness. That will always remain with me. It's always the simple things that Johnnie did that make me realize what I want in a man. Johnnie always expressed one very important fact, to never short change myself. He wanted me to seek out and *I* find happiness. My mind's a million miles away, blocking all that is insignificant. I vaguely hear Javis ask, "Are you okay?" his eyes heat my skin.

I come to.

"Did you say something, Javis?" I turn looking him in his brown eyes.

"Are you okay?"

"Oh, yes, I am."

"You seemed to have been in another world," he says as he overlaps his hand on mine.

"Javis, I was briefly, but thanks for asking." I smile.

E<small>IGHT</small>

BUNDLES OF SOILED clothing overflow out of the bathroom hamper. The bathtub has a dirt ring around it. There are streaks of black markings on the kitchen floor. Papers lay scattered upon the end table, sofa, and on top of the TV. Tiny dust balls are bunched up on the floor. Caked up food is stuck to the pots and food particles are clinging to the dishes and utensils. One week old sheets spread over the mattress. An untidy bed needs making. Clothes need to be picked up off the floor. I am in no condition to clean up. I lie on the sofa and look around the living room and find one of my black shoes by the front door and the other is leaned on its side by the sofa. I have on the same clothes from two days ago. A half-empty bottle of Alizè, White Zinfandel, and Sangria sits on the end table with an unopened bottle of Chardonnay in the ice bucket, and a wine glass has rolled underneath the table.

I got pissy drunk. The severity of my best friend dying was too great. I must've collapsed on the sofa in a deep slump of mourning. Knowing full well that come the next day I would be smacked in the face with reality as I sobered up. I didn't care. I didn't want to feel anything. I wanted no more pain.

My head is throbbing, clanking, kicking, punching, stomping, as I awake at 5:30 a.m. There is a deep sensation of inebriation circulating throughout my body. A potent whiff of odor bypasses my nose as it scrunches up making my stomach want to puke my guts out. I am barely able to move my intoxicated body and each time I try to grasp the back of the sofa to pull up I slip back into my imprinted spot. I bury my fingers into the leather and persistently try to pull myself up, sitting there for a few moments waiting for the room to stop spinning. Unsteady, I stand. Feet are tailgating as I slowly walk into the kitchen to check the garbage, but it's not that. Dawdling, I check the mousetrap in back of the refrigerator, but the trap is empty. I huff when I shove up the kitchen window and stick my head out thinking that it might have been a garbage truck nearby and possibly the odor has seeped through the window, but there is no truck. The smell of rottenness filters throughout the entire apartment. It sickens me. I reach into the cabinet to get a can of Lysol disinfectant and spray profusely, but the odor lingers. I light six sage and tobacco flower scented candles in the living room and the fragrance from the candles and the odor combined just sicken me even more. *I need to get out of this house.* I decide to go to the park and unwind.

I go back into the kitchen and walk into the closet to get my cooler. I open the freezer and reach for the bag of ice and empty it into the cooler. Then I open the refrigerator and reach for three spring waters and put them inside, I grab a magazine, blanket, and pillow. I take a shower and squeeze into my worn-out looking Paris Blues jeans and coral T-shirt. Massaging my scalp with jojoba oil I push my hair back with a headband and open the door to head out.

As I wait for the elevator, I am pleading with God that I will never drink like a fish again if He will take the spinning, nausea, and headache away. My hangover is my punishment. I haven't drunk any type of alcohol in so long that I got tipsy right away. I get on the elevator and lean against the back wall.

Outside I click the remote for the trunk to open and put the cooler in the corner, along with the rest of the items, and then drive up to Garrett Mountain Park in West Paterson. I catch sight of a police officer on a horse hiding behind a bush trying to catch speeders. I watch couples holding hands walking along side by side. Children run and play, and fly kites. Men are challenging each other to games of basketball. I park my car, and pop open the trunk to get the blanket, pillow, magazine, and small cooler. I find a good spot and make myself comfortable under a large shaded tree. Relaxed, I flip through my "O" magazine until I come across an article about relationships. It grasps my attention right away because the men are talking about how they met the love of their lives. They speak about how they consider their women to be their partners. I am really into the article when I hear a deep, sexy, baritone voice.

"Excuse me, Ms., you happen to have any water in your cooler?" his eyes are glued to me, waiting for a response.

I look up and say, "Yes, I do."

"Sorry for interrupting you, I just spilled some mustard on my shirt and I wanted to try and get the spot out before it set." The man seems a bit embarrassed.

I reach into the cooler and grab a bottle of spring water and hand it to him. He places the bottle on his blanket and pulls off his shirt. I can't help but ease my eyes to look at his body. My eyes enlarge. His chest is chiseled with rippling dark skin. His body is a piece of art. His baldhead accentuates his strong features and his mustache adds definition to his face. I figure he's about six feet and possibly in his early forties. He's in excellent shape, no potbelly, and strong tight stallion legs, nice pumped up biceps, and to top it off he has all of his teeth. His feet look like he frequently gets pedicures. *Huh, I am very impressed.*

"Where are my manners, my name is Blu McDowell. Excuse me Ms., I don't even know if you're married, have a boyfriend, if he's here with you or not. Here I am invading your space. Forgive me." He kneels down hiding his charcoal-colored knees in the green grass.

"I'm Avery Love. Unfortunately, I'm not that fortunate to be married," I say as I lay my magazine on my lap and gaze into his walnut black eyes.

Blu extends his hand and our palms grip. It breaks that awkward feeling. We are now on a first name basis.

"Blu, your name is very unique."

"Yeah, I hear that all the time. It was my mom's

favorite color." He smiles with a reminiscing look on his face.

"Avery, your name is different, but I like it."

His perfectly arched thick brow rises as he strokes his chin.

Initially I am distracted but then I come to and promptly speak to keep the rhythm flowing.

"Yes, it is definitely different. Unfortunately, I don't know why Poppa chose the name."

"What do you do for a living, Blu?" I ask.

"I'm self-employed. I have a home-based company in Graphic Design. I also do photography as a hobby." He wipes the mustard off his shirt.

"What about you, Avery?"

He lifts his head up and looks me straight in the eye. I stall for a brief moment. The look on my face is a dead giveaway that I am caught off guard.

"Well, right now I'm...um...um...unemployed. I'm taking some time to figure out what I want to do as far as a career. I was a paralegal at one point in time." I feel ashamed so I lower my head.

"Avery, you are soul searching for that passion that lies beneath."

"Yes, but I haven't found that niche as of yet."

"Don't rush it, it will come in due time." He smiles showing off his deep dimples.

Our conversation has become compromised. We don't disclose our life histories.

"Avery, you seem very mysterious, but I find that to be attractive," he says as he invites himself onto my blanket.

I blush.

Blu seems to be genuine, constantly looking deeply into my eyes when he speaks. There is instant chemistry. I am a little awkward, because he is staring at me but I don't turn away because that would be rude.

"I love your hair," he continues. "You know everyone can't wear their hair short and natural. You are a very confident woman, I can tell."

Blu nods his head three times and makes some

kind of humming sound, muuuumhummmm. He reminds me of Ma'am when he does that because when she felt she was right, she would make a humming sound afterwards.

I blush, again.

Blu is intriguing. We talk about the article that I am reading. We seem to have different views, but the one thing that we do agree upon is compromising in relationships. It's getting late so I talk about packing up and heading home. Blu opens his black backpack and pulls out a business card. On the back he writes a phone number. My cheeks are within the red family shade. It has been sometime since a man has even looked my way. I feel slightly attractive.

As I reach for the card I say, "Blu, I will call you near the weekend." I gather my belongings.

"Okay, I will be looking forward to your call, Avery."

He picks up his shirt and stretches it over his head.

As I walk away, Blu calls out my name, so I stop, turn around and stand with an innocent, girly look on my face.

"Get home safely," he says sitting on his blanket and stretching his body out. I take a deep breath, smile again, and start walking towards my car.

I am beaming on my way home. I know that first impressions are not always what they seem, but I feel hopeful that Blu is a man who follows his words. My judgment of character is a bit stale so I have to count on my better judgment before I make a huge leap of faith. Man, I really wish that Johnnie were here because he could sense a dog from a mile away. I just don't wanna get hurt. Having my guard up too high will only scare a good man off and having it down too low will only leave room for someone to break my fragile heart. I decide not to concern myself with it. Blu and I have just met. As long as he does what he says he does and means the words that he speaks, I'll be fine. We'll be fine. I'm not asking for too much, at least I don't think I am.

I arrive home around 8:45 p.m., hoping the stinky odor is gone from my apartment. As soon as I open the door I can still smell it, but it's not as fragrant as before. I open all the windows, kick off my shoes, and go into the kitchen to get a strawberry Ensure. In the bedroom I lay on my bed deep in thought.

The foul odor finally dissipates. I still don't know where it came from, but I hope it doesn't come back. I watch a little TV while drinking that same can of strawberry Ensure.

Mugginess is stagnant in my apartment and I know that it is going to make it difficult to sleep tonight. I stack my pillows and put them at the foot of the bed, closer to the window so a breeze can stroke my face and arms. I place my fan on medium to cool the rest of my body down. It's so hot that the bedroom walls are even moist. I set my clock and wrap a silk scarf around my head, still thinking. It's time for me to get positive, cease the stressing, and try and give an honest effort towards happiness. It's time for a self-makeover.

I reflect back to the way I used to be. Damn. My shallow ass was a sight to be seen. I was selfish most of my life. I didn't show concern for anyone. I remember three years ago when a woman at the job family was burned out their home around Thanksgiving time and the office was collecting donations: clothes, money, shoes, and coats. Someone had approached me asking if I wanted to donate anything. I responded by saying, "Donate! I ain't no Thrift Shop." When the boy across the street was riding his bike a car hit him. I looked out the window seeing him stretched out in the middle of the street and I mumbled under my breath, *he should have been watching where he was going and wearing a helmet, dummy* and I shut my window. When this homeless man asked me for some change, I went ballistic responding, "You want some change, how about changing your lifestyle and *GET A JOB,* change that!" When people died it never fazed me because I didn't know them. If someone was ill it never distressed me and I didn't find it necessary to ask if that person needed anything. Those caring feelings were never in me. I could have cared less.

Up until I met Johnnie it never mattered unless my name was mentioned. I was a selfish, heartless, cold and callus, prissy bitch. Even when Poppa died I cried, but I didn't feel I released a cry of sorrow. It was more of a sigh of relief because *I* could not stand to see him like that everyday. He slowly reduced down to a skeletal frame, eyes wide, face sunk in, and his bodily functions malfunctioned. He was decomposing and the foulness lingered from his breath as I leaned in to kiss him. And in my mind I was kissing him "goodbye" still bitter about my past. I was livid and deep within I didn't care if he died. He hurt me deeply. And when I looked at him it was a constant reminder that he soon would be leaving. He was stabilized with morphine to ease his pains and it put him in a comatose state. Seeing him weak, helpless, and the look on his face defined what he was feeling within, lonely. The same feeling I had been introduced to when he kicked me out. Cancer was eating him up. That was the first time I'd ever seen Poppa weak. He could not speak with his words of wisdom, book educated he was not, but his life experiences would entrance one to listen to his stories. I interlocked my fingers with his and it seemed to connect us for a brief moment. His hands were cold as his breath was hot. He was burning up inside as if he were about to combust. I traced the scar on the right side of his head where his tumor resided, softly stroking light as a feather as his eyes remained closed. His chest lifted and paused, lifted and paused erratically. His coloration turned purple. And inside I was gloating. He gripped my fingers tightly as if he were hugging me goodbye. And then he was gone. His spirit rose out of his temple soaring to a better place. At least that's what I hoped. I didn't scream, panic, or lose control. I became a hardened shell. I simply dampened a washcloth and patted his forehead, draped a white sheet over him and played his favorite gospel song by Smokie Norful, "Still Say Thank You." I turned and looked at Ma'am as she was sitting in her recliner, her arms crossed with her fingerprints imprinted on her shoulders rocking back and forth humming a southern hymn. I sucked my teeth and went into the kitchen to make a sandwich. Ma'am was emotionally broken down and after each day, week, month she worsened. Hopelessly lost, she died four months later of a broken heart. I was resentful because she left me all alone. *Old Biddy*! She could've fought those demons that brainwashed her into thinking she was weakened by the loss of her *husband*. Instead she relinquished herself with open arms, having no consideration for *me*. She didn't even ask how I felt, or talked to me about how much she yearned for him. She didn't give me any indication. She didn't give a damn. Just one day she was here and the next day she was gone. I despised her. But looking at a reflection of myself, I'm just like her in a small sort of way. I harbored these feelings for many years, vindictive of those who still had their loved ones around. No one understood what I was going through because I wouldn't let anyone close enough to analyze and come to a resolution to the problems that I was encountering. I'll admit that I used every bit of God's blessings, looks, body, and intelligence to achieve the status quo in men. I had no daddy so I made them my "sugar daddies" without being compensated monetarily. I was seeking revenge on all men because of my ill feelings towards the man who conceived me, and later tossed me to the curb as if I was nobody, nothing. The only one that really made me shed a tear was LoJac and the tears were not for him, the tears were for me. I never wanted to get too close to anyone because everyone I ever really loved was suddenly taken from me. I'd promised myself that the only person I would depend on was me. The material things that I never had, I would purchase just for the sake of knowing that I could afford it.

Ma'am and Poppa could not afford extravagant

things to lavish me with. They did the best that they could to raise me. It was very difficult for Poppa to find work because of his lack of education. Ma'am was a seamstress for a living, hoping to one day own her own boutique, but she took ill and that dream was like sour grapes—bittersweet. Making a difference was important to me. I struggled after being forced to leave home at the age of seventeen. College was a priority. I needed a new surrounding of my own. *Launching a career with high expectations would promote higher growth*, I thought. I wanted it so bad that I could taste it on the tip of my tongue. Busting my ass, meeting deadlines, giving all of my energy to show my capabilities, it was all in the palm of my hands.

It frustrates me now because my life could have been so different. Living the life I should, instead of hibernating, scared to allow folks into my life. Scared that they will turn their noses up and step around me as if I am insignificant. Transparent as they divulge to the world, "Warning, Warning Avery is HIV-POSITIVE!" Amber lights flashing, stating slow down and get the facts. Too many folks are walking blindsided, confused and misinformed. Information is being amplified through billboards, school awareness, television, radio, pamphlets, newspapers, and advocates—products of living proof.

Although I have not screamed out to the world, it's known. My doctor knows; the Image Center knows; my Pharmacist knows. Word of mouth travels and soon everyone who's concerned will know. I am no longer a woman. I am a woman who's HIV-positive and my life expectancy has a question mark. But everyone's life expectancy has that. Everyday folks are walking daily in shoes that fit quite comfortably, until others step in those same shoes that become a size too small. They suffer immensely. It makes me appreciate my life. Loving it unconditionally.

I sit back and think about the abandonment by my loved ones, suppose no one shows up at my wake or funeral service. Yeah, it could happen. I witnessed it in plain view with Johnnie. And I pray that as long as I have air left in my body that will not happen to me. I'm battling with myself. Life and death are dueling. Almost like a tug-of-war with my soul. Death squeezes, twists, all of my inner strength. Life coaches me to *believe* that I feel no pain. That it's a figment of my imagination. That I'm strong-willed. Life builds me up with faith. Life encourages me, while death discourages me. They rumble within my mind and I feel unshielded. I'm angry, weeping in my size eight shoes. If you choose not to touch me, sit next to me, you have that choice. If you choose not to speak, look, or even breathe near me, you have that option. All that I ask is to allow my life to matter. Empathize. It doesn't matter if I'm a stranger or not, 'cause I'm still a human being.

I cannot fathom the thought of my parents not being supportive of me at this point and time in my life, if they were here. In my mind I want to do more to bring some serenity in folk's lives. Release their inner fears, replenish their souls, and educate by telling their stories candidly. I feel the changes flourishing within myself. Take it from someone who has been so shallow transforming into someone who comprehends through the eyes of Johnnie. He has influenced me in such a short time frame. And I feel like I'm ready to explore the world on a higher ground. I want to bring some peace in my life and extend my hands out in support. Support those who are hungry with expression, feeding their souls with the artistry of poetry and nourishing their inner spirits with hopes and promise. All this time I had it in me, that soulfulness. I want to extend my arms like wings and fly towards my sole purpose. I want to be able to reach folks in a profound way. And the bottled up creativity inside me is flowing: the arts, poetry, music, photography, and theater. Everything has hit me all at once so I reach for a pen to write it all down. Thoughts run through my head non-stop. For once I'm enthused about something meaningful. And I feel like it has a lot of substance. I've been feeling empty since Johnnie has been gone and my energy level has been doused to a meaningless drip. Feeling pity for myself, and reflecting on how I feel inside. The enthusiasm that Johnnie has ignited burns out as a gush of wind circulates. I need that push, that persistent motivation that he has delivered, making me feel invincible.

Stretching, as my mouth spreads widely. Mentally I'm exhausted as my eyes blink. I lean back against my pillows, positioning my body into a comfort zone. I am swept into a dream that's vivid. *Johnnie's at the foot of my bed tickling my feet as I awake sitting up against my headboard. He looks healthy like he did when we went to the company Christmas party. He's smiling so happy to see me and I reach out my arms to hold him, but there's no one there. I know he's here. He expresses his thoughts of my idea. I am shocked that he knows what I am thinking. I can see my thoughts become reality as he shows me the final outcome. Everything's in great detail, from the building, to the street name. Everything seems so easy. Confirmation has surfaced. "Love, go for it!" I feel confident with his assurance, trusting in him and mostly in myself. He drifts off in the mist of air as I am still reaching out for him. Reaching, but there's no one there.*

I turn on my side catching a glimpse of a piece of yellow paper dangling on my nightstand. Curious of what it reads, I lengthen my arm and pull it towards me. The handwriting is Johnnie's and it reads *Ground Floor of Flava*, symbolizing the roots of our beings within an atmosphere that's tranquil while inhaling the aroma of flavored gourmet coffee. I smile and my eyes tear up. I look up at the ceiling and say, "thank you." It's not a figment of my imagination. Johnnie was really here in my room. I felt his aura all around me. His scent was alluring. It was real. It was so real!

It's 4:30 a.m. and I'm wide-awake, thinking, thinking about all the inspiration Johnnie has left for me to fulfill. Through his life and death, he still has an amazing influence on me. He had the confidence, the belief from within. He put his best foot forward, exerting all of his energy to confirm what he already knew to be true. Success reeked from his pores and he was always in control of his destiny. He felt; taste, spoke, and most importantly pursued it. I have not known anyone with so much faith. Johnnie came to me for a reason, maybe he sees this idea becoming a success, but I will never know unless I go for it. I can't believe I'm up with all of this weighing heavily on my brain. I guess because I was never the type of person who believed in spirits. It always seemed unrealistic and spooky. The "afterlife" didn't seem sensible. Ma'am and Poppa's spirits never came through so I always believed when you died everything died with you, spirit and all. I felt a lot of bitterness back then and maybe that's why they never came through. Ma'am always used to say that if you talk to spirits they can hear you. I envisioned Ma'am and Poppa in heaven holding hands, walking through the park laughing full of happiness.

I look up at the ceiling with watery eyes and say, "Ma'am, Pop, I love you." This is a profound moment for me because I can't remember the last time I actually told them how I sincerely feel. My heart expands as if it's being pumped with air. A smile spreads over my face because for once I feel the dead skin cells shedding and new skin forming. Underneath I am yearning for the love of another, but for many years I had built a strong wall of protection. My solid walls blocked all whom dared to enter. When the quarters became too close, it was time to bail. And to be candid, I am not convinced that the men in my life will stay. I consciously leave my door ajar, just in case they decide to walk out; the sensation won't be as pungent.

NINE

GOD'S HOUSE used to be my home away from home. I used to be a member of Temple Cross Baptist Church on Giltroy Street. Every Sunday morning I was up with the roosters. And times when Poppa and Ma'am couldn't attend, I would go alone. It never fazed me that I spent so much time in God's house because I felt as if I belonged. Ma'am used to be an usher for several years and Poppa was in the choir. Poppa used to sound like Marvin Sapp. Hmm. I can hear him singing, "You Are God Alone." Everyone loved to hear him sing solo. He often sung in acappella and the whole congregation would be in tears. Poppa was soulful and his voice shook your body because his spirit was powerful. It made him cry. I haven't stepped in Temple Cross Baptist Church in some time.

I remember back in the day, I was eagerly listening to what Reverend Giltroy had to say because his sermons showed relevance to my life. He was an elder man who was the spitting image of Ossie Davis, full of compassion and integrity. His words used to pierce within and the sweat dripped down his face because he released all of his energy for the Sunday service. The choir uplifted spirits as everyone clapped in support. Folks would stand stretching their arms out praising the Lord and inviting Him into their hearts asking to be healed mentally, physically and spiritually. I felt comfortable back then, more at peace. Yes, I belonged.

Eventually things changed when the beloved Reverend Giltroy took ill and later departed to our heavenly Father. Despair climbed upon my shoulders and pushed me down until I stopped walking through His heavenly doors. Depression set in and I returned, but the connection that I once had seemed to dissolve and the volume of His calling drowned out becoming voiceless. Spiritually I was severed in two and a little birdie whispered in my ear, "Trust within to guide you." I traveled from home to home to find my paradise, which was like trying to find a needle in a haystack. It was challenging, discouraging, and I felt powerless. From that day forward I kept God in my heart in my own way. That's not to say, that I won't return back through His doors, I just need to feel at home when I do. I got disgusted by the things that I'd witnessed as a member. Things that didn't add up to me, like hearing folks screaming and shouting as they caught the Holy Ghost when it seemed to be on cue. Church was more of a spotlight for fashion and gossip. The collection plate traveled around in the beginning of service for tithes and offerings. And I used to wonder where the money was going. At times the ceiling was leaking, paint was peeling, stairways were crumbling, the air conditioning wasn't working and the heaters were as cold as the snow on the ground. There were bake sales to raise money as well as rummage sales. I didn't mind giving my ten percent, but it would have been nice to see where the money was going. I couldn't see it, but I could clearly see that the new Pastor was driving around in a spanking new Bentley. I just needed confirmation that my hard-earned money was going towards a cause that was preached so energetically in service. Pastor's sweat dripping armpits, hair dampened, voice hoarse, and the movement of his feet as he caught the Holy Ghost, but nothing was being manifested as far as the upkeep of the church. I quietly left one Sunday with no desire to return. Not through the new Pastor's doors.

Call me old-fashioned, but I need things laid out right in front of me to make me comprehend. If it couldn't be produced then it left me to believe that something was fishy. And that smell was definitely not a pleasant scent. I guess if the Pastor would have attempted to do something maybe I would have been reluctant to leave, but each Sunday seemed worse than the last. And my gut instincts were telling me that I needed to change my sense of direction. I never thought it would be to walk out of those doors and not enter into another home. But to be perfectly honest, I haven't been able to find one to measure up to Reverend Giltroy. I know that I shouldn't compare, but people are just that, people. And if my spirit was not connecting that was a clear signal that I needed to find comfort elsewhere. It just happened to be that I've found it within my heart and these four walls, at least for now.

I will honestly admit that I used to be bitterly angry at God. Yes, it's true. I blamed Him for allowing this to happen to me because I thought we had a good understanding of each other. I was reading the Bible, attending service, giving ten-percent, attending Sunday school, Worship, and anything else, and He in return would protect me. He reneged on His part. I shut Him out of my life after the ordeal and I literally felt my spirit dying. That was when I started hibernating because I thought if He allowed this to happen to me, He wouldn't protect me from anymore harm. My head was spinning and I was so lost within myself. I didn't have anyone that I felt I could trust to divulge my deepest secrets to. Things come back to you when you least expect it, but this was the worst of the worst because I did nothing to deserve it. This horrible person, who brazenly came out of nowhere and destroyed my life because he wanted something he never stood a chance in having, ME! He beat it out of me, and stole my precious gem for his perverted pleasure. And after all that was done, I blamed the Man upstairs for not penetrating through to that animal to acknowledge his weakness and seek help. Apparently, the bastard must've felt as I temporarily felt about Him. He let me down and I could not forgive Him for quite some time. My blinders were shut so that I couldn't even see that even though I shut Him out, He never left my side.

Tⁱⁿ

A SHARP PAIN hits me in my chest. I become motionless. I don't want to move because I fear the pain will increase. Slowly, I lean back against my goose down pillows and run my fingers through my hair. Watery eyes display my discomfort. I try to think of something pleasant to take away the pain, before it intensifies. I wait a few minutes and then I rise from my bed and go to the bathroom. I look in the mirror and at that very moment, I swear, I witness a flash of my life fast-forwarding in my eyes. Both of my hands cling to my face. I get paranoid thinking my life is being cut short. That my time is coming soon and I betta' get ready to meet God or Satan. My hands shelter my mouth, body shudders, feet weaken, and I fall to the tile floor and weep.

I can hear my alarm clock sounding off in the bedroom and with very little energy I struggle to get on my feet and return to bed. My body withdraws, fatigue sets in, and I feel myself folding instead of flourishing. I have taken a step backwards and I can't understand why. Things seem to be looking up for me and I feel alive, but my mind is playing tricks on me. I have to pinch myself to make sure I am not already dead. Confusion spots my face. *Johnnie I need you.* Damn. Johnnie would know exactly what to do. He would know exactly what to say and how to makes things better. God, I miss him so much. I close my eyes trying to stop the tears, but they just run down my face faster and faster. I feel helpless. And my body curls into a fetal position like I want to surrender. I make it to my bed and lay still.

I doze off and when I awake its 11:00 a.m. I just recline, still thinking. Thoughts are playing, pausing, rewinding, fast-forwarding, and re-playing in my head. I snap and grab my hair and try to stop all of the madness that's occurring. I let out a scream. I scream so loud that it echoes throughout my apartment. *I'm losing control of me. What's wrong?*

I go into the bathroom to take a long, relaxing bath. I try not to think too much, but I have no control over my mind. *God help me?* I need to get myself together. After my bath, I sit in the living room and try to distract my thoughts by watching TV, but for some unknown reason Ma'am and Poppa appear in my head and I start shaking out of nowhere. My stomach hurts badly. I curl up on the sofa and flashbacks of my childhood run quickly across the TV screen, and then it stops. Then there are more flashbacks and then it stops when Johnnie dies and I completely lose it. I sob uncontrollably, wiping the drippings of snot from my nose, and holding my stomach as if I am constipated. I get up off the sofa and go to the bedroom to get dressed, but my body is weak and I end up lying back down. By this time I am so distressed because I've never experienced symptoms like this before. Emotionally I'm disconcerted, twitchy, and unsure of my own capabilities. *Oh, God, please help me?*

I reach for the phone to call Dr. Fulmore's office, but then I hang up. I plead with God to save my life because I honesty think it's fading before my eyes. I sit still for a moment contemplating seeking help. *Am I losing my mind and possibly having an emotional break down?* I can't very well answer myself. I pick myself up and reach over for the phonebook that's lying on the side of my desk. I search through the yellow pages for the physician section looking for a Psychiatrist and I pick up the phone and call. The phone rings twice and then a woman answers.

"Peabody & Grayson office, how may I help you?"

"Hello. I would like to make an appointment."

"Ma'am, who am I speaking with?" The woman asks in a pleasant tone.

"Um...um, my name is Debra. Debra Matthews."

"Ms. Matthews, May I ask what type of insurance you have?" The woman coughs.

I am silent for a moment, playing footsy with myself, "Um, I have Mountainside Blue Shield PPO." I suddenly feel even sicker to my stomach and I hang up the phone.

Why did I hang up? I get off the bed and sit at my desk to write in my journal, but I have nothing to say. I am at a loss for words. And that's a clear indication that I am suppressing a lot inside that will eventually erupt into something I may not be able to handle. I decide to attempt to call a Psychologist before it ends up being too late.

"Cristal & Johnston Associates, how may I help you?"

"Hi. MynameisAveryLoveandIwouldliketomakeanappointm entassoonaspossible." My words run together as I speak quickly, I lower my head waiting for the woman to respond.

"Okay, Ms. Love, I do have an opening tomorrow at 3:30 with Mrs. Cristal. If any cancellations come in today, I'll be more than happy to give you a call. May I have your daytime phone number?" The woman has a strong southern accent.

"Well, my daytime number is my home number, which is ...." My eyes wander around my bedroom as I give her my number.

"Okay, Ms. Love, please try to get here fifteen minutes early just to fill out the paperwork. Our location is 99 Northfield Ave, in West Orange, New Jersey." The woman speaks quickly before she says, "Hold please?"

I patiently listen to a recording of music playing over the phone until she returns.

"Ma'am, thanks for holding. Did I give you our address?"

"Yes, you did," I say, while twirling one section of my hair.

"Okay, you are all set for your appointment. You

have a nice day."

"You too."

As we hang up, my heart's beating erratically. I need to lie down, but think I should call my insurance carrier to make sure Dr. Christine Cristal is in-network. I don't. I don't care because I had to build my nerve just to call her and she's who I am seeing regardless if I have to pay cash. I return to the living room, turn the radio to a jazz station and sit on the sofa with my feet up. I wrap my arms around my knees; rest my chin upon them, just thinking. I listen to music because it seems soothing and I just sit there in a vegetated state. I don't move for what seems like hours and by the time I come back to earth it's after two o'clock and I am still immobile. I am locked in a zone. This is the very first time I have experienced something like this.

Ring...ring. Ring...ring, Ring...ring.

I don't move.

A chilling feeling comes over me so quickly. I think about Johnnie's memorial service. I think about hugging him and smelling his body scent, and seeing the look in his angst-ridden eyes. I think about our conversation in the park and somehow everything transforms into Poppa. And then it transforms into Ma'am. Everyone that I have loved has died. And I'm all that I have. That frightens me. *Who will miss me?* I bury my head in between my knees and start crying so full of grief. Deep inside I am hoping that Dr. Cristal's office will call me today because I really need someone to talk to. I can hear my stomach growling, but I have no appetite. I don't even get up to get a can of Ensure out of the refrigerator. I can't stop the thoughts, the emotional roller coaster that I am feeling. I feel so cheated. And that's when everything comes to light. Everyone I've loved has died and the feeling of not being missed enters my mind. I don't have anyone in my life at this present time that would miss me. And if I should die tonight or tomorrow, who would know? There are no neighbors I associate with. I don't have any acquaintances. The only person I truly speak to is the mailman. And that isn't very often. I finally get up and grab a piece of paper and pen. I write out a Living Will, just in case I die in my sleep and the only reason I am found is because of the stench that stinks up my apartment and lingers out into the hallway. I don't see it happening any other way. It takes me nearly two hours to write.

I decide to leave everything to Mr. Clyde, my pharmacist. I choose Mr. Clyde because he has been like a father to me. He's always concerned about me, making sure I don't lose too much weight. He's just a thoughtful and kind man. I feel very comfortable with my choice. After I write everything out I walk into my bedroom and reach for an envelope in my desk drawer. I seal the Living Will inside and set it down on my nightstand right beside my bed. On the front of the envelope I write, "LIVING WILL" in big bold letters with a permanent marker. My body's weak so I snuggle up on my bed underneath my comforter and fall asleep.

I am knocked out when I realize its 9:00 p.m. I lay in bed for a few more minutes until I notice the light on my caller ID blinking. I lean over to look at the display and Dr. Cristal's office has called. I pick up the phone and listen to the message that the receptionist has left. It looks like I missed the opportunity to go in for an appointment today because she asked me to call back before 5:00 p.m. I have no choice, but to wait until tomorrow. I delete the message go into the living room and sit down to watch TV. I hear my stomach growling so I get up and go into the kitchen to get an Ensure out of the refrigerator. I return to the living room and continue to watch TV. I haven't taken any of my medicine today, nor have I eaten anything. I feel like I'm sinking and if I continue there won't be any of me left. I will have shriveled up and go stir crazy in a week or so if I keep this up. *I need help.* Mentally I repeat to myself, *Girl, you're going to make it. Just keep on trying. You've come too far to stop now. You're not a quitter, you're a survivor. SURVIVOR.*

Instantly someone or something has just heated

my body as if I am having hot flashes. The chill in my feet changes and instead becomes so warm that I have to take off my socks. My hair's damp, forehead's moist, and my whole body seems different. And then someone or something embraces me. I know that I am not going crazy. I can sense something in the room with me. There's a fragrance that I have never smelt before. It's not a strong scent; it's mild, delicate, and sweet. My eyes are heavy, very heavy. And I can swear that as I lean back I am being tucked into bed like a child. I have no control over what is happening to me. My body is comfortable, very comfortable. And then the room goes pitch black.

In the morning the sun peeks through the Venetian blinds. I stretch my body hearing the leather on the sofa crunch. My mind is clear and I am famished. I get up and go into the bathroom to freshen up. In the kitchen I make a decent breakfast, drink a can of Ensure, take my medication, and clean up my mess. I go back into my bedroom and sit on my bed. I smile because I am grateful. Yesterday, an unusual experience helped me get through a very difficult time. I know that no one will believe me, but it was real. I was hopeless. I was ready to throw in the towel and surrender. I was so weak. I continue to smile and say, "Lord, I thank you. Yes. You saved me. You lifted me up out of my misery. You saved me from death." I shake my head and swallow hard full of appreciation. I feel full.

Noon has snuck up on me as I sit watching TV in my bedroom. I start to think about what I will say or how I will start the conversation with Dr. Cristal. This will be the first time that I have ever gone to see a Psychologist and I am not sure what to expect. I find myself actually trying to convince myself that I don't need to go. That God has helped me through it all, so all will be well, but my inner voice (Avona) says, "Girl, you could have a relapse. You best go and seek help." That's all I need to hear for me to get my tail out of bed and start preparing for my day. By the time I get through with everything it's going on 1:00 p.m. and I still haven't taken my shower, done my hair, or ironed my clothes. My pace has slowed down as if I am trying to miss my appointment on purpose. But something nudges me hard and I put some fire under my ass. I must admit I am concerned about going because I don't want this total stranger to think that I am crazy. I don't want her to prescribe me medication that I will have to take for the rest of my life. I'm taking enough medication as it is. I decide to just bite the bullet and see what this woman has to offer. See if she can root out the problems that I'm experiencing. I stretch the ironing board out in the living room, get my jeans and shirt, and return back to the living room to iron my clothes. My appearance isn't as important to me as me finding out what's going on with me.

It's almost two o'clock and I still haven't taken my shower. I'm moving like a snail, edgy as can be. I finally go into the bathroom, take my shower, get dressed, moisturize my scalp, and pick out my hair. I apply my makeup lightly, spray a pinch of perfume, and slip my feet into my mule shoes. I look presentable enough for me. Trying to waste time, I sit by the window in my bedroom and watch the movement in the streets. It's a very hot day, so I reach over to my dresser and grab my sunscreen and apply it to my skin. Time's moving slowly, but I am eager to head out so I grab my purse, keys, sunglasses, and leave.

As soon as I open the lobby door the sun greets me with hotness. When I get into my car I turn on the radio and the temperature is a scorching 98 degrees. It's that miserable heat where your body will still feel dehydrated even after drinking several bottles of water. I roll down the windows instead of turning on my air conditioner and drive off.

When I arrive at Dr. Cristal's office it looks like a house converted into an office. At the door to the house I am greeted by the secretary. She has mocha skin, with a narrow nose, small thin lips, large eyes with thick-framed glasses, a thick full-figure frame;

hair colored in honey blonde streaks, curled in a Halle Berry style that does not accentuate her face. She is not attractive, but she's friendly. She smiles showing a big gap between her two front teeth and hands me some papers on a clipboard. I sit down and fill out the forms. I feel out of place and I'm sure it shows on my face. *I'm seeing a psychologist.*

After I finish filling out my paperwork I hand it back to Gretchen, the secretary, with my medical insurance card. She makes a copy of my card and gives it back to me. My eyes roam around the nicely decorated office. It has pastel yellow paint, with a border of wallpaper at the bottom. A fruity fragrance lingers. I place my finger in my mouth and unconsciously bite my nail. I see the woman look up, and then I stop. She smiles as she answers the phone.

About twenty minutes later a tall, slender, dark-skinned woman, with gumball eyes, and long, silky, straight hair, comes walking out with a white woman. They shake hands. The white woman speaks with Gretchen, while the dark-skinned woman looks over a sheet, and then calls out my name. I make eye contact with her, stand, and then go into an office that looks more like a comfortable living room. The woman introduces herself as Dr. Christine Cristal and we shake hands. She invites me to sit on her plush red sofa that has big, multi-colored throw pillows, as she sits on the opposite end. She looks over the paperwork, and then she puts the chart on her lap, and puckers her blackberry, lipstick lips.

"Ms. Love, what brings you here today?" Her eyes show concern.

It's difficult at first for me to open my mouth and then I let it rip.

"To be perfectly honest, I really don't know what brings me here." I let my head fall.

"Can you explain what you're feeling inside?" she asks as she crosses her legs.

"I feel pain, lots of pain. He, he, he...did this..." My eyes immediately tear up.

"Who is he? What did he do to you?" she asks.

"I don't know him. He just came out of nowhere and...and...raped me."

Dr. Cristal gives me her undivided attention and says, "Ms. Love, do you want to talk more about it? I won't pressure you."

"No. I'd rather not. Not yet."

"Okay. I'm going to ask you some questions and I want you to take as much time as you need to answer them." She pulls out a pen from her ivory suit jacket.

"What was your upbringing like? Was it pleasant?"

I raise my head giving eye-to-eye contact and then respond, "Yes and no. I mean it was pleasant in the beginning while I was in elementary school and my four years of high school, but then things changed after I graduated from high school. Um..."

My emotions flare up and the tears start to flow.

"What happened to you after high school, Ms. Love?"

"Poppa..." I raise my hands to cover my face.

Dr. Cristal hands me a tissue so I can continue.

I stroke my weary face.

"Ms. Love, I'm not going to rush you in talking about it but eventually you need to express it."

"Ma'am said nothing." My face falls into my palms.

"You mentioned Ma'am. Is she your mom?" Dr. Cristal asks.

"Yes. She was always quiet, a wife who stayed in her place. Poppa was very stubborn, mule-headed and Ma'am never spoke up, no matter what. I had to struggle out in an unfamiliar world with no one to guide me. I changed, grew strong, and independent. I despised him and her for not speaking up. I didn't keep in touch with them for many, many years, until Poppa took ill." I dab my eyes with the tissue.

"Your Poppa took ill and how did you feel when you found out?" Dr. Cristal asks as she leans back on the sofa and uncrosses her legs.

"I thought about my last conversation with him when he was gripping my hand as I watched him take his last breath. How I showed no emotion. I was bitter. I cried out of anger. Poppa suffered. He literally suffered. And at the very moment I thought about how I suffered. How I tried and tried to please him and nothing seemed to be good enough. It couldn't have been good enough. I was the only one in the whole family who graduated from high school and to me that was a huge accomplishment, but obviously he saw it differently." I grin hiding my pain.

Dr. Cristal continues to write in her note pad.

"How did Ma'am react?" She scratches her scalp.

"She suffered and I could have cared less."

"Why? What type of relationship did you and Ma'am have?" Dr. Cristal lowers her head and begins to write again.

"We weren't close. We were never close growing up. And I always felt a little neglected. Sadly to say, I don't know why."

My eyes sharpen exposing my evil twin.

"Dr. Cristal, I have so much anger built up inside of me. I thought it had disappeared once they both died. Now it is all coming back. Things are so...so distressing. I lost my best friend recently and the open wounds are splitting more and more. It is all coming back." I place my left hand up to my eyes and pinch the corners to catch the tears from falling.

"You lost a friend? How?" She stops writing and just listens.

I start to cry with such sorrow. It painfully releases what is burdening me.

"My best friend, Johnnie, had AIDS. And I never got to tell...." I pause.

"And you never got to tell, what?"

"I never got the chance to tell Johnnie face-to-face that...." I sniffle and dab my nose before it starts to run. "That...that... that...I'm HIV-positive."

I shut my eyes waiting for Dr. Cristal's

response. Inside I am sick, not knowing if she will pull away from me and ask me to leave. She's quiet for a moment. Then she stands and walks over to her desk. She writes on a post-it, sits down and hands it to me. It's an address.

"Ms. Love, I would like for you to come to this address tomorrow evening at 6:30 p.m.? It's a spiritual group meeting I've started years ago, helping people like you to cope with living with HIV/AIDS. We meet at a school once a week. It looks like our time is up this afternoon, but I would like you to come back for another session, only if you're comfortable." She smiles.

"Yes. I would like to come back. And I'll try to make it tomorrow."

Dr. Cristal walks me to the door.

"Thank you, Dr. Cristal."

I walk towards Gretchen to schedule my next appointment.

As I walk out of Dr. Cristal's office I feel so different inside, a feeling that I can't explain in simple terms, but I am so enthralled by her ability to make me talk. Talk about things that no one else knows. This is a new experience that I believe will put me back on track. I just don't know how long it will take. But I have the patience to continue my journey.

Eleven

I AWAKE PRAYING.

"God, please watch over me? I think that I'm losing control of my life or the devil's playing his shrewd games, again. I'm contemplating whether I should go to this appointment with Dr. Cristal today. I feel like a quack seeking help from a psychologist, but I guess You know what's best because I've already stepped into her office. I hear You Lord. I should listen to my instincts and follow Your advice. Pride should not stand in my way. You're absolutely right, Lord. You won't put no more on me than you think I can handle. Thanks for listening."

The remainder of my day I lay around in bed moping and thinking. I am thinking about how I opened up to Dr. Cristal and wondering what she honestly thought of me when I told her that I was HIV-positive. I don't even know what made me blurt it out like that. It just rolled off my tongue like POW. And I couldn't very well change it after the fact. What's done is done.

I lean my neck back to stretch the kinks out. I go into the bathroom to wash my face and brush my teeth. And then I think about Dr. Cristal telling my personal business to someone. I don't know how close her relationship is with her secretary, Gretchen. She could possibly be talking and not thinking and let it slip out of her mouth. Anything's possible. I can't help, but be skeptical. Things are different now than when Johnnie was here. I could trust him with my life. But Dr. Cristal's a total stranger. I guess it will take time to trust her and believe what she says to be the truth. I decide to take a chance and let go.

Blu McDowell slithers into my psyche and I replay him slowly taking off his shirt. All I can say to myself is, "Showtime!" I mean, I've seen many men in my day, but Mr. McDowell was an unexpected package with a big red bow tied around him. It's already Thursday and the weekend's so close that I'm eager to call him, but I don't want to seem desperate. I'll wait.

My mouth is watering for a BLT so I go into the kitchen, and pull out a package of turkey bacon, lettuce, tomatoes, mayo, and reach on top of the refrigerator for my wheat bread. I eat, take a shower, and get dressed in my olive slacks and poncho blouse with open toe sandals. I comb out my hair, put on my teardrop diamond studs, gloss my lips, outline my eyes, and brush a smidgen of green smoke eye shadow on to enhance my look. My face glows and I feel so invigorated. Looking at my reflection I can honestly say that I look rested for the first time in a long time. Although I am concerned about others finding out my secret I have to let it go and face it. I will certainly know if Dr. Cristal has deceived me by the feeling in the pit of my stomach once I walk into her office. I'm sure her secretary, Gretchen, will have a disturbing look on her face if she knows. But right now I can't worry about that. I have too many other things going on. I have an appointment with Dr. Fulmore, so I best get moving.

I dangle my purse from my shoulder, take my keys off the key hook, turn the doorknob and take one final look around the room scanning to make sure I haven't forgotten anything. As I start to walk towards the elevator, I realize that I did forget something, my umbrella. It's only water so I don't even bother to turn around and go back. At the front door of the lobby, I hear loud, hard drops pounding violently outside. Stepping out the door I see big droplets that flood the sewer and the kids from the block are throwing rocks in it. The rain saves me fifteen dollars from not having to wash my car which I can use for gas. I hurry and run to my car hoping not to get soaking wet. My windows are difficult to see out of so I turn the windshield wipers on high. It's really difficult driving, but I take my time and make it to Dr. Fulmore's office in one piece. The ankles of my pants are stuck to my legs as is my poncho so I try to fan it hoping it will air dry. The rain starts to come down even harder. Like Ma'am used to say, "God sho' is venting today."

Dr. Fulmore's office is almost empty. There's one other woman sitting near the entrance. She looks like she may be seven or eight months pregnant. Apparently she's waiting for someone who's already inside seeing the doctor. Her feet are so swollen that she has on bedroom slippers. I glance over at her while signing my name on the list, and then I smile and put my head down because I feel a little uneasy about her catching me staring at her. I grab a magazine and then sit down and wait for my name to be called. The pregnant woman is intriguing, mainly because I am fascinated because I wonder how it feels to have a child inside the womb. I keep staring and each time I get caught, I bury my face in the magazine. *It must feel weird and exciting all at the same time.* She's brave wanting to bring a child into this world. Instinctively, I don't want my child to suffer because of my circumstances. I mean, I'm sure women in my situation still have a family after they know that they are HIV-positive, but I personally do not want the added pressure on my shoulders. But everyone's different and has different outlooks on having a child being HIV-positive. As much as I want to ask the pregnant woman some questions, I cannot find the words to stir up a conversation. Instead, I continuously peek over my magazine until I get up to ask Violet a question.

"Hi Violet, how long do I have to wait to see Dr. Fulmore? I think my appointment was at 1:00."

"Avery, I don't see an appointment for you today. Are you sure it's for today?"

"You know what Violet, maybe I have my days mixed up. I've been in sort of a funk lately so I might have thought it was today."

"Well, since you're here, do you need to see Dr. Fulmore?"

"Actually, I do because I've been experiencing that sharp pain again in my chest."

"Okay, I'll squeeze you in, Avery."

About twenty minutes later the medical assistant, Praise comes out and calls my name.

Rising like a sergeant and heading for the door I follow Praise. Every time I see her I compliment her on her name. We talk for a brief minute, as she looks over my chart. I step on the scale and after Praise checks my blood pressure, she asks me to wait in room number five. About ten minutes later, Dr. Fulmore enters the room as cheerful as always.

"How is everything, Ms. Love?"

"Oh, everything is okay, Dr. Fulmore."

"How have you been feeling?"

"I've been feeling all right, but I had that sharp pain again, yesterday."

"Okay, I am going to listen to your chest; take nice slow breaths, in and out. Avery, have you been skipping any of your medication?"

"No, Dr. Fulmore."

"Have you been strenuous with your physical workouts?"

"No, I've cut back quite a bit. I have been under a lot of stress. There are some personal things going on in my life right now."

"Okay, okay, as a precaution I want to schedule another image of your chest."

Honestly, I'm feeling like it's not okay because I dread going there, but I need to follow Dr. Fulmore's orders. I take a deep breath and take it all in. *It's not the end of the world and I would rather be safe than sorry. I am not going to stress. I am not going to stress.* I head toward the door to exit the building. Violet raises her voice stating that she will leave me a message as to the day and time for me to go to the Image Center. I nod in acknowledgement and leave with a look of concern on my face. I dread coming to the doctor and being in the position that I'm in, but what can I do? My life's different now and no matter how bleak, I still have to accept all that comes with it.

By the time I arrive home my caller ID is

blinking red with a message.

"Hi Avery, its Violet, I'm calling to let you know that I scheduled an appointment for today at five o'clock. If that is inconvenient for you call the Image Center and reschedule, okay. Bye."

Damn! Violet sure doesn't waste time. I might as well head back out because it is already 4:15 p.m. I go to my walk-in closet and grab my olive green raincoat and walk back out into the black clouds hoping that the sun will finally come out. It's pouring continuously with little intervals that mislead me into thinking that it will stop. My windshield wipers are on full force and it's still difficult for me to see. I strain my eyes while driving for fear of having a collision. A half a block from the Image Center the sky opens up with a gleam of sunshine. I park my car in a spot near the door and enter with a sick feeling in my stomach. Chills run down my spine as I sit in the corner chair waiting for one of the technicians to call my name. Jazz is playing overhead and its light to my ears, almost too relaxing because I feel myself drifting off into a brief catnap. The sickening feeling I am experiencing has ceased and a comfort feeling returns. I am mindful of what I am thinking because I have made up my mind to start being positive. I want goodness to filter through instead of being tarnished with negativity every time things get tense. Something spiritual came over me yesterday, giving me the feeling that I can achieve greatness. I can accomplish every goal, and jump over every hurdle that tries to inflict pain in my life. For once I feel powerful and in control. I sit for fifteen more minutes and then a male voice calls out,

"Avery Love."

A white man stands with a chart in one hand and a gown in the other.

"Hi, I'm your X-ray Technician, Karel."

"Hello, Karel."

Karel escorts me into this cold, quiet room with lots of x-ray equipment. I think about my first experience with that unpleasant woman. I don't even recall her telling me her name.

"Ms. Love, here is a gown for you to change in."

He excuses himself from the room giving me privacy to change and then he knocks before entering to make sure I am ready. While he's setting up we casually talk until he alerts me that he's ready to take my x-rays. I feel comfortable. Karel has a friendly disposition, warm and very flattering. He explains what he is about to do beforehand. I feel safe and respected. He doesn't make me feel like I am contagious just by looking at me. He doesn't make me feel unimportant. Karel makes eye contact when he speaks and the rich green color in his eyes exemplifies worthiness. He does not give me a sigh of discouragement when viewing the x-rays and his tone does not change to a pity pitch. He remains relaxed and it gives me a ray of hope that when circumstances seem bleak, there are good people who can change your mindset to think optimistically.

Around 6:00 I head for Dr. Cristal's spiritual group meeting. I open the door to the school and enter the gymnasium. My eyes widen. I become teary-eyed. There are so many people sitting in a circle. The realization of others walking in my shoes becomes real. I am awakening in more ways than one.

T WELVE

IMPULSIVELY I WANT to call Blu McDowell but a part of me doesn't want to come off as desperate. The anticipation grows in me and I can't contain myself. I pick up the phone and dial his number craving to hear his sexy, baritone voice but his answering machine picks up instead. I frown.

"You've reached the residence of Blu McDowell, please leave a brief message and I will kindly call you back."

"Hi, this is Avery. Avery Love, the one you met at Garrett Mountain Park. I just called to say hello. When you find the time, please give me a call back at...Goodbye."

I stand still for a brief moment feeling strange about just calling a man. It has been some time since I've even spoken to a man, other than Johnnie. Warmth flows over me and then quickly disappears.

Today will be my day of pampering. In the bathroom I run the water to take an oil bath. I light four tea light candles and surround each corner of the bathtub. While I am doing this I hear the phone ringing so I dry my hands so I can quickly grab the phone but I am minutes too late. The answering machine picks up. After a few seconds I press the button to listen.

"Hi Avery, it's Blu I was checking my messages and heard your angelic voice. When you get a moment give me a call back."

My body grows hot just hearing his voice. I turn to walk back towards the bathroom when the phone rings again. I pick it up on the third ring.

"Hello."

"Hello, may I speak with Avery?"

"This is she."

"Hi, it's Blu. I just left you a message a few minutes ago, but I was so anxious to speak with you. I feel like a teenager meeting a girl for the very first time." He laughs. "I don't know why and maybe there is no explanation for it, but you've been on my mind since we've met. I couldn't call you because you never gave me your number so I had to patiently wait for you to call me."

A smirk spreads over my face.

"Well Blu, I guess that anxiousness got the best of both of us."

Blu laughs loud like I just told a Bernie Mac joke. I guess this is his way of breaking the ice.

"Yes, I was thinking about you and was a little hesitant in calling because I didn't want you to presume me as being zealous. We both sound like teenagers."

Our laughter breaks the ice and our dialogue flows. We talk for about an hour and then have to cut our conversation short because he has to meet with a client. He says he will call me either tonight or tomorrow. Then we say, Goodbye.

Once I hang up the phone my body tingles. Blu's flattery has me cheesing. My face lights up. I head back towards the bathroom, turn on the nozzle for the hot water and just sit there. I have a flashback of when Blu pulled off his shirt at the park. The ripples on his flat board stomach are like ripples of jet-black water. I try to reach out to touch him as if he is standing before me, but catch myself. I shake my head, *he is so fine*. I sprinkle some dried rose petals in the water and turn off the knob. I put my left foot in only to quickly tug it out because the water is too hot. I sit on the toilet seat massaging my foot still swimming with thoughts of Blu. After much lusting, I take my bath. I envision Blu there with me as he graciously massages my feet, kissing my pinky toe and slobbering all over my big toe with his warm, juicy lips. I drift off only to come to in a bath alone. How pathetic.

Stepping out of the bathtub I liberally mask my skin with Mango Butter. I slip on my panties and bra and walk into the living room and sit down on the sofa. The light is lit on my phone.

"Hi Avery, this is Dr. Fulmore, I received the results back from your x-ray and again everything looks fine. If you experience any other problems, please feel free to give me a call. You probably just need to relax and stop stressing. God Bless."

I decide to make an appointment to get my hair done with my stylist, Aja.

A delightful gentle wind of honeysuckle seeps through my kitchen window and cascades throughout the apartment. Yesterday's rain has cleansed everything and has given today an afternoon of highlighting glory. In my bedroom I get dressed, pick up my flip-flops, drop them in front of my bed, slip them on, pull the strap to my backpack and exit the apartment.

I open the lobby door with full force as if I am making my entrance for a large audience, and stepping out into the world of change. The air has a sweet smell to it. High beams of sun tan my face, neck and arms. I have forgotten to put on my straw hat so the ends of my hair have lightened over the day. I watch bare bodies of men pass with the smell of Usher and XX-XY Hugo Boss as I enter my car. It makes my flesh shiver. Looking at their buff bodies, biceps protruding, genitals' dangling as some wear Speedo's as they ride bikes. I wet my lips several times, until they gleam with a natural gloss. *Hmmm, doesn't he look delicious? His hands caress my nipples and he palms my breasts squeezing intensely. His breathings erratic, like a porn flick and the hot air flutters against my ear. A tickle, but no laughter's exchanged, only the sounds of me feeling pleasure. My mouth opens wide. Ah...Ooh...Ah...Ooh...but no sound escapes from my mouth. My lips pucker. His big, strong, masculine hands boldly creep down to my inner thigh. He's teasing, tantalizing slowly against my safari. We are beading with sweat and our bodies are sticky, flooding with our juices. Two sticky, hot, honey buns. His whispers are in two different languages in my ear. Ooh. His language of love makes me thirsty for him.*

Intensity heightens as my legs extend in mid air, inviting him to enter me. We have been longing for this moment, as my eyes close; I feel his muscular body shading mine. He speaks softly, "Avery, open your eyes?" I open them with a crease in my forehead because his strokes are intensely hitting the right spots. His thrust grows stronger and stronger and my moans grow louder and louder. We're in rhythmic tune; beating hearts feeling as if it will combust through our chests. His eyes droop with a sexiness that makes me hungry. I'm starving. He moistens his lips and the sweat drips profusely from his face and onto my breasts. The bed squeaks as the moment approaches. He utters softly, "Avery, Avery, I'm cum...'!" We climax simultaneously. He peels himself off of me and lies beside me. Both of us are breathing heavily, catching breathes in between. If we smoked we would have been puffing away. Our hands interlock and we slowly fall into a satisfied sleep.

Reality sets in. I feel a wet puddle in my panties so I open the car door, walk through the lobby door, and take the stairs to my apartment door. I walk to the bathroom to freshen up. I feel embarrassed for myself, for the lusting and craving like a nymphomaniac. My body craves for men. I think of investing in a vibrator but I'm so used to the real thing that it may short fuse me if I don't have an orgasm. I like the sensation of a penis stroking the insides of my walls. My vagina starts to throb and then the phone rings. I answer the phone with my buttocks exposed.

"Hello."

"Hello, may I speak to Avery?"

"This is she."

"Avery, this is Blu."

"Hello."

"Was I interrupting you?"

"No, no, I just walked in the door because I..."

"Well, I had sometime in between my day and I just wanted to hear your voice."

I smile.

"That's nice to know, Blu."

"Avery, do you have any plans for today?"

"Well, actually, yes, I'm about to go to the hair salon."

"Oh, okay."

"Why is there something wrong, Blu?"

"No, no, I just..."

"Yes."

"I just wanted to know if maybe you wanted to have a cup of coffee later this afternoon."

"That would be nice."

"Well, when you get back from the salon give me a call and I'll come pick you up."

"Okay."

"I guess I'll see you later."

"Sure."

"Bye."

"Goodbye, Blu."

My temperature rises. Woo! That man does something to me every time I hear his voice. It just runs down me and makes my feet tremor. I go straight into my bedroom to get a fresh pair of panties. After freshening up, I jet out the door.

The corner of Bloomfield Ave in Montclair is hectic. Traffic's heavy. It seems that everyone and their mommas are out. I quickly find a parking space, put on my sunglasses and exit the car. "Villa of Locks" is packed. Gawking eyes steady me as I enter the salon. Women look me down and are mumbling underneath their breath. Eyes cut through like a machete from women that I don't even know. I look around for Aja, my stylist, sign my name on her list and grab a magazine. Aja's an extremely beautiful, African-American and Japanese woman with straight silky hair that makes men drool. Her eyes are slightly slanted giving her an exotic look. She's tall, lean, and sexy. She can be feisty, too. She has been doing my hair since I went natural. I won't go to anyone else.

The inner traffic of wet, twisted, coiled, and dreaded locks is finally dying down. Aja walks up to the receptionist station and greets me with a smile letting me know that I am next. I twirl the ends of my hair somewhat impatiently as I am tired of all the looks from women who are straight up "ghetto". *It's a damn shame when you have to speak loudly to get your point across when the other person's sitting right next to you.* While patiently waiting for Aja a young lady walks into the salon. She looks about seventeen, tall with athletic looks. Her dark pigment complexion reminds me of a dark chocolate Hershey bar, and she has the prettiest eyes I have ever seen. She distributes flyers for AIDS Awareness. They are called "Red Alert." The flyer briefly explains what the Hotline Service provides and advertises equal opportunity employment for the Hotline Service Center. It's a service that gives folks with the virus options to release their frustrations through the service. I see myself listening to a voice of reasoning, comprehension, and compassion. The structure of the service helps those who feel defeated. Truthfulness seems to be the key to facing this illness. More often than not, folks don't truly have anyone to confide in. There are those who have chosen a certain lifestyle and then those who have no say in what was inflicted upon them.

The young lady seems well-educated. She distributes ink pens and red ribbons to anyone who donates a dollar to the cause. I reach into my backpack and hand her a ten-dollar bill, she says, "thank you," and then she circulates throughout the salon. It kinda puts a damper on my natural high. I start to feel guilty. The words, "I can relate," want to come screaming out of me, but the timing and my surroundings will not allow me to do that. I want to educate her with the reality by saying, *Honey you are looking at a product of living proof,* but deep inside I don't want her to know. I'm undetected and I'm content with that. The young lady has mistakenly scratched my hand with her fingernail when she takes the money. The last thing I want to say to her is that I'm HIV-positive. She might have a panic attack or freak the hell out because she has come in contact with me. I don't even want to go there.

I hear someone scratching their throat and the distraction makes me come out of my deep fog. I notice Aja and stand up to follow her in the back.

"Avery, what's up?"

"Hello, Aja."

"Boy, you must've been thinking about something awfully good, girl."

I smirk.

"So Avery, how have you been?"

"I've been fine."

"You haven't been coming to the salon; I think it has been maybe six months since the last time I did your hair."

"Yeah, you're right it has been about that long. As you can see it needs some TLC."

"Girl, you ain't said nothin' but a word, Aja to the rescue."

Aja leans me back in the chair and saturates my hair with warm water. She liberally applies some nice smelling shampoo, which tingles and exfoliates my scalp. She forcefully massages my scalp and I feel like I am in heaven. She rinses and then repeats the process again. She says I need a deep conditioner and that I will have to sit under the dryer for fifteen minutes because my hair is a little damaged. She applies the conditioner, puts a plastic cap over my head, and escorts me to the dryer. She hands me an Essence magazine to read and moves onto her next client. The noise level has died down enormously. Some of the "ghetto" women are either under the dryer or being shampooed, which separates their damn mouths from talkin' about nothing. The hot air from the dryer is intense and starts to burn my earlobes, so I wave to attract Aja's attention so she can bring me some ear protectors. About twenty minutes later she comes and removes me from the dryer and leads me back to the sink. She rinses the conditioner out of my hair and then takes me to her workstation. It will probably be another twenty minutes to a half hour before I actually get out of here. I think about calling Blu from the salon, but then I decide to wait until I get home. Aja's pretty quick; she doesn't talk much when it comes to making her bread and butter. Her philosophy is to, "get you in and out making between seventy-five and up per head." I would be the same way. Aja knows her stuff and she's good. And her competitors in the salon know it to be true. Her list of clientele stretches to the point that her co-workers are envious.

"Avery, looks like you have some split-ends. Do you want me to trim your hair?"

I am in deep thought again but I finally come to.

"Aja, I do have a date today, so I guess trimming it would be fine."

"Who's the lucky guy?"

"Oh now, Aja, nothing has changed with me. I never kiss and tell."

She laughs and says, "Gurl, I feel yah. These trifling asses out here will steal your man right from under yah. They have freakin' radar on a muthafucka like they know when he just got paid an' shit. I call them the "greenery bitches," 'cause that is the only time their asses want to be bothered. And as soon as that muthafucka is broke, shit, off they go, to another desperate-horny-two-timing-low-life-of-a-man. That type of shit would get an uncouth bitch knocked the fuck out by me. Shit, I'm a bad bitch." She laughs again.

Three o'clock approaches and I'm just getting out of Aja's chair. She gently massages some fragrant oil into my scalp. I give her the usual ten-dollar tip. Pleased with the outcome I hurry to get home to freshen up, call Blu, and meet him for coffee.

Arriving home at 3:30 p.m. I still have to take a shower and change my clothes. I feel pressed for time when I enter my apartment. I linger to catch an uninviting smell.

I go into the kitchen to make sure it's not the garbage, and it's not. I check the mousetrap again and it's empty and then I check the bathroom just in case the toilet has overflowed. But nothing is out of the ordinary. I light some scented candles, kick off my shoes and check my answering machine to see if anyone has called. I have one message from the pharmacy. Ah, shoot! My refill must be in. Damn. I was right over there. I call Mr. Clyde to let him know that I will be there to pick up my prescription in an hour. As I start to call Blu to explain that I have something I need to take care of, and ask for a rain check, the phone rings.

"Hello."

"Hello, Avery, its Blu."

"Hi, Blu, I was just about to call you. Um, it looks like something came up and I won't be able to meet you for coffee. Is it possible for us to meet another time?" I am biting my lip and tapping my feet.

"Sure. Um, Avery, do you think we can possibly meet later this evening? I was really looking forward to seeing you."

I blush.

"I don't see a problem with that. So, let's try this again, shall we. I'll call you from my cell phone to let you know that I am on my way home, give you my address, and you can meet me. Okay?"

"Okay, sounds like a plan."

As I hang up the phone a smile spreads across my face, like dominos spread down the line. I like the fact that Blu seems very understanding. His tone is very mellow, even though he has a deep voice. I rush to the pharmacy; pick up my prescription, briefly speak with Mr. Clyde, not even giving him enough time to give me my usual Ensure and hightail it back to my apartment.

I call Blu from my cell phone and give him my address. My mind quickly drifts back to when he took off his shirt and my body grows warmer. By the time I reach my building I need a fire hose to cool me down. My body is a blazing inferno. I park my car across from the building. Upon exiting the car I hear a deep, baritone voice call out my name. I take a deep breath, and turn around slowly. *Damn, he's fine.* Blu has a

Denzel Washington kind of walk and his bright smile lights up my insides. I walk over to greet him in the center of the street and we hug. His scent provokes me, but I keep my composure. We ride the elevator to my floor and as I try to unlock my door I simply can't because my hands are so moist that Blu has to open it for me. I lower my head in embarrassment, but then raise it because I am flattered that he understands. He opens his arms to say, "*ladies first.*" Before entering my apartment I am hoping that the foul smell has disappeared. I smell it faintly, but Blu does not say anything. I invite him to have a seat.

"Blu, would you like something to drink while I freshen up?"

"No, thank you."

He sits down on the sofa. I put on the CD player, while I hurry to take a quick shower and change. Our voices echo from the bedroom to the living room until I run into the bathroom. He smiles at my passing by and watches my derriere shake. My insides melt like ice. In just that second I want to leap on him, arouse him with my eyes and lure him into bed. My body starves for his touch and my imagination takes me to a place that I haven't been in so long. *I want intimacy.* I freshen up quickly and put on some wide legged jeans and a spaghetti strap mauve top with my open toe slip on sandals. I spike up my hair, add a little mascara, liner, shimmer shadow, and a thin layer of Bobbi Brown neutral lip-gloss. As I open the door Blu's eyes widen.

"Avery, WOW! You look amazing." He rises to his feet.

I blush.

Boy, I tell you that "WOW!" makes my whole night. Blu opens the door for me and we interlock our fingers and walk towards his silver Mercedes. It feels surreal for me to be going out on a date. I am nervous as we drive to a quaint little café on Bloomfield Ave in Montclair, Indigo Smoke. Before we leave the car Blu reaches into the back seat to grab a brown bag. He gets out of the car first, so I remain seated until he opens my door. We walk hand and hand across the street to the restaurant. Inside, the setting is that of an ex-large living room, with lots of tables and chairs. On each wall there is a huge print photo; decorative vases with branches intertwine as art pieces. The ambiance is inviting and it feels as if we are in the heart of New York City. To top off the night they have a live Jazz band, a vocalist who's a toe tapping, finger snapping, Anita Baker, Leela James, and Sade all in one. Blu asks the waitress, who introduces herself as Mahaley, for an ice bucket and he chills the bottle of wine he brought. We are feeling so relaxed. Mahaley takes our order. While we wait the vocalist sings another song that is so full of soul. First we have an appetizer of barbeque wings and then we move on to our main course. I indulge in the whiting fillet with tomato salad and a side order of mashed potatoes. And Blu has the salmon croquette with a side order of macaroni and cheese and mashed sweet potatoes. The food is outstanding and the ambiance sets a mood that has already been stirred up in me at my apartment. We talk for hours as he gazes into my eyes and gently inserts a yellow flower picked from the vase on our table, into the left side of my hair. My pulse throbs and oozes out down to my feet. He touches my hand and caresses it back and forth with his thumb. It gives me a tingle. *I'm sure he could tell that I am feelin' him.* My feet move to the drumbeats of my heart, legs spring, arms expressing my enthusiasm, hips swaying, back jerking, breasts shaking, as my bare feet praise my sisterhood. I am woman. I am powerful. I am eccentric, alluring, and...and...very horny. Right then and there on the table I want to make love to him. Ooh! My twin, Avona, is vividly persuading me. *Do it, girl. Do it! Get bold, and just do it!* But I am not courageous. So I remain seated, staring into his memorizing eyes.

After dinner we drive up to the Great Falls on McBride Ave in Paterson, and we look down at the murky water. We talk some more on the bench nearby.

He gently lifts my right hand, gives it a moist, brown sugary kiss, and then leans in to give me a kiss, but I rudely turn my face and his lips meet my cheek. I put my head down, looking at my watch and state that it's getting late, and that maybe we should be going. He has this perplexed look on his face, but does not ask any questions. He opens the car door for me and we drive home. At my building, I look him in his eyes.

"Thank you for a wonderful evening."

"Avery, you don't have to thank me for showing you a wonderful time. I did it because I wanted to. This is who I am and I appreciate the woman in my life. This is just the tip of the iceberg." I smile, as the warmth of his words flow through my veins and we say good night.

My eyes tear up as I slide my feet up to the stairway to my building. I turn around before entering the doorway and watch his car pull off. A part of me wants to kick myself, but then the other part is content with my decision. It's all about timing and the timing was not right for me. I don't want to be brash and allow one kiss. It may mislead him into thinking that I want more. My body's yearning for the contact, but my heart and conscience want to reveal the truth. The truth is that I'm HIV-positive and I need to allow him to make the final decision. I'm so torn that my heart hurts.

The after-effect of this wonderful date, I fear may turn into the last. And the thought of when to share my news with Blu only distresses me more. It's not an easy decision to make and just because we had one date doesn't mean that he's the one. I certainly need to be sure before I expose myself. I am sore inside so I allow the tears to release from my eyelids because I need an outlet. Sitting on the edge of my bed, I adamantly decide that I will share my news with Blu on our next date, if one should occur. Lying back on the bed ogling at the ceiling, I ponder my wonderful evening. Blu is a true gentleman and a part of me wishes that he wasn't, so that I can find an excuse not to see him again. I feel like calling him and allowing my running mouth to explain my behavior, but I know my words will get tongue-tied so I change my mind. I peel off my jeans and top. I am fully exposed in my bedroom wearing only my bra and panties allowing the air to hit my hot skin.

In the kitchen, I open my pills and pour a small glass of water. As I open the refrigerator it reminds me that I need to clean it out. I discard containers that look like there is mold growing on them. The coolness from the refrigerator chills my thighs. Blu has really opened me up to the reality of dating again and I don't know for sure if I'm actually ready. The thought of another woman in his arms does not sit well with me, so I know that I have to divulge my secret and hope for the best. I have to ask myself do I feel Blu is worth my time? Do I feel that he is a sincere person who will understand my reasoning for not being forthcoming right away? My biggest issue is how he will react. In my mind I envision him standing with glossed over eyes and a quiet face. He will reach for my hands and he will state that we will get through this together. Dammit! A part of me wishes he already knew, but I know in my heart it is not the appropriate time. The phone rings.

"Hello."

"Hello, it's me, Blu."

"Hi."

"Look, Um...Look. I just called to say that I don't know what I did wrong, but I want to apologize for it. I have never encountered someone rejecting me before. I must admit it really put a damper on my ego. I was surprised because you seemed into me. We seemed really in tune at the restaurant, so I guess I'm just calling for an explanation as to what happened."

"Listen, you didn't do anything wrong. There are things about me that you don't know."

"Well, I'm listening."

"It's not that simple, Blu. I can't discuss it like this. We have to be face-to-face." I pause, move my mouth away from the phone, and sigh.

"Is it that bad? You sound so serious." His voice has a hint of frustration.

"I sound serious because it is serious. I just feel that you have a right to know before we go any further." A lump in my throat forms and I try to hold back the tears.

My heart races, palms are sweaty, my body is hotter than ever, but I am trying desperately not to crack over the phone.

"Blu, when can we meet?"

"I'm flexible."

"Let's make another date for tomorrow. Maybe we can catch a movie?"

"That sounds fine. Are you okay?"

"Yes."

"Are you sure, Avery, because my instincts tell me that you aren't? I'm concerned."

"I'm okay. I'll talk with you tomorrow. You have a good night."

After we hang up I am sick to my stomach. My nerves are shot, so I make myself some peppermint tea to relax. How am I going to look him in the eye and say what I need to say? How will the words come out without me being tongue-tied? I massage my temples. I am a nervous wreck. Johnnie pops up in my mind and makes me think about what he would say if he were here. He would take me in his arms and gently stroke the edges of my hair and say, "Avery, either way it will be okay. Don't sit around moping and stressing over it. Just do the right thing." I smile because I know what I am about to do is the right thing, but the outcome is my biggest concern. I'm flustered. I decide to soak my body in a bath of honey milk and allow time to help me come up with a good approach. *What would be a good approach to tell someone that you are HIV-positive? There is no good approach, you either do it or you don't.* I get into the bath and rest my head on the bath pillow. I shut my eyes and let my thoughts go to another place in time.

It's amazing how the mind can play tricks on

you. I think about myself in another place in my life. I am not HIV-positive. I have a husband, a house, and a daughter. We are happy. I feel like I have it all in the palm of my hands and then reality sets in. I am soothing myself in a honey milk bath alone. Emotionally, I am overwhelmed. Dating. I mean, I know that it's a screening process to see if there's a match, but damn, does it have to be so difficult? I am so tense that the bath doesn't seem to loosen me up. I get out; look at my reflection in the mirror, hoping to see something that will make me feel better. I don't. I pull down my towel, wrap myself in it, and go into the living room to turn the CD player on and listen to Heather Headley. I make up my mind to leave the door half open and accept whatever happens tomorrow. It's 12:45 a.m. and I definitely am not tired so I grab Toni Morrison's book 'Love' and read until my eyes shut down.

THIRTEEN

"AGE IS NOTHING but a number," but when the big 40 starts creeping up, it makes me realize that I'm not getting any younger. In my early-mid twenties my life seemed promising. My future was bright. Now, looking back I really had a gold mine, but I don't honestly think I appreciated it. I took life for granted and I really didn't look beyond the bright lights. I was building a career, dating whomever and doing whatever, without question. The thought of wanting a family never crossed my mind, building a foundation with someone definitely never crossed my mind. It was about me and only me. I came home every day to an empty apartment. I ate alone, went to sleep alone, cried alone, and continued the same cycle day in and day out.

To be truthful the slightest bit of intimacy, having someone to come home to, sharing my space and building a foundation would make a world of difference to me. I'm lonely. I waited too long to finally realize what's important. I blocked myself in a cubicle of me. I never allowed anyone to get close enough to love me. Out of all the men that I've dated, I've never been in love. And the only time I've ever used the "L" word was with Johnnie. But that kind of love was a friendship love. I've never experienced love from a man where I could feel it throughout my body; see it in his eyes, in his touch, and through his cries. It just has never happened. That's my fault because I kept men at a distance. I bounced. It was the only way that I could assure myself from being hurt. The only man who truly hurt me so deeply was Poppa and that has scarred me for many, many years.

The walls tumbled down on January 9th and I had no one to rescue me. There was no one to call from the hospital to pick me up, or help take care of me after my attack. No shoulders to cry on. I went home to an empty apartment. Shaken up, afraid of my own damn shadow because in my mind I believed my rapist was still watching me. He knew my every move and just when I wasn't covering all of my tracks, he may strike again, but this time he would mean business and finish me off. I was frantic, jumpy from any and every noise that creaked, banged, or crackled. The memories didn't go away. They were branded in my brain forever rewinding and fast-forwarding in slow motion recapturing every scene.

At 2:00 a.m. I roll over, set my alarm, turn out my nightlight and go to sleep.

The snooze button goes off and I jump out of my skin. The room is cool from the window being open all night. I hit the snooze button, and close the window. In the bathroom, I look in the mirror, take a deep breath, and just stand still wishing I had never talked to Blu last night. Sudden warmth comes over me. Anxiously, I want to get it over with. *Maybe I should ask him to meet me at Lucille's Soul Food and Breakfast Diner on West Broadway here in Paterson?* I stand tense by the phone, and call Blu's number, but I simply hang up because I don't have the courage to follow through with my plan. Something weird comes over me so I pick up the phone; call the number again. One ring, two rings, three rings, and then Blu picks up.

"Hello."

His hello is a whisper.

"Hello, Blu, its Avery."

"Is everything okay, Avery?"

"Yes, I'm sorry to call you this early, but I was wondering if it was possible for us to meet this morning at Lucille's Diner on West Broadway? Do you know where it is?"

"Yes. I would love to meet you, but Avery, I insist on picking you up."

"Are you sure you want to do that?"

"Yes."

"Okay. Um...will you be ready around 10:00?"

"I will be there at 9:59 a.m."

Blu chuckles and it makes me feel at little better. I smile as we hang up. After my shower I go into the bedroom, open my closet and reach for my DKNY denim dress, which I adore. I scan the closet looking for shoes and a purse to match. I dab a small portion of fragrant oil on my hands and massage it all over my body. I place everything on the dresser: keys, purse, and cell phone. My stomach's growling loudly so I drink an Ensure; sit in the living room watching the morning news waiting for Blu to arrive. My teeth are chattering because I am so nervous. The scent of fear is all over me and I cannot disguise it. I am sipping sparingly on my Ensure, looking at the clock, and finally flinching when the buzzer finally goes off. I tug at my dress, and answer the intercom by pushing the open door button, and I wait. I am still like frozen ice. A gush of cowardice circulates around me and I want to panic. I am breathing heavily, heart is pumping, palms are moist, and my mouth is dry. I can feel Blu getting closer to the door and then when he rings the bell and I stiffen up. By the second ring I have regained consciousness and open the door to greet him with a smile.

"Good morning."

"Good morning, Avery. Are you ready to go?"

"Sure, I just need to grab my purse."

In the bedroom I grab my purse, keys, and cell phone, and then I drop them all. *I'm so clumsy.*

While kneeling down to pick them up, Blu calls from the other room, "Avery, are you okay?"

"Yes, here I come, Blu."

My butterflies in my stomach seem to have turned into flies. It's difficult trying to keep my cool, but I am doing the best that I can under the circumstances. We head out and Blu closes the door.

It's a gorgeous day and as I look up at the blue sky my spirit is lifted. We compliment each other's outfit. I must say, we are both stylin'. He suavely reaches for my hand as we walk towards his car and then he opens the door for me. As he shuts the door he strokes his hand against my leg. I giggle because it tickles. In the car he reaches into the backseat and pulls out some beautiful yellow roses. They are so pretty. I have the biggest smile on my face. He leans over and gives me a kiss on the cheek and we drive off. I feel like he's too good to be true.

When we arrive at Lucille's, Blu opens the door and we walk in holding hands. The waitress greets us with a smile and escorts us to a table. She hands us a menu.

"What would we like to drink?" she asks.

"Apple juice, please," I say.

"Orange juice," he says.

We stare into each other's eyes and Blu gently massages my hands.

"So, Avery, what is it that you have to tell me?" At this point I feel my words may come out in a stutter, so I pause. And as I am about to speak the waitress comes with our food. *Perfect timing.* Our eyes meet; we season our food, say grace and eat. After the meal, I get up to pay for breakfast. We stand in front of Lucille's long enough for him to reach in for a kiss and again I turn away.

Blu puts his hand up to his mouth and blows his breath out to see if there's an odor.

"Avery, what is it!"

I can hear the frustration coming through full force. I ask Blu if he can drive up to the Great Falls on McBride Ave, in Paterson, so we can talk. Blu nods his head and opens my door for me. I am nervous. Mouth is parched. I feel the perspiration under my armpits. The parking lot we pull into is empty. All that can be heard is the birds chirping.

Blu turns and looks me dead in my face and says, "Okay Avery, what is going on? Please tell me?"

I can't look Blu in his eyes at first, but then I turn to face him with tears already falling down my face. My mouth is so dry that I moisten it with my saliva. I start off rambling, confusing myself. Then, out of nowhere, I become assertive and start to speak from my heart.

"Blu, when I first saw you I thought you were a nice looking man. I was instantly attracted to you. When you gave me your number I was flattered. The reason I was so flattered was because I haven't been around a man since my best friend Johnnie."

I pause.

"Blu, the reason why I am always turning my face when you reach in to kiss me is because there is something I feel you need to know about me first."

"What? What is it, Avery?" he asks, reaching for my hand.

I see frustration building. It is in his eyes. And then I just put my faith in God and allowed the words to come out.

"Blu."

I swallow.

"Blu."

I scratch my throat.

"Blu."

I take a deep, deep breath and say, "I'm HIV-positive."

My eyes widen. Blu snatches his hand away, and moves quickly away from me. His eyes bugle out. He opens his glove compartment and grabs his sanitizer hand gel, massaging it between his fingers, inner palms, and the outer surfaces of his hands. I swallow hard as the tears continue in slow motion down my face. He is making me feel worthless. He turns to look at me with sharpness, and then turns away. A roar of scathing bullets release from his mouth as if I am being shot in the face, eyes, and one last bullet finishes me off in the left temple.

"Avery, when the hell were you going to tell me?" He turns away. "Were you going to wait until after I started having feelings for you and then drop this time bomb on me? Oh, no maybe you were going to wait until after we..."

He plays with his upper lip by pulling it, and then he turns to look at me again and I swear his eyes seem to have changed colors. He starts rubbing his crotch area. It's like his whole persona has changed.

"I ought to whip my dick out and piss on yo infected ass," he says smugly, while gripping himself like he's opting to masturbate.

My ears can't believe what he has just said to me. The distraught look upon my face stresses it. *What happened to the "gentleman" that was wooing me? The nice guy? The respectful guy?* My head is spinning.

"*BIIIIITCH, GET THE HELL OUTTA MY CAR!!*"

I literally flinched.

"*GET THE FUCK OUT!*" he yells as his finger points to the door.

As I open the car door Blu shifts his gear into reverse, and backs up. I quickly jump out before he pulls off. My heart races. He is a different person, totally out of control. He won't even allow me to explain anything. He left me standing there with bloodshot eyes. My heart shatters and I feel like I shouldn't have said anything. But then there was Johnnie, his truthfulness led me to believe that it was the right thing to do. *Look where it left me. I am alone.* My head hangs low as I wipe the tears walking from block to block. *I don't wanna feel the pain that I'm feeling. Stinging me like a green hornet. I want it to stop. I want it to go away. I wanna die.*

When I reach my apartment building I feel lightheaded and my body is limp. I place my key into my door, and open it. With my back against the door I slide all the way down to the floor and I start to ball. Blu has hurt me something deep. I cry even louder to express my inner pain. He treated me as if I am nothing—a nobody. And it didn't faze him. I sit there for an hour numb with disbelief. My eyes are swollen and the expression on my face tells a tale of truth. I feel lost. So lost that I want to stand before an on-coming train and let it take me out. The light in my living room flickers on and off, but I don't think anything of it. But then it keeps happening. A warm sensation surrounds me as if someone is in the room with me. It's as if arms are embracing me. I smell the scent of Polo Black and I smile and cry all at the same time. I get off the floor and go to sit on the sofa. Often, I talk to Johnnie and this day is no different. I look up at the ceiling and say, "Thank you. Thank you for being the only man who never hurt me." I stretch my body across the sofa and listen to the outside world. I glance over to the edge of the end table and pick up Mr. Clausen's business card. I also think about the young lady in the salon who was handing out the flyers and look over by the phone to see if I still have mine. My mind is on speed dial. I sit up and grab a piece of paper and a pen and begin to jot down ideas for a business. Johnnie has given me a location in Montclair. I think about giving Mr. Clausen a call on Monday to see if he or maybe someone he knows could assist me in creating a business plan. I feel a little better because deep in my heart I know that I did the right thing. The soreness is still there and it will probably be there for a few more days, but eventually it will fade.

I sleep through the night, no night sweats, hallucinations, or chest pains. It is just a peaceful night's sleep. It is a blessing to feel energized and alive. I haven't felt this good in so long that my body doesn't even know how to respond to the feeling. I sit up and start to think about my business name. Do I want to call it Ground Floor of Flava or do I want to call it something else? I want something that will represent Johnnie and me. Everything that I do will always include him. I peel a piece of yellow post-it off and reach for a pen and write different names down until I decide on Anonymous. I immediately think of myself. It's a touchy subject to expose to everyone, but it feels right to me. It feels right to my spirit.

I get out of bed to get a bigger piece of paper and write down what type of business I want, whether it should be a Coffee Shop with Spoken Word, or a Gallery of Arts for amateur artists trying to get noticed. There is a building that Johnnie suggested I need to go check out before I call Mr. Clausen. I run into the bathroom and turn the nozzle of the shower, then run back in the bedroom and snatch some undergarments before I run back to the bathroom and jump in the shower. Idea after idea travels through my mind like a rush. This positive energy surges through my whole body and it takes control. My concept for Anonymous consists of a circle of positive juices, all blending together like a tropical mix. It won't matter where you are from, your color, or gender; it will only be a matter of substance. That substance will make it unique. Real names are not important because you will be able to be whomever you chose to be without conflict. Whoever you envision yourself to be that's who you are. Discrimination will be prohibited. It doesn't matter if two people have the same anonymous name, simply because they will have the same hunger to appreciate the differences in their artistry. And that hunger will feed a thousand soulfully. Instantly, I have captured the whole essence of Anonymous and it is riveting.

I hurry out of the shower. I have started something and I don't want to lose my train of thought. I feel it will be easier to have a gallery of arts for talented unknown artists all coming together giving a piece of their souls. I'm excited as I walk into the bedroom to get dressed.

Just yesterday my life seemed so depressing and full of confusion, but today things are being put into proper perspective. It seems so ironic how life can transform a negative into a positive so quickly. A part of me felt like crawling under a rock when Blu displayed his terms of endearment, but God's so powerful and He and only He can make things prosperous if only I adhere to His calling. I feel a calming, sort of spiritual energy all through my apartment as if something or someone is rescuing me from a week, month, or year of heart wrenching distress.

Ring, ring, ring.

"Hello." There's no one on the other end so I

hang up. The caller ID displays a number that is *unavailable*. I finish getting dressed and reach for my notepad, pen and backpack and head for Montclair. I snatch the post-it with the address on it from my dresser. A tingling sensation runs through my arm. It feels unfamiliar. Like an awareness of what's taking place. It's not something I can describe in simple terms, but it's a spiritual feeling that makes me feel connected. Certain things cannot always be explained and maybe this is one of them.

In the kitchen I make a sandwich, pour some milk into a container and wrap the sandwich to go. I don't feel the need to put on any makeup so I walk straight out the door, into my car and drive off. The address on the post-it reads 1140 Bloomfield Ave, which I'm familiar with because my stylist's salon is on that particular block.

The day keeps changing. One minute the sun is out and then it peeks back in and the sky gets gray like it's gonna rain. I roll down my driver's side window letting the air mildly surge through my natural tresses as I listen to Michael Baisden, Love, Lust, & Lies.

When I arrive in Montclair, I stop in front of the building, look up and down the street, and park. I stand in front and jot down the number displayed on the window for leasing. Placing my face close enough to the glass I see how big it is inside. Impulsively, I call the number and a woman answers.

"Thank you for calling Tribe Realtors, Charla Jenkins-Rollin, how can I help you?"

"Hi, my name is Avery Love, and I am inquiring about the building on 1140 Bloomfield Ave in Montclair."

Mrs. Jenkins-Rollin gives me a brief description of the place. She says it's a two-floor property and that there are four vacant apartments above. She stresses that the building can be leased for just the commercial space or the entire building is for sale for an asking price of three hundred eighty-nine thousand dollars. I nearly bite my lip when she gives me the figures. I know that I cannot afford it, but I still want to see the inside so I ask if it's possible if someone could come and show it to me. She seems very enthused and says that she will be delighted to come and show me the place if I am able to give her twenty minutes.

"Sure," I say and I wait in my car for her to arrive.

Twenty-minutes have passed when a champagne-colored Jaguar pulls up in front of me. I wait for the woman to exit her car and give me eye contact, which signals me that she could possibly be Mrs. Jenkins-Rollin. I get out of my car and greet her with a smile. We shake hands and formally introduce ourselves.

Mrs. Jenkins-Rollin has a pleasant vibe to her. She's a petite woman, possibly in her mid-forties, with a caramel complexion. Her short, tapered, natural cut is polished and complements her features. She wears a soft pastel pink Isaac Mizrahi designer pants suit and she speaks very proper. I feel a little awkward because I look shabby, because my intentions were to just take a glimpse of the building and not really meet with anyone. My main concern is at times folks can be judged by their appearance and mine unfortunately screams, *broke!* I keep my head held high, speak with some common sense and make eye contact hoping to camouflage my outer appearance.

"Ms. Love, this place has been vacant for little over a year. The owner took ill and could not continue with his life-long business, which was a delicatessen. He was doing very well until he had a stroke and could not work the long hours. So he decided to try and sell the place. Unfortunately, no one was bidding."

She opens the door and we step into this room and an aura comes over me and I know this place is meant for me. There is a stairway that spirals upwards. The rooms are enormously large and should fit about one hundred to one hundred fifty people just on the first floor. I know that I can convert it into a gallery. The dust makes me cough a bit, but as I look around everything seems promising. I close my eyes and envision a stage for Spoken Word, the left wall for photography, the right wall for paintings, and in the center will be a setting of table and chairs. The hardwood floors are refined and beautiful. As we walk upstairs I picture more artwork along the brick walls. Upstairs could be a social setting where folks could mingle and relax. I picture everything, every room concisely in my head. Mrs. Jenkins-Rollin speaks about square feet and I see her lips moving, but her voice is muted as I am in my own world. And then I hear her say, "What are you looking to do with the place?"

"Huh?"

"What type of business are you looking to turn this into?"

"Mrs. Jenkins-Rollin, I was thinking about a gallery of arts."

"What a wonderful idea, Ms. Love."

I nod in agreement. The price without the vacant apartments is three thousand a month. I don't want to react with her looking me in my face so I crack a smile and we walk out. She hands me her business card and asks me to think about it and to give her a call if I am seriously interested. *I am very interested, but how I can afford three thousand a month.* I am not going to allow the price to discourage me. I get back to my car and I search for Mr. Clausen's business card and give him a call hoping to set up an appointment. A young woman answers the phone stating that Mr. Clausen is currently out of the office, so she takes a message. I have so many different ideas in my head it just isn't even funny.

Since I am on the block I decide to stroll into the salon to say hello to Aja. But before reaching the salon I stop at His and Her Incense Boutique. It's nicely decorated and the scents lure you in as soon as you pass by. I sample some of the oils that appeal to me and others just make me feel nauseous. A man's standing behind me.

"Pardon Me," I say.

He says, "Beautiful, you are not in my way."

I smile.

He walks around to glance at the soaps, bath beads, fragrant oils, candles, lotions and foot butter. My back's hot as if someone is right behind me. The heat is intense and then the same man approaches me.

"Excuse me Ms? May I ask, what is your name?"

I look him in his hazel eyes and say, "Avery."

"I'm Travar Atkin." He reaches out his hand.

Travar's definitely attractive, with strong features and a whitening smile. His height has to be close to seven feet and his biceps are chiseled. He has long dreadlocks that dangle down his back, but they need a bit of grooming. His goatee is outlined with sharpness on his honey skin. He's a pleasure to look at. And I must say I am lusting as I suck on a piece of apple jolly rancher. I pretend that I am nibbling on a succulent part of the turkey. The wing that doesn't have much meat, but leaves a flavorful taste in your mouth as you nibble all the skin off the bone. When I look at Travar my mind is in the gutter. And I don't feel dirty about it because I am physically attracted to him. Every body part of significance is tingling in agreement. I have to focus while Travar is speaking and it is quite difficult. The man is beyond fine! He kind of reminds me of Shemar Moore, but with dreadlocks.

"So Avery, do you live around here?"

"No, I don't."

"Well, I live right up the street on Sutton. Are you familiar with the area?"

"Some parts."

"What brings you over this way?"

"Damn. Travar, you sure ask a lot of questions."

"Oh, I'm sorry, didn't mean to pry."

"No, it's okay. I didn't mean to come off rude."

"No harm done. Is it possible for me to get your number? Maybe we can go out to a movie, dinner, whatever?" He cracks a smile.

I must admit I am hesitant at first. Blu travels through my mind. *This might end up being a re-*

enactment of the 'Blu episode' and I really can't stand for that to happen again. So I figure I will ask for his number just to see if he will hesitate in giving it out, but he doesn't. Boy, do I feel stupid. Travar is very forthcoming with his home, cell, and business number on his business card. Damn. I have pie on my face. He says that he's a Promoter who is always searching for new talent in the entertainment business. How ironic? I don't mention anything about my idea for my building. I've learned to never really talk about things until I know for sure that I can make it happen. He and I walk around together as we buy a few items in the store. As we leave we stand in front of the store making small talk.

"Avery, give me a call tonight?"

"Okay." I start to walk off with my camera in the back of my head snapping snapshots of his tight ass.

I walk two stores down and enter the salon to say *hello* to Aja. She seems extremely busy so I wave and leave to go home. I get in my car; pop in one of my Jill Scott CDs and drive away.

The day is young and I do not know what to expect from the rest of it. Everything is very pleasant and my spirit is on high. Instead of going straight home, I drive up to Garrett Mountain in West Paterson, park my car, and lay my plaid blanket across the grass thinking about *Anonymous.* My cell phone rings and it's a callback from Mr. Clausen's office.

"Hello."

"Hello, this is Mr. Clausen, how have you been?"

"I've been fine."

"Is everything okay, Ms. Love?"

"Yes, I was actually calling on a business matter that I am hoping you can assist me with. I'm thinking about starting my own business and I want some insight on structuring everything. I thought since Johnnie trusted you, you would be the perfect candidate for me."

"That sounds delightful, Ms. Love. How does

your schedule look tomorrow?"

"Open, Mr. Clausen." I chuckle with enthusiasm.

"Let's meet, say around, 9:30 a.m."

"I will be there."

"See you then, good day."

"Goodbye."

I roll on the blanket with excitement. I don't care that folks are watching. Stimulation runs through my blood vessels with the anticipation that everything, no matter how difficult it may be, is coming together.

Looking around I see a couple so full of intimacy. Not the kind of intimacy that is distasteful, but the kind that floods with compassion and understanding. I can tell by their body language, eye contact, holding hands, kissing in public, that they are absorbed in a deep found love. I stare at them and a part of me is slightly jealous. The bittersweet taste is on the crevasse of my mouth, but then I'm distracted by someone's radio loudly playing "Always and Forever," by Heatwave and the scene just makes complete sense. Love is in the air. Love for another or love within self. All the pieces make sense and that is what changes my whole mindset. My time is coming and I want all of me to be in focus. I fold up my blanket and walk towards my car to go home, relax and write out a business plan.

I am famished when I walk in the door so I go into the kitchen to make myself a turkey and Swiss cheese sandwich. My mind drifts to Travar. I smile. *My, my, my...God truly blessed him.* Walking past my phone I pick up the flyer that the young lady distributed at the salon. It seems weird, but I feel connected to this flyer like I am supposed to be doing something to help out. *What can I possibly do?* There is a phone number as well as a website address on the footnote. I explore the site on the Internet and read about the history of *Red Alert.*

A young gentleman named Xavier Combs III is the founder of the non-profit organization. He reveals a candid story as to why he founded this company in

1999. It was the bereavement of his only sister, aunt and later a best friend. Since they were all women he felt compelled to do something to make folks aware of the situation. They all contracted the disease in different ways and they all had different views on the impact of how it affected them in society. He said that he was astonished by their stories because they felt they had nothing to lose by being brutally honest. He spoke of his sister who contracted the disease from her boyfriend. He stated it nearly crushed him to watch her perish right before his eyes. His aunt was a heavy heroin drug user. He stated that he despised her, but appreciated her honesty. She died. His best friend was in her last year of college about to graduate with honors, when she took ill. She needed a blood transfusion. Her parents were both deceased and she was the only child. He stated he felt helpless, wanting to help out but could not because he was not a match. She was given the blood transfusion only to find out months later that she had the AIDS virus. She was devastated and no matter how much he was there for her, he could not stop the inevitable. She couldn't handle the drastic changes and later took her own life by hanging herself. All these women were between the ages of 20 and 43.

I become tearful as I read so I pick up the phone and speak to a representative. I schedule an appointment to meet on August 16th. The representative asks me how I had heard about the organization and I briefly explain that I have one of the flyers.

After I hang up I sit still staring at the computer screen.

Fourteen

I AM RELUCTANT to admit it, but I am indeed my Ma'am's shadow. When I was seventeen a huge change came about for me. Poppa. Poppa was the kind of man who was very set in his ways. He was old fashioned. Folks perceived him as being very outspoken and very direct. He did not have a soft touch when he approached issues. Not Poppa. Seventeen was my senior year. I graduated in the class of 1986 from Parrington High School in Wayne, New Jersey. Poppa felt that at that age I was considered an adult. The day after graduating he walked in my bedroom and handed me an envelope. I ripped it open quickly thinking it was a graduation gift. Only to realize it was one thousand dollars. I turned and looked him in his eyes and said, "Poppa, what's this for?"

"Avery you are an adult. It is time fo you tuh venture out intuh the world of opportunity. I wan' you tuh see—touch it and hold ontuh it as if it were your last breath tuh take."

I looked at him and frowned.

"Poppa, I just graduated yesterday. I don't even have a job, apartment, or anything. What is one thousand dollars going to get me?"

"Avery dat's wha' you are gonna find out."

He was assertive and the look in his eyes meant he was serious.

"Twelve o'clock, please, have your things packed and head out."

"Poppa, I can't possibly be ready by twelve o'clock."

"Avery, you have no choice. Twelve o'clock head out!" He said with authority.

I looked him dead in his eye and felt as if I did not even know him. I felt empty inside. Tears formulated and rolled down my face, as I started getting my belongings together. I just shoved them in my luggage, cussin' him under my breath. My body was tender like someone had just cut through me with a keen knife. I was numb to the core. And Ma'am. Ma'am never spoke on how she felt about the situation. She didn't even come up to help me pack. She would not dare try to override Mr. Love's final word. Oh, no. Not her. I suffered for many years after that. And flash backing to it now doesn't lessen the soreness in my throat.

The whole idea of me getting my hands dirty in running a business scares me tremendously. I have nothing to fall back on if I fail. No. There's no cushion of security. It doesn't matter how *beautiful* one perceives me to be. It has nothing to do with my big breasts, wide hips or nice rump-pa-dump. It has nothing to do with any of that. It's merely about nourishing my whole being to make this dream a reality. I must devote, commit, and most importantly ask for help from total strangers. I need to build trust in relationships in a working environment that is acceptable for everyone. Selfishness has no role in this and if it did it would only disrupt and everything accomplished would come crashing down. I am so used to depending on me and I know that this is going to be a whole new world for me. But I'm optimistic. Walking through a door with an open mind is now how I see it.

I've been up thinking all night. I am so anxious to speak with Mr. Clausen. I hope he can guide me in the right direction, advising me by giving me the positives and the negatives of opening a business. I need to relax. A bath of hot bubbles of bath bead oil will help to alleviate some of my anxiety. I pull out some floating candles and a large clear bowl, add some water to the bowl, place the candles in and light them. Then dim the lights and turn the radio on low. I ease into the bath. I'm enjoying the moment of tranquility. While lying in my pool of serenity I think about Johnnie at Nuyorican Poets Café. Man, I feel so lucky to have had such a beautiful and loving friend. Most folks go through their whole lives wishing, hoping for a best friend. I really want this process to be a tribute to Johnnie.

Soaking for a half hour was enough. I towel dry and go into the bedroom to sprawl my naked butt onto my bed. Then a few seconds later, I stand up and look in the mirror, seeing a woman who has come a long way. I see a woman glow, not because of a man giving her a compliment, but because she is finally truly finding her way. Confidence sneaks through my pores and outlines my face. I envision myself either sinking or swimming towards something great. I am serious enough to put the money that Johnnie has left me to support this need, want, and desire to have something of my own. I crave it for the both of us.

Tomorrow's all planned out in my head. When I meet with Mr. Clausen I want to portray the look of a businesswoman. I want to be dressed up in business attire. When he first met me it was under unfortunate circumstances, but I want him to see that I have my head together.

Morning is upon me and I feel absolutely incredible. Like a new woman I leap out of bed and go into my walk-in closet and reach for my navy blue pin-stripe suit. I will look sharp. I damn near sprint into the kitchen as if I have already drank some Red Bull. I make some eggs whites with cheese, a couple pieces of turkey sausage, toast to a toasted golden brown and pour myself a tall glass of apple juice. It smells like Ma'am's kitchen and I sit and I let myself enjoy it like I am eating some of Ma'am's peach cobbler with vanilla ice cream on top. That woman sure knew how to cook!

After finishing breakfast I am getting ready to meet Mr. Clausen. Now its 8:30 a.m. Time seems to fly by so quickly when you move around like a snail.

The lobby is quiet. When I open the door I feel a slight chill in the air, but it feels pleasant. Opening the door of the car I place my briefcase in the backseat. I take off my blazer and hang it on the hook so that it won't get wrinkled from my seatbelt. I hear Johnnie preaching to me about being prompt. I smile because it is as if he is sitting beside me in the car saying, *Gurl, I taught you well.* I laugh out loud and turn on the radio. It doesn't take long to reach Mr. Clausen's office.

I walk in and greet a young woman whose name is etched on a piece of carved wood in bold letters. It spells out Tia Smith. She has shoulder length dirty blonde hair with blue eyes, thin lips and a tapered nose, and very deep dimples that you could stick your fingers in. I introduce myself.

She says, "Mr. Clausen is expecting you." I only sit for a moment and then she calls me and I follow her to his office with my head held high.

Mr. Clausen looks different because he isn't dressed in a business suit. He's more or less business casual with his khakis and Grant Thomas polo collared shirt. His salt-n-pepper hair is still very distinguished and I find him to be very attractive for his age. He greets me with a smile and says it is a pleasure to see me. He has a strange look in his eyes like he is checking me out. I smirk because I am flattered. He offers me a seat and then leans back in his executive chair. He looks so relaxed and it makes me feel more comfortable.

"Ms. Love, would you like a cup of tea or coffee?"

"Tea would be fine."

"Tia, would you kindly bring Ms. Love, a cup of tea, please?"

"Sure. Ms. Love, how many sugars would you like?" she asks.

"Oh, two is fine, thank you."

As Tia walks out of the office Mr. Clausen asks, "Ms. Love, what would you like to discuss?"

Opportunity is knocking so I immediately jump in.

"Well, as you know, Johnnie left me money for whatever I want. Well, I'm seriously thinking about opening up a business." I sit erect with my legs crossed and a look of confidence written on my face.

"What type of business?"

Mr. Clausen seems very attentive. I reach into my briefcase and show him my business plan, and a blueprint of how I want the place to look.

"Well, Ms. Love, you seemed to have been soaking your idea." And he cracks a smile.

"Yes, I have."

"May I ask, what brought this on?"

"Well, I just feel like this is something that would bring some joy into my life. Reaching out to other people would be a healing for me, and then I thought what better way to give tribute to Johnnie."

Mr. Clausen nods his head.

"Well, have you found a location?"

"Actually, yes, in Montclair, on Bloomfield Ave."

I give him the business card of Mrs. Jenkins-Rollin and explain the leasing price, describe the two-levels, and I even mention the possibilities of buying the whole building. He pauses, places his hand by his mouth and massages it like he's deep in thought.

"Johnnie left you one hundred thousand dollars, correct?"

"Yes."

"The asking price for the building is three hundred eighty-nine thousand dollars, correct?"

"Yes."

"And if you just lease the commercial space it will be three thousand a month, correct?"

"Yes."

"What type of business, would this be?"

"It will be a gallery for the arts so people can come and enjoy music, photography, paintings, singing, and poetry. It will give them a lounge to come to and unwind in after work or on the weekends. I want to have desserts, appetizers and have even considered people being allowed to bring their own food if they choose to."

"I must say, Ms. Love, that's certainly a wonderful idea."

Mr. Clausen continues to massage the creases of

his mouth. He throws out several options: bank loan, grants for small business, and combining the use of the money I have from Johnnie.

"Now, I know that one hundred thousand is not a lot, so I've considered trying my bank as well as any grants or other possibilities."

Mr. Clausen nods in agreement and states that he will be thrilled to assist me with the process. He advises me that his fee will be one thousand dollars. I feel that I can trust him, so I write him a check. He states he has a lot of networking power and he knows people that can help us try and get this off the ground. After discussing business, he looks me over and says, "Ms. Love, you look delightful."

"Thank you, Mr. Clausen."

We shake hands and he personally walks me to the door and says that he will be in touch very soon. I keep my composure, but once I am in my car I take a deep breath and exhale slowly. This is a major deal and I am praying that everything runs smoothly.

On my way home I decide to stop at Wachovia Bank to look into filling out an application for a small business loan. The determination of the loan will leave me with options of leasing or buying, if I'm approved. That will give me some idea and maybe the difference can be approved by a grant. I hand my application to a young obese man with freckles, small eyes, long pointy nose, with bold red curly hair. He's sitting behind a desk that reads: Customer Service Representative.

He looks over my application and then says, "Ms. Love, someone will either contact you by phone or send you a letter in the mail about your qualifications."

"Thank you."

"You're very welcome."

I am boosted with the assurance that I am going to be approved for the loan. I walk out of the bank feeling high, and kick my heels to a new beginning.

The sweet smell of rain is in the air and I do not want to get caught in it. The sky is dark. It is about to pour. I am ten minutes away from my apartment but I lead foot home in seven. I dash out of the car and run into the building before the dime size drops soak me. I can't wait to get into my apartment and peel off this suit. I am so used to dressing comfortably in my jeans, dresses, and Capri's. And my feet are crying for mercy in these shoes. As I open the door the shoes go flying; the blazer is being pulled off, the blouse buttons are being unloosened, and my pants are inching their way down my legs before I even get to the bedroom. I feel like I am suffocating. It pays to look the part, but it is torture. I walk around in undergarments letting my skin breathe.

It is now 11:30 a.m. and I have no plans. There is no place for me to be, so I sit on the sofa and watch TV before dozing off into a catnap. I awake close to ten minutes to two I yawn, stretch and try to get the stiffness out of my body. I hear drops falling against the window as if they are knocking to come inside. The sky is in tears, releasing big drops that pound on top of cars as it washes the dirt to the ground. Streets are flooding because the sewers are clogged with debris. Watching from the living room window I can see the rain slow down and then thicken as if it's playing tag, like it's trying to catch folks off guard and get 'em soaking wet. The streets are not filled with folks loitering trying to make a hustle. It is quiet. Travar invades my mind. I search aimlessly for his business card, Travar Atkin. I pick up the phone and give him a call and as I am about to give it one last ring he picks up.

"Hello."

"Hi Travar, this is Avery. I don't know if you remember meeting me at the His and Her Incense Boutique in Montclair?"

Travar laughs in amusement. I'm lost because I cannot figure out what I have said that is so funny.

"Yes. Avery, I remember," he says comically in a Jamaican accent.

"Why did you laugh?"

"Because you're already prejudging me before you really get to know me. You're thinking that I have soooooooooo many women that I can't even recall meeting you just yesterday. Insult me a little harder, why don't you."

"No, I wasn't trying to imply anything of the sort."

"So Avery, do you have a last name?"

"Yes, my last name is Love."

"Avery Love, it has a ring to it." He laughs.

Surely, I must have missed the punch line.

"Tell me a little bit about yourself, Ms. Love?"

"What do you wanna know?"

"How do you make your living?"

"Currently, I am unemployed, but I have some business prospects in line."

"What do you do for fun?"

"Well, Travar, I don't know because I am more of a homebody. I enjoy writing and reading."

He interrupts me. HOW RUDE!

"That is boring, boring, boring, and drum roll please, BORING!"

Travar has hit a soft spot. So I decide to defend myself.

"What is so boring about stimulating my mind?"

"Aren't you a testy one? I like it."

I chuckle because he sounds like Jim Carey.

He laughs.

I cannot help it, but I start laughing because I can clearly see that Travar is a comedian. He definitely has a great sense of humor and it just reels me in more. Travar decides to go in for the kill with the next question.

"So Avery, what type of men do you normally date?"

I'm quick on my feet with the answer, "Good-looking."

"Okay, okay. I feel yah. At least you have a sense of humor; most of these women that I've dated are so high maintenance that they can't even crack a smile afraid that they will crack their makeup or something. I have been wondering where all the "real sistas" have been hiding."

"Well, us sistas been wondering where all the real men have been hiding. It works both ways."

"True that, true that. Avery, you are all right in my book."

"Oh, I'm glad I get your stamp of approval." I roll my eyes and pucker my lips.

We both laugh.

Although it is raining outside it is bright in my apartment. My spirit is on high and nothing is bringing that high down. Travar is stimulating, but I have learned not to allow my guard to fall so easily. His boyish charm and amicable ways are only an invite, but it doesn't mean that I have to accept. Yes, his package is all that and a plate full of smothered barbeque ribs. But I am in control, at least over the phone. He is definitely the prime rib where you find yourself licking the sauce off of your fingers. All of my little lusting thoughts are between me, me, and me. I grow hot and the tingling sensation pulsates throughout my body, with a rush. I can't imagine how I will be face-to-face, but I am not intimidated.

"Avery, let me just cut to the chase, would you like to have dinner with me?"

I smile.

"Yes."

"Great! How is tomorrow at 7:00?"

"Fine."

"What type of food do you like?"

"I'm open."

"Well, how about a home cooked meal?"

I have a 'live one'!!! HCM (home cooked meal) it is not a figment of my imagination. I have a 'live one'!

I am very flattered. I leap on the invitation to come over for dinner. He probably doesn't realize it, but when a man says he knows how to cook that is like buying a woman platinum diamond stud earrings, at least for me. I feel like I just hit the jackpot. Dang, he is fine, and he knows how to cook, is employed, and has his own apartment. "Shoot!" It doesn't matter if he has or doesn't have a car. Four out of five is like hitting the freaking lottery. Travar gives me his address again. I jot the address down on a piece of paper, but we talk an hour longer before we say goodbye.

In my mind I have highlighted the important points of the conversation. Travar seems down-to-earth, not arrogant even though he is fine as hell. I turn the volume up on the TV to watch Oprah.

I remember back in December of 2003, Oprah went to South Africa to give Christmas gifts to all the children in different villages. I had no reaction. I just knew that people were dying from AIDS. Children were left to fend for themselves, sick, hungry and cold. My whole outlook on life was put in a different perspective once I saw that show. But it didn't pierce to the core of me. What really hit me was when the hospitals had no medication to comfort their pain. The mothers, fathers and children were suffering. Anguish resided in me because they had to leave their children who depended on them. Now they were depending on their children. There were young and older children who had to work to support the family. I had no reaction when watching the show back then, but now my heart cries, silently. People are dying, dying a death that is silent at first and then progressively explodes within weakening the immune system. It is traumatizing, especially for those who live in *poverty* because they have no means to get the proper treatment and quickly they dry up looking way beyond their years. Eventually they surrender. It may sound harsh, but it is reality. People are left counting the blessings of yesterday because their todays are agonizing and tomorrows are not promised.

In this life I have to think of everyday as *my* last and stop putting off things that I want or desire. I need to stop waiting for that so-called 'right time' because that time may never be right. I have to take a leap of faith and hope that I am making the right decision. And if it is not the right one, then I will need to trust and believe that another door will open, whether I walk through it is totally up to me. But best believe if I don't another shall. Missed opportunities happen quite frequently when fear straps one down, because it can have anyone believe that they are unworthy. You can crave a stomach of fullness and only receive crumbs of a life that isn't even enough to feed a damn mouse. But common sense tells us to continue to search for nourishment.

FIFTEEN

I SIT IN the living room contemplating if I should stay home or go to Travar's house for dinner. I want to but I'm wondering if it's a wise decision. Physically, the attraction for him is intense; so intense that it makes my toes wiggle. His voice penetrates through tantalizing parts of me that have taken men months to entice. I can't figure it out and truthfully I don't really want to know. I feel like maybe I am setting myself up for disappointment. Why am I about to torture myself? *Control, keep everything in control and it will be okay, Avery.* Convincing my mind doesn't necessarily mean my body will listen. I am a woman who has needs and those needs have not been dealt with in what seems like a decade. I can't turn my feelings on and off like a water faucet. I can't stop the tingling sensation. I can't stop the thoughts. I like a good smelling man with nice masculine hands massaging all of my tension away. I like a man nibbling on my earlobe, while whispering sweet nothings. I like flowers, candy, and jewelry. Point blank, I like men!

I already said that I will be there, so there is no need to change my mind with all the trouble he is going through to prepare dinner for me it would be inconsiderate to cancel. I have to put myself in his shoes, so I decide to go. I have six hours to prepare for dinner so I lounge around the house. I really want to look sexy this evening. Normally I don't go out of my way, but I feel sexy, and hope to reel him in. He may misunderstand my intentions and call me a tease and that is possibly true, but if he knew my situation maybe then he would understand how I am feeling. I don't want to make the same mistake I made with Blu. I'll spill the beans tonight. This is a sticky situation and I truly wish I do not have to be a part of it. I just wanna enjoy the company of a man without having to concern myself with whether I will see him again after I divulge my secret. This shit puts a damper on everything. I must think positive. *This evening will not be like it was with Blu.* I'll leave before things get out of hand.

I diligently try to choose the right outfit for this evening. What color will bring out my eyes? Maybe rust, off-white, midnight blue, or the basic black spaghetti strap dress would be appropriate. It is unanimous; black will set the evening off right. I run a hot oil bath of ocean, jasmine, and lavender all blending together making an insatiable fragrance. I close my eyes in front of the mirror and ask myself, *what do you want to come of this evening?* My body is yearning for lovemaking. *Am I going to be able to be honest with Travar to see if he would fulfill my request?* I'm horny, so horny that his smell may moisten my vagina. I had already ordered my Reality Female Condoms and received them Express mail. Who's to say if or when they will be used? But I am taking the initiative to protect myself, as well as Travar. I soak for about thirty minutes and try to insert the little rascal, but it is quite frustrating. After about three good tries I think I have it down. But I am a little anxious to know how it is going to feel during sex. I start to get dressed. I slip on my silk undergarments, zip up my black Oscar de la Renta dress that hugs all of my curves and then strap on my sexy black open toe Jimmy Choo's. I apply my MAC smoky eye shadow and a natural Bobbi Brown peach lip-gloss. I dab a tiny spot of DKNY Be Delicious behind each ear and around my neck and even dab a bit on the berry bush. I put on my 24-karat gold rope necklace and teardrop diamond studs, and spike my hair. I am absolutely stunning and I feel incredible. I call Travar to let him know that soon I'll be on my way.

I grab my Oscar de la Renta clutch bag and keys and leave out. I stop at the liquor store to pick up a bottle of wine. In the store I have a strut in my walk that makes all heads turn. Yes, I am feeling myself. The dress puts some oomph in it. But by the time I have reached Travar's street a feeling of nervousness and butterflies in my stomach come over me. The feeling increases when I ring his doorbell. My feet tap, and my fingers play make-believe piano along my hip. The door opens. Travar stands there and doesn't say a word. I turn and look the other way because I suddenly feel uncomfortable. He has this look in his hazel eyes that indicates he is stunned. I smile.

Travar says, "Um...I'm Um...Um, I'm sorry for staring, but you look scrumptious." His eyes are burning through my skin.

I'm flattered. The look on his face makes me feel sexy as hell. And I must say he looks good 'nough to slop with a biscuit and scoop with a teaspoon of honey. He's casually dressed in black slacks and a sexy periwinkle shirt. He holds my hand as he welcomes me into his apartment. Inside I realize that he has similar taste. His apartment is gorgeous. I hand him the bottle of Yellowbird Merlot that I bought. I scope out his tall windows, and scented candles, silver and gold ribbons around the assorted arrangement of flowers on the dining room table, with a setting of black china, and a silver bucket chilling a bottle of Dom Perignon. I smell the aroma of the food. It is heavenly. Miles Davis is playing in the background, which really sets the scene. My eyes are getting misty because he went through all this for me. I am speechless. We sit on his raisin-colored leather loveseat and he pours us a glass of Dom Perignon while we wait for the dinner to finish. When he looks in my eyes I am falling. Hell I fell. His body scent of "Nude Boy" is seductive and I want to reach out and kiss him. My heart is dancing and in between my legs it's moist and creamy. I can feel my lips sticking from the cream. I exhale trying to show restraint. Travar moves closer to me on the loveseat. I'm on fire. We toast to friendship. *Damn. I want him. I want him badly.* I never feel this comfortable with anyone, other than Johnnie. The evening is really starting off well. He checks on dinner, while I use his bathroom. It's too good to be true; this man has the cleanest bathroom I have ever seen for a man. When I return, he serves dinner. I ask if he needs any help but he tells me that I am his guest and he wants to wait on me.

Oh...my... God! I know I just hit the damn lottery for sho'.

"Ms. Love, your dinner is served." He holds out his left arm with his right arm holding the folded towel that dangles as if he's a waiter. I smile.

He escorts me to the table, pulls out my chair and sits on the opposite end. The table is delightful with lasagna, chicken Parmesan, salad, dinner rolls, and a strawberry cheesecake for dessert. I get up from my chair, walk over to him and kiss him on the cheek to show my appreciation.

He stares in my eyes and says, "Avery, you look very beautiful."

I am already melted but the butter is bubbling on a high flame of lust.

"Thank you, Travar."

In between my legs is burning hot cream that is coating my lips. I am foaming at the mouth.

"You look edible, if I may say so myself, Travar." I lure him in by wetting my lips.

I swallow hard trying not to become teary-eyed. I truly believe that he feels I am beautiful just by the look in his eyes.

After dinner, we sip a cup of gourmet coffee and sit on the loveseat talking and cuddling. He unbuckles my shoes and massages my feet. *Oh...my...God! The man massages feet. I've died and gone to heaven, for sho'.* He starts kissing me on my neck, while his other hand strokes my thigh. My body grows fiery hot. I want to just spread 'em and invite him in. I tease his earlobe and find it's his sensitive spot. Travar moans and I start kissing his neck. I feel the bulge in his pants knowing that things are heating up. My conscience is speaking, damn near screaming at me. *Avery! Avery! Stop!* But I ignore that inner voice because I want him so bad. I want to feel him inside of me. We continue on until he has my right breast in his hand, sucking on my nipple. I moan.

"Travar, please stop." He knows that I don't mean it. I know that I don't mean it. I don't want him to stop. If anything, I want him to keep on going until he pops my precious gem allowing me to release my built-up juices onto him. The look in his eyes alerts me that he is into it and trying to stop him now is going to be difficult. But I have no choice in the matter. Damn.

"Travar, please stop?"

"Avery, what's wrong?"

I get a little choked up because he is staring me in my face. I clear my throat several times before speaking. Taking deep breaths, I pause, deep breaths, pause and then begin to speak. I dangle my head low and then lift it back up. *I am a strong woman. I can do this.* My eyes wander the room for my purse, shoes, and keys before actually saying what needs to said.

"Avery, what is it?"

"Um. Travar there is something you need to know about me. First, you made me feel like a queen this evening. Dinner, the candles and dessert; everything was beautiful. I want everything to remain beautiful this evening, so what I am about to say can either change that or the evening can continue on." My eyes are watery and a tear falls. He looks concerned and takes my hand. I lose it at that point and just start crying an ugly cry.

Travar stands, wraps his arms around me so gently and says, "Avery, whatever, it is we can get through it."

How I've longed to hear those words.

I hold my head high, look him in his hazel eyes, and say, "Travar, I'm HIV-positive."

His eyes became watery and he put his hands up to his head. He sits down slowly. I can tell he is in shock. More like a silent shock. And I see the tears drip down his face. There is silence between us and only the music is playing. He doesn't curse, yell, or scream. He has no reaction. He sits there staring at the floor with tears flowing, dripping one-by-one. I remain standing, and then pick up my shoes, purse, and keys and walk towards the door.

But before I walk out I say to him, "Thank you for treating me like a lady."

I walk out of Travar's apartment never anticipating seeing him again.

SIXTEEN

MY BODY CRAVES for the touch of masculine hands caressing every inch of me. I lust for Travar wanting friction between our bodies. I want him to stroke my walls peeling away the layers of mutilated flesh. Underneath are pieces of tortured, ripped dangling pinkish chapters of history. I want him to soothe me by lubricating his latex against my canal as my juices flow turning my anguish into bliss. Selfishly, I want his heart to beat rapidly, licking, rhythmically grinding, and squeezing the juices as he outlines the outer surface, with a sigh of climaxing.

Bewildered with remorse I want to pick up where I left off and console him. How much do I want to extend my arms and have him reach for my embrace. He has opened locked gates that have hindered me for months. Our eyes synchronize, we are connected. I want to wash the pain away and rekindle the passion that is within the depth of our souls. He feeds me in a way that no other man has ever fulfilled my insides. I yearn, hot and bothered by the thought of his touch. His fingerprints are still on my breast. His saliva is stained upon my nipple. Lingering in the mist of air is the scent of "rude awakening" as I divulge my biography that left him in a stagnant state. Time will heal that pain that I have inflicted. Time will allow him to appreciate the woman that I am who *unselfishly* reveals what would inevitably pardon us.

Withdrawn, I fall down the slope of repenting. I am trying to find some inner peace to say, "I'm only human." Nevertheless, pain has been inflicted upon someone else at my expense. *Why did I even say anything?* Consciously, I had no choice in the matter. I'm not the same person I used to be back in the day. It's not just about Avery anymore. I care. I realize there is no need to beat myself on the head and try and knock some sense into this pitiful mind of mine. I can sleep knowing that I had the sense of stopping it before things really got out of control. We came so close to having a major collision of bodies, sticky, sweaty, and exploring hidden spots of pleasuring. I exhale just thinking about his honey complexion smothering me like I am glazed ham. I feel reluctant to move forward because I have taken a step backwards. Not fully pursuing, but coming so damn close.

I sit in silence thinking about Travar's mental state. He may have difficulty trusting women because of me. I see him in my head sitting with his hands covering his eyes. I see the tears falling. His silence kills my spirit and tears it into bits and pieces of regret. A part of me desperately wants to go and knock on his door and ask for another chance, but I don't think he will accept me. I sense that he is still numb and in a shell of solitude.

I cannot and will not allow this distress to overcome so much of my progression. In time Travar will encounter another prosperous love. Oh, how I wish it could be me. I have to focus on what lies ahead; my business opportunity will allow me to generously give back to others. But deep in the pit of my being I want love from a man. It seems important to be able to open my heart to someone who is willing to embrace it. Having a partner will add to my journey of fulfillment. I see it plain as day; he recites poetry flowing from his tongue and it fills my body as he creatively makes love to me. He bottles my scent for safekeeping and tastes my skin with fragrant oils. He details my body identifying in the darkest of night. He sniffs the smell of my vagina and grooms it to his liking. We stare into each other's eyes hypnotized. I am melting as I massage his biceps, back, buttocks, legs, and feet with my Avery oil. Moisture drips from my face as I am immensely aroused. I have chiseled his body down to its anatomy, detailing every essential particle. I grip his locks and lick the saltiness off of his chest. Oh yeah, and we become one under the moonlight.

I envision all of this in my head because that is what I would have liked to happen. Unfortunately, I'm left with a thong of wetness, and a bottle of Alizé.

Seventeen

"RED ALERT" is in bold on my caller ID, which reminds me of my appointment with Mr. Combs III. I almost forgot about it with everything that has been going on. Eagerly, I've been waiting for the bank to call or a letter to arrive. Ma'am taught me that when you least expect it, doors open from unfamiliar places. My patience has worn out its welcome and all I want to do is call to check on the status, but I don't. Instead I monitor the mail and screen each call knowing that it won't change the present situation. I have to stop staring at the phone because it will never ring. Normally, news catches you off guard whether it is good or bad. Patience grows slowly and does not compliment the fast pace of my mind. I want things yesterday. I know everything is systematic, a process that has to follow red tape. Background checks, credit checks, loans, rent and other assets are all a part of the prolonged journey on the Yellow Brick Road. I block my mind and try to preoccupy my thoughts with structuring the dialogue for an innovative interview with Mr. Combs III. I am concentrating on intellectual responses transposing my positive energy onto him. Impressions are like walking on a tightrope hoping not to fall in embarrassment.

I can literally feel the sincerity in this man's voice. This is a man with a plan who has carried out all his ambitions in perfect detail. Ultimately, it makes me contemplate if this is something that I really want to do. I want to devote my time and energy for the right reasons. Although this job probably wouldn't be paying what I am used to making, I still want to put my best foot forward. At this very moment it feels right.

I am on pins and needles and the tingling sensation flows throughout the palm of my right hand. Possibly something good or bad is coming my way at least that is an old superstition. I remember Ma'am used to always say that when her palm was itching that something good was coming. Her tone was soft spoken, but you could tell by her voice that she truly believed it. I never questioned her because she always had this look on her face that glowed. As I grew up and heard it many times, I began to see why she believed it.

It's definitely time for lunch so I go into the kitchen to make a turkey and Swiss cheese sandwich and pour myself a tall glass of apple juice.

Ring, ring,

"Hello."

"Hello, Ms. Love, this is Mr. Clausen. I am calling to touch base with you about your business prospects. I have contacted a couple of colleagues of mine. We are structuring a business plan that you may want to consider for possibly a business loan and grants. I would like us to meet within a day or two once I receive some more information. I also called to schedule a meeting with Mrs. Jenkins-Rollin to see the foundation for myself with one of my colleagues who is a contractor. In the interim, how are things with you?"

"Things are fine. I went to my bank to see if I could get a business loan, filled out the application and I am diligently waiting for a response."

"Good, good, that is a step in the right direction. We will touch base soon. I have a meeting so I will talk to you in a couple of days. Have a nice day."

"You too."

Mr. Clausen is a man of his word and that confirms to me that I have made the right choice. I drift off thinking about Johnnie, wanting him with me so we can pursue this together. He would have been ecstatic. His creative mind really helped the process. Johnnie had that go-getter attitude that captivated folks. Success illuminated throughout him and I truly believe he was destined for it. I look up at the ceiling and start to talk to him; it's not unusual for me to do this because I feel within me that he can hear, see, and probably feel when I'm sad, happy, emotional, and weak.

I often wonder what the "other side" is like. It is probably a ray of sunshine throughout the year. I wonder if it's like being in New York City because Johnnie loves the excitement, the view of the lights, and the city itself. He would be bored if there is no action going on up there. I can see him now, chatting with God about re-decorating heaven. Every time I envision it puts a smile on my face. I feel myself growing at a particularly slow pace and that is fine. Sooner, more so than later, my destiny will surround me and I will be blissful with Johnnie standing right beside me. I feel it in my bones that something good is coming!

Eighteen

BEEP, BEEP, BEEP. I keep hitting the snooze button on my alarm clock, but the damn thing won't shut up. Sleepiness must be getting the best of me because I don't realize that it isn't the clock after all. It's a garbage truck outside backing up. I almost want to yell out the window, "Can a sista, please get some sleep around this joint!" But I am too classy for that this early in the morning. Yawning, I stretch out my arms and take a good look at the clock; it is 9:10 a.m., my eyes widened as if to say, "Oh Hell!" August 16th has come so quickly. I have a ten o'clock interview with Mr. Combs and if I don't put some fire under my ass, I will be late. I get out of bed, grab some undergarments, and run to the bathroom to take a shower.

It's approaching 9:30 and time is of the essence. I do not want to be late for this interview. My ensemble is almost complete as I run my fingers through my hair and apply my makeup. After I look over the finished package I rush towards the kitchen to grab my medication, a slice of potato bread and wash it down with orange juice. I can feel my heart pounding. *I can't be late.*

Its 9:50 and I'm hoping that I can make it there in ten minutes since the office is on Hamburg Turnpike in Wayne. Lead footing it, I reach the block and swerve into the parking lot. Checking the time, it is 9:57, three minutes to spare as I open the entrance door, hearing only the clicking of my shoes on the marble tile. It is a long corridor. I'm breathing heavily as I greet the receptionist. I give my name and time of my interview, and she hands me an application and pen.

"Excuse me, Ms. Love?"

I stand and approach her station.

"We had to change your interview time yesterday to 10:30, instead of 10:00. I'm almost certain that we left you a message in reference to this change." The woman looks quite puzzled.

I laugh and say, "You did," it was my error for not listening to the message because I remembered the time.

We both laugh, especially me because I am running around like roadrunner trying to get here on time. I sit back down and continue filling out the application. My adrenaline is on high and it takes time before it slows down to its normal level. Calming myself down, I listen to the music coming from out of the speakers overhead. Surrounding the office are pictures of Maya Angelou, Rosa Parks, Frederick Douglas, George Washington Carver, Dr. King, Malcolm X, and many others. The clock that stands behind the receptionist station is an old antique that is polished and rich with taste. There is an oversized Oriental rug in the center that complements the entire room. The chairs are soft leather mahogany, which enhances the red oak wood receptionist station. The setting is very relaxing which alleviates some of the pressure.

At 10:20, I hear the clicking of shoes. The footsteps come from the long corridor, and that's when I see a Caucasian man, about six-feet tall, with a lean stature, and a close barber's cut. He's wearing a tailored three-button heather blue suit and an expensive pair of bloody red Italian leather shoes. He greets the receptionist and then he calls my name in a voice not unlike Tavis Smiley. I smile in acknowledgement. His eyes are light brown. He asks me to follow him half way down the long corridor. He opens the door for me and then we have a seat. His office is divine. There are pictures of women, men, and children in a collage in this large display. The heading reads, "*This is my Life*." He has a library in his office filled with lots and lots of books. Mr. Combs greets me with a smile.

"Ms. Love, tell me what brings you to *Red Alert*?"

I look Mr. Combs in the eye and say, "Compassion."

"Interesting."

He stands and walks toward his library to lift a book. Then he turns around.

"Ms. Love, may I look over your application?"

I hand it to him with my resume attached and the tip of his fingers touch mine. His hands are warm. He reviews my application and resume and asks about my time as a paralegal.

"What did you like or dislike about that position?"

"Mr. Combs, there is nothing to dislike about it, actually I absolutely loved it."

My eyes light up when I speak about it. And Mr. Combs is very perceptive because he notices the sparkle.

"Why did you stop?"

"Circumstances beyond my control."

"Circumstances, can you be a bit more specific?"

I don't want to get too personal, but I have no choice in the matter.

"Well, I had a best friend who took ill." I cross my toes while speaking. "He needed me so resigned from my position to be his care provider."

I want to beat Mr. Combs to the punch, so I continue on. "I resigned because there was no definite time frame as to when he would depart. I didn't want to put pressure on myself. I felt other opportunities would come, and even thought about pursuing my own business. He was my family, all I had."

I could feel my emotions surfacing so I stop talking.

"Well, Ms. Love, you are an extremely compassionate woman. I think you would be a wonderful asset to my establishment."

I bat my eyes twice because I cannot believe what I have just heard. I know that I have a perplexed look on my face. *That's it? That's all I needed to say?*

170

What happen to the drill sergeant questions? What happen to making me feel uncomfortable as he stares into my face as if he is trying to look through me?

"Welcome aboard, Ms. Love."

"Thank...you. Thank you, Mr. Combs."

He continues to speak about *Red Alert*. He gives me a brief history about his upbringing. "Ms. Love, my mother was Caucasian and my father was African-American. We resided on North Eighth Street in Paterson."

I am taken aback because I cannot tell that Mr. Combs is biracial.

"The neighborhood was predominately white and it was difficult at first having a black man living in the neighborhood. I lived there almost all of my life until my parents were killed in a car accident. My sister and I were left to care for each other. I, being the oldest had to continue my schooling and also work full-time to provide for us. Property values decreased and the homeowners blamed it on the minorities who rented. The homeowners put up "For Sale" signs and sold their homes and moved to the suburbs. We had to move in with an aunt on my father's side and she exposed us to a lot of African American culture. I found it to be exciting, interesting, disturbing, and emotional. I later went to a Passaic County Community College and majored in Business Management. My sister had a flair for Interior Design and landed a great job in Manhattan part-time while she finished high school. She enrolled in college and before she had a chance to graduate she found out that she had AIDS. She had a cold that lingered. She kept putting off going to the doctor. And when she finally went, after taking a blood test, the results determined that she had contracted the virus. She was only seeing one person, which was her boyfriend. I found out later after her passing that he gave the disease to two other women before expiring."

Mr. Combs massages his face and sighs, a deep sigh.

"That is what compelled me to start this whole

process in 1999. We are a family here; we look out for one another. We learn, encourage, and prosper because of it."

He seems distant and then he slowly reels himself back.

"I'll have you meet with one of the managers sometime next week. Her name is Careen Walker. She will go over your benefits, vacation, sick days, personal days, Policy and Procedure manual, and Acknowledgement of Confidentiality form. Our starting salary is thirty five thousand annually, with raises every six months based on performance. There is a lot of growth potential here. Our hotline service center is located on Valley Road, which is actually not far from here. We have mornings, evenings, nights, and overnight positions. We have a staff of maybe ten people to a shift with backup on standby. We mostly take incoming calls from women, men, teenagers, and some elderly who are living with HIV and AIDS. We are listeners, filling them with hope and promise. It's somewhat like a mediator helping people fight off their demons. Ms. Love, your position will be very emotional. It can be stressful. We do provide counseling for our employees at no cost to them. And always keep in mind every job is not for everyone. Our most important rule is "confidentiality". We don't disclose information about our callers. And if it happens that would be grounds for immediate termination. If you ever feel the need to discuss any issue, you can always speak with Careen. Do you have any questions, Ms. Love?"

"No, sir, um... Mr. Combs."

"Okay. Careen will be contacting you once she has a full ten people to start the next shift. It may take about a week to interview a couple more people."

"That is fine."

"Ms. Love, it was certainly a pleasure meeting you."

"I feel the same way, Mr. Combs."

We shake hands and he escorts me to the door.

Driving home exhilaration showers over me, but I am disappointed with myself at the same time leaving a feeling of blah in my stomach. I don't want to deceive Mr. Combs, but I could not find a way to disclose my status. I need to keep it under lock and key. What business is it of his anyway? He can't change my situation. Here I am trying to make excuses for my insecurities.

A block from my apartment I see the mailman entering the building. Hopefully he has some mail for me. I parallel park by the entrance door, and greet him as he is walking out. Checking my mailbox there is a letter from Wachovia Bank, and I quickly open it.

"Ms. Love, in review of your application for a business loan it is with regret that we must deny your application due to your credit history."

There goes the domino affect in my forehead. *Deny! What?* I hurry upstairs to call the bank. Something is definitely wrong. While calling I realize on the letter the asterisks following the last four digits of my social security number are incorrect. They transposed the numbers. A Customer Service Representative answers and I explain my situation. She advises that I should go to the branch where I applied for the business loan and explain my findings. I hang up the phone and walk right back out the door.

Slipping in my MaryMary CD, I drive off with a look of frustration on my face. By the time I reach the bank I have cooled down enormously. I sit in the lobby area and wait patiently to speak with a Customer Service Representative. Finally, an older overweight man approaches me asking if I need assistance.

"My name is Wayne Davidson, how can I help you?"

"Avery Love. Less than a week ago I applied for a business loan. Well, Mr. Davidson I received this denial letter in the mail today, and I found that the last four digits of my social security number are incorrect. Secondly, my credit score last time I checked was above satisfactory, so this letter could not possibly be for me."

I hand the letter to Mr. Davidson and he reviews the information.

"Ms. Love, may I ask you a few questions?"

"Sure."

"When was the last deposit made on your account?"

"It was sometime this month."

"Do you have your social security card?"

"Yes."

"May I see it, please?"

"Sure."

I reach for my purse, pull out my wallet and hand Mr. Davidson my social security card.

"Ms. Love, this is definitely an error on our part. I need to bring this matter to my manager's attention so that we can expedite correcting this issue. You may need to give us a few more days to process your application to see if you qualify for the business loan."

"That's fine, I just need to know if it is going to be approved or not."

"Sure, Ms. Love, we will work as quickly to accommodate you. I apologize for the inconvenience. You have a nice day."

"Thanks, Mr. Davidson."

Finally, I am able to go home and kick off my shoes and take this suit off and relax.

I am exhausted from running around and starved all at the same time. As soon as I get home I put on some sweats and a T-shirt and walk in the kitchen to make a sandwich. I turn on the little TV in the kitchen and sit and eat. I feel my eyes droop so I turn the kitchen TV off and go to the sofa in the living room. I get comfortable by curling up. Next thing I know, the TV is watching me.

Night comes. Most of the day I have slept away and my body feels worn out from too much sleep. It's 10:30. Damn, I must have really been tired. I need to get up and walk around so I go into the kitchen. Suddenly I have a craving for some Butter Pecan ice cream, knowing that I don't have any in the freezer.

The craving provokes my mouth to water. I need to have that ice cream so I slip on my mule shoes and step out to Pathmark.

The supermarket parking lot is full. I guess everyone needs a night snack. I rush out of the car and into the store. I glance down each aisle and realize I should pick up some garbage bags and dish detergent. In aisle ten I accidentally brush up against a young man's arm because this ignorant lady has her cart slanted in the aisle.

"Excuse me."

"Pardon me, ma'am." The young man says.

I really don't get a good look at the gentleman, but I know he isn't originally from Paterson. He has a thick southern accent. I focus on getting my ice cream, garbage bags, and dish detergent. I go down aisle twelve and search in the cold for my Haagen-Dazs Butter Pecan ice cream. Finally locating it, I hurry to open the glass case, grab it, and close it back quickly. I shiver for a moment and then I notice the same young man is behind me.

"Boy, Sis, it must be cold in there," he says.

"Yes it is." I laugh a little embarrassed.

"By the way, my name is Zaelyn."

"Hi Zaelyn, my name is Avery."

He doesn't look that young after all.

As I'm walking off I hear Zaelyn scratching his throat multiple times, so I turn around to see if he's okay.

"Are you okay?"

"Yes, ma'am, there's just a little tickle in my throat."

I turn back around and walk towards the express line at checkout. Five seconds later Zaelyn is standing behind me. He tries to make small talk, but the line is moving so quickly and he cannot speak that fast. I smile because it's quite funny. As I am approaching the cashier and place my items on the counter I turn around to take a glimpse of him. He looks to be somewhere in his late thirties early forties. I turn back and greet the cashier, pay, bag my items, and walk out. Zaelyn has a small basket filled with items and he's hurrying to place them on the counter. Before I reach my car I hear him calling out my name. I stop in the lighted area and wait for him to approach me. He's walking at a fast pace.

"Avery, I know that you don't know me, but I wonder if, well um, well first...you married?"

I blush.

"No, I'm not."

Before he asks the next question I say, "I don't have a boyfriend, either."

He smiles.

"Well, um, would you possibly, um, like to join me for coffee, brunch, or lunch? I'm not married and I don't have a significant other. Here is my card, call whenever you like."

I smile and reach out for his card. After we say good night, I jet back home.

Zaelyn definitely has a different approach than most of the men I've been meeting. I find it to be kind of cute. He sort of fumbles over his words. His nervousness really does show. Now, that can only mean that he is either not used to approaching women or he is just a shy kind of guy. He is about the only one who has ever asked if I am married. I really like that. I tuck his card in my back pocket, reach over into the passenger side and pull my bag towards me as I exit the car.

It is now 11:15 p.m. and I am wide-awake. I help myself to three scoops of ice cream, slip in my *13 Going on 30* DVD and sit back to enjoy the movie. I wonder what it would be like if, like the movie, I could slip back and forth in time. What kind of choices would I make? Life is not life if we don't have choices.

Nineteen

I'M TURNING OVER a new leaf on life and trying to maintain some sensibility in the process. A part of me wants to call Mr. Combs and divulge my secret. But business is business so I have to keep an open mind and hope for the best. It can become more harmful than good because even though he is the founder, he may not want anyone who is HIV-positive working for him. This is personal and I am not about to take that chance. Hopefully, I won't have to work there very long. Inside I feel split. How hypercritical is it of me to be trying to console people through a hotline service when I can't even expose myself? The other part of me is saying it is none of their business because I am not sleeping with them. I am not harming anyone. I am basically trying to survive and make a living like everyone else. There is no easy way to handle this whole life issue bullshit. It frustrates me because I have to dodge, duck, and be in denial for others. Let's get right down to it, it's not for them, it's for me because I am so damned tired of hurting. Folks may change once they find out that I am ill. I have experienced it twice with Blu and Travar and the outcome was not blissful. Right now I have to do what I have to do to get my business started. If it is wrong, let it be wrong and I'll have to live with the guilt.

I reach into my pocket and feel a piece of crumpled paper. It's a receipt from the supermarket as well as Zaelyn's business card. He has his own contractor's business, "Homes Improvements." It's catchy. I feel a little hesitant in trying to get to know someone because my track record has not been good lately. Being honest can surely put a halt on someone's love life, but it is still the right thing to do. I know I just contradicted myself, but work and love are two completely different things. You can't live off love.

Nothing is easy and if it was I would be the first to question it. Life is about struggles, experiences, and carrying those life lessons around in your purse and wallet for future reference. I want love in my life, but not at the expense of hurting. I used to be so closed minded, obnoxious, and insensitive. I must admit if Johnnie didn't come into my life when he did, I probably would have been a lost cause. I found in the depth of my being a soft spot to care for others in a way that I didn't know I could. Being HIV-positive has awakened me in a way where I can see life changes. It may sound a little stupid, but it has changed me for the better. It's helped me to learn how difficult it is to forgive. It has opened me up to appreciate the simple things, more so than before. It allows me to feel compassion. Most importantly, it gives me the strength to want to live. I have stopped hibernating behind closed doors and withering away with the help of Johnnie. This is now the life that I have to live. And if I don't find acceptance in it anyway possible it will be a real, as Johnnie stated so bluntly, detriment to my spirit.

My sense of purpose is in arms reach. I can almost taste it in the crevasse of my mouth and it tastes so good. I've come too far to stop and I don't wanna stop. I want, need, and ultimately deserve to have this job, business, and to live a prosperous life. I'm claiming it all.

The streetlight outside blows out and it is dark and dreary. The music of nature is singing as the crickets vocalize out loud. The folks across the street are still up because I can see the television on. The night is muggy. Two standing fans, a ceiling fan, and a little portable fan in the kitchen are all running on high. I have to strip down to my birthday suit. And I am miserable. This brick building is well insulated. It's comfortable in the winter, but brutal in the summer.

It is 3:30 in the morning and I am taking a cold shower to cool off. Wrapped in a towel I lay in the buff on the bed as the air rotates from the two fans. It is a freakin' sauna in here! The sweltering heat moistens my body as my eyes close and I fall into a drowsy sleep.

The last Monday of August has the smell of cinnamon and nutmeg. I crave French toast with maple syrup and a sprinkle of confectionery sugar with a bowl of fresh strawberries. I sit up and lean against the headboard thinking about how to start off my day. Stretching out my arms I yawn so loud that it could have wakened the dead. I am well rested, ready to take on the day in full force.

It is 9:15 a.m. and I have to call Dr. Fulmore to schedule my two-month appointment. I also need to contact Mr. Clausen to see where we stand as far as *Anonymous.* Contacting the bank today is definitely on my priority list. *Boy, I have a lot to take care of.* That's a good thing because normally I can't think of a thing to do.

I start thinking about returning to the workforce. My days are spent mostly conversing with Sis and moping around my apartment. This will be a fresh start for me and a chance to do something worthwhile.

Sirens set off in my stomach so I go into the kitchen, and check the refrigerator to see if I have any eggs, milk and butter. I search the cabinets for syrup, confectionery sugar, cinnamon, nutmeg, and vanilla extract. I look on top of the refrigerator to see if I have enough bread left. I am in business! My black skillet is hiding in the rear of the cabinet. I pull it out, wash it and place it on the stove. Under a low flame I put one tablespoon of butter in the pan, whip my eggs and sprinkle in my seasonings. Dipping my bread in the mixture I place it into the pan. My mouth is drooling. Within minutes I can smell the aroma of French toast. I don't have any fresh strawberries so I slice an orange instead. I give Dr. Fulmore's office a call before I eat.

"Dr. Fulmore's office, Violet speaking, how may I help you?"

"Hello, Violet, its Avery."

"Good morning, Avery."

"I want to schedule my two month appointment with Dr. Fulmore."

"Avery, did you get Dr. Fulmore's message a couple of weeks ago?"

"What message? He left me one stating that everything looked okay on my x-ray." My face is flushed.

"I know but he called you right after that and left a message about noticing a spot on the x-ray that he wanted confirmation on. He asked that you call him back to schedule another appointment with the Image Center."

"I never got another message from him. Could it be possible that he left the message on someone else's answering machine?"

"It's possible because that day he was running around here short staffed with an office of patients waiting."

I frown. It is inexcusable not to follow-up on the call and make sure I receive the message. I can't believe this shit! Suppose there is something major wrong?

"Violet, go ahead and schedule an appointment with the Image Center!" I say in a hostile tone.

"Sure, I'll call you back."

"Okay!"

I slam the phone down. My body trembles. I feel panic hoping that there is nothing wrong with me. My mind is distracted as I sniff the scent of my French toast calling, "Avery, Avery." I sit down and dig in filling my belly to the brim. Breakfast hits the spot.

Before I can even exhale from being so stuffed, the phone rings.

"Hello."

"Hello, may I speak with Avery Love, please?"

"This is she."

"Hi, Ms. Love, This is Tia, from Mr. Clausen's office, he wanted me to give you a call to see if you could meet with him on Thursday, Sept 2nd at 10:00 a.m?"

"Tia, it is funny that you should call because I

was going to call him today. Thursday is fine."

"Very well, I will let Mr. Clausen know."

"Okay...Goodbye."

I might as well stand by the phone because all I need is the bank to call stating that I am approved for the business loan. That will definitely make my day. For a Monday it is pretty busy so early in the morning. Everything seems to be coming together. I'm hoping Mr. Clausen has some good news.

Glancing over on the end table I spot Zaelyn's business card. It's early in the day so I give him a call on his business line.

"Hello, you have reached Zaelyn at Homes Improvements, please leave a brief message. Have a blessed day."

"Hi Zaelyn, this is Avery Love, the one you met at the supermarket. I just called to say hello. When you get a chance give me a call. My number is ...."

I guess I have gotten over that discouraging feeling of meeting men. There is no reason for me to prejudge Zaelyn because of past encounters. Opportunity only comes around once in a while. Lately I've been listening to my instincts. And it advises me to take things in stride with both eyes open.

Ring-ring, Ring-ring, Ring.

"Hello."

"Hi Avery, it's Violet. I scheduled you for this afternoon for 3:00 p.m. Are you able to make that appointment?"

"Sure."

"Well, you know the routine. Once he gets the results back he will schedule you to come in."

"Okay, Violet. Thanks."

Twelve o'clock is right on point. I open the window to allow some air to flow in. The air smells like cucumber and cantaloupe, delicately sweet. The block is alive and hectic. Kids are outside playing and getting wet by the fire hydrant until someone calls the City and someone comes and shuts it off. They just wait until they leave and then turn it back on. There seems to be a lot of traffic through the block. Cars are passing by honking for the kids to get out of the way. The kids are enjoying the cool water in the hot sun. I hear a woman across the street talking to her husband. I hear the mailman whistling as he walks toward the building. Everyone seems to be in good spirits.

One-thirty is approaching. I lay my clothes out. My spirit is lifted and I am feeling really good like I am overcoming some of my battles. I still have a long ways to go, but deep within I am climbing.

Life is so profound. Looking back on where I once was to where I am now is phenomenal. Progression is in control. I am evolving with time. There are times where I feel like life is pressure. Pressure to stay afloat. I've been trying to keep distance from drama, confrontation, and meaningless bullshit. I often wish to have a companion, preferably a female. I had the greatest relationship with Johnnie, but I've never allowed close interaction with a woman. That would be nice. My biggest problem is meeting someone on my level. She can't be clingy, needy, or dramatic. I'm seeking a hanging partner. Someone who is well connected, refined in her demeanor, and trustworthy. I can care less about attractiveness because I am more interested in a good sense of humor along with personality.

I do some light cleaning, dusting, vacuuming, and tiding up. Walking in the bathroom I hang up some fresh towels. The whole apartment smells summery fresh.

Two o'clock is near so I take a shower. After, I walk around the apartment in my thong and bra. It is a struggle putting on my denim Capri's. Sistah must have gained a pound or two. I slide my mustard spaghetti strap top overhead. Slipping on my denim sandals I admire the purse that matches. I massage my scalp with sage oil. I'm comfortable and at ease about going to the Image Center. Normally it is a fight with my internal thoughts. I just hope Karel, the technician is there.

I quickly gather my things so that I will not be late for my appointment. I rush out the door and into a world of sunshine. As I walk towards my car I feel eyes strangely heating my back. I turn around to see Blu scoping me out with his dark eyes. He has a look of disgust on his face. My hands shake as I try to put my key in the car door. Finally, after three tries I inadvertently scratch the paint on the side, pull the door open and sit down looking straight ahead. Two seconds later a young, high yellowish woman in her mid-thirties comes out of a fenced house and he gets out to greet her. He cuts his eyes to see my reaction while he tongues her down. Nonchalantly, I act as if I don't care, but in actuality I feel stunned. Seeing his face puts a sour taste in my mouth. I don't want to react because it will only stroke his ego. My biggest concern is that he will tell his new flame about my illness. But then I think about it for a moment. That will only complicate things more for him because he will then have to convince her that nothing took place between us. *How many women today are going to let that slide without questioning*? There is a lot of room for questioning. Blu probably will not want to set up any barriers for himself. My instincts say that he might start a rumor with a male about my illness before he would ever tell a woman he is dating. He is water under the bridge so I am not going to let him discourage my progress.

On my way to the Image Center I keep repeating, "Strong, powerful, and resilient." I have to convince my brain that I have it under control. These words soak in so easily and I believe that I am as tall as an oak tree. Two blocks from the Image Center while idling at the traffic light, there is a man with mud-like complexion in a hunter-green Audi. We are side by side as he turns and winks with this huge smile on his face. I blush because it has just brightened up my gloomy day. I tell you God works in mysterious ways!

I pull open the door of the Image Center and a scent of citrus passes my nostrils, and I sneeze three times because the scent is potent. I reach into my purse for a tissue, walk towards the receptionist station to sign in and sit down. As usual it is chilly. The hairs on my arms are standing up and my nipples protrude with hardness. I know I have forgotten something. In my mind I pretend that I am in sunny Barbados, the sun screening my skin evenly. I'm walking with sugary sand between my toes in my two-piece tropical bikini, swaying my hips as my buttocks rise high and low. I feel men glancing at me with provocative thoughts in their minds. Their eyes tell all. They are sizing me down 34, 26, and 34. Of course, I have a great imagination because my hips are too voluptuous and my ass has too much junk in its trunk to be a 34. I smile because the thought is humorous.

"Avery Love." A familiar voice calls.

I enter the doorway to meet a familiar face. I swallow with a lump lodged in my throat. It is her, standing there with her petite frame, flush complexion, and assertive look upon her face. The Sergeant is what I call her. Her tone is sharp and direct. She constantly looks around when she speaks as if she has a wandering eye. That drives me crazy. Feeling insignificant is not a great feeling. *I will not allow her to make me feel uncomfortable, again. She is now going to experience what I've felt.* The Sergeant hands me a gown extending her arm with great length, like I am contagious. *That is it!* I have to defend myself. My forehead wrinkles, eyes are direct, and lips twist.

"Excuse me, but what is your name?"

The drill sergeant looks a little flustered.

"What is your name?"

"Ms. Sweet," she replies.

I smirk because she is surely not the depiction of her name.

"You know, Ms. Sweet, I've been here twice thus far and my experience the first time was discomforting. You made me feel unwelcome. I know that you know I am HIV-positive, but it doesn't give you the right to remind me of it. I am a human being, just like you. I deserve eye contact, to be treated with a professional demeanor and compassion. Your display was dry, uncompassionate, and disturbing. If you don't have compassion for the ill why be in the profession?"

Ms. Sweet keeps her head high, looking piercingly into my brown eyes and says, "Ms. Love, I apologize for my unprofessional behavior."

I walk away to get undressed and put my gown on.

She seems sincere. I'm sure it was difficult for her to admit that she was wrong, but she swallowed her pride and took responsibility for her actions. I'm impressed. I feel powerful, but don't feel above her, nor do I want to be. I had to take the initiative to speak up and stop being treated with unworthiness. No one should accept that type of treatment no matter what their circumstances. My tone mellows.

"Ms. Sweet, I accept your apology."

The creases around Ms. Sweet's eyes are warm and bright. A rosy tone accentuates her cheekbones. All she needs to complete the look is to possibly give some vibrant color to her hair. A makeover would give her a youthful look. Ms. Sweet and I talk briefly while she takes my x-rays. And after, she excuses herself from the room to allow me to get dressed.

As I am about to leave, Ms. Sweet calls out my name. She takes my hand and overlaps it with hers and says, "thank you." This is a moment I will never forget. My visit ends on a good note.

When I arrive home at 4:15 p.m., I check my mailbox before heading upstairs. There is what looks like a bill from the Image Center, as well as a letter from Wachovia Bank. I rip open the envelope from Wachovia; unfold the creased letter only to view in highlighted marker, "missing information". The bank wants proof of my current employer. Damn. I can't check off self-employed because I'm not. I've been living off of my savings since I've left the law firm. I massage my left temple because wanting this business is giving me a migraine. I have my interview with

Careen Walker from Red Alert tomorrow and maybe she can provide me with a letter to forward to the bank as proof of employment. It definitely can't hurt to ask.

Entering the door to my apartment a gush of heat greets me. It is stuffy. My nostrils are dry inside and I am congested. The windows are pulled up halfway but all that sweeps through the screen is hot air. Immediately I turn on all three fans and start stripping down to my bare skin. I sit on the sofa to recapture the conversation I had with Ms. Sweet.

Ring, ring, ring,

"Hello."

"Hello, may I speak with Avery?"

"Speaking, who's calling?"

"This is Zaelyn Homes, the guy from the supermarket. I received your message earlier, but I could not detain myself. I've been thinking about you since you called. Um, were you busy?"

"No, I'm just relaxing on the sofa."

"Avery, is it hot enough for yah?"

"Yes, too hot for me."

"Today is a hectic day for me because I'm short staffed. I'm trying to pick up the slack but it is too much for one or even two people. Business is good, so I won't complain."

"Zaelyn, it will work itself out."

"Listen, um, I plan on leaving here around seven o'clock. Would you be interested in having dinner with me this evening? I know that it is our first time actually speaking, but it will give us an opportunity to see if we connect in person."

"Well, I didn't make any plans, so okay. You want to jot down my address?"

"Sure."

I give him my address and then we say our goodbyes.

My day is so full with all the calls, to the little mix up with Dr. Fulmore, and to the discussion with Ms. Sweet. Life is full of surprises.

Cuddling on the sofa seems safer than crawling

into my bed. I stretch out comfortably, but for some reason I cannot get relaxed enough to close my eyes. My mind flashes back to Blu and Travar. It is a distraction because within a couple of hours I will be on a date with Zaelyn. If I keep harboring on my past relationships I will never encounter the kind of love I deserve. I sit up and think about the pros and cons of going out this evening with Zaelyn. I realize it's something I want to do. I pull back the comforter and stand to prepare myself for a wonderful evening. It is ten minutes past six o'clock so I enter my walk-in closet to decide what to wear. I definitely don't want to over dress or under dress so I do a combination of both. I lay out a pair of black slacks, light silk lavender spaghetti strap top with a shawl, a nice African necklace with earrings to match, and some lavender high heel mules. I'll use the bath oil called Sassy that I purchased from the His and Her Incense Boutique. Running my bath water, I dab a few drops to allow the fragrance to cascade throughout the apartment. I light one oversized candle and set it on my vanity so it can exude the fragrance of sweet honey.

Ring-ring, Ring-ring, ring.

"Hello."

"Hello, Baby."

"Hi, Zaelyn."

"I called to let you know that I will be leaving a little later. By the time I get home and freshen up it will be past 7:00, so do you think that you will be ready around 8:30?"

"I think I can be ready."

"Okay, I'll see you then."

"Okay."

After we hang up I grow excited. I slither in my bath water like a snake. I squeeze my sponge and wet my arms and legs, chest, and neck. The water is hot and it feels so good. Leaning back in the water I rest my head on my pillow and meditate.

My mind travels many miles away while I'm soaking. A gush of confidence absorbs my body, assuring me that this evening will be a success. I get out of the bathtub, dry off, and go into my bedroom. It is sauna in here. Sitting on my bed I massage some gold shimmer cream on my arms and around my neck. I rejuvenate my feet, legs, and buttocks with some oatmeal lotion. My makeup is delicate and natural. After painting my face I get dressed. I hear drum rolls in the mirror because I look so good. I anticipate Zaelyn's reaction as his mouth hangs open, eyes bulging, and speech stuttering. I laugh out loud just from the thought of it.

Eight-thirty is a couple of seconds away and I am in control. The buzzer goes off and I answer the intercom and buzz Zaelyn in. A few seconds later he rings the bell and I answer the door. His mouth hangs open, eyes bulge, and he starts stuttering trying to compliment me but his words overlap each other. I smile because my premonition was right on point.

"Zaelyn, would you like to come in?"

"Yes ma'am."

"I just need to grab my purse."

As I'm walking towards the bedroom, Zaelyn says, "Oh, you won't need your purse."

I am flattered, but I get it anyway. Poppa didn't raise no fool.

Zaelyn opens the door for me and we stroll out.

I am checking Zaelyn out as we walk side-by-side and he looks polished down to his shoes. He is wearing a casual camel linen suit. He has on a soft beige shirt and his dark skin tone brings everything out. Dark chocolate shoes are polished to perfection. His hair is clean cut, and he's nicely shaved, and smells like fresh ocean oil. Woo! Temptation is on my back saying, *Chile, whachu gonna do? His dark chocolate is sinfully good 'nough to nibble.*

Once we get downstairs and out the front door he softly lifts my hand and kisses it. Man, his lips are soft and moist. I am slowly being taken in. He opens the door to his Acura RL and I let my buttocks sink into his butter soft leather seat. The inside of his car is clean as a whistle and smells like delicate ginger.

Zaelyn takes me to a famous restaurant on 42nd Street in New York called BB King's. The restaurant is very warm and inviting, especially with the live entertainment. We nibble on a fruit, veggie, and cheese platter, until our main course arrives. Zaelyn orders us white wine. I am so intrigued by his southern demeanor. He kind of reminds me of Poppa. He takes the initiative to handle everything and I sit back with appreciation of it all. Finally, I have a real man.

Zaelyn gives me a bio of his life.

"Avery, I'm a practical man, dedicated to my work because I thrive on succeeding. I'm hardworking, wholesome, and religiously faithful. I built my company from scratch with commitment and persistence. I'm originally from Williamston, North Carolina. I've met quite a few women back home and they were slow paced like an evening breeze. I enjoy fishing, taking quiet walks up to Garrett Mountain Park and watching DVD movies. I'm pretty laid back and non-confrontational."

He smiles.

I'm entranced by his vibrant smile that enhances his chubby cheeks. His dark brown eyes, blue-black complexion blends flawlessly. He has to be about five-feet-ten inches with a medium build, and a rotund stomach. He is family oriented and is ready to settle down, wanting three to four children. He seems too good to be true, but I'm infatuated with his confidence.

"Avery, you look lovely, simply lovely. I mean, when I saw you I said to myself, that is a beautiful woman. I see your features in my head and my knees buckle every time. I knew that I wanted to get to know you mo' on a personal level."

Zaelyn's compliments weaken me. I am swimming in him without a lifejacket. I know that falling for this southern man with a humble manner can be detrimental. He is sweeping me off of my feet with his charisma. What is a girl to do? Instinctively, I want to pursue this further, but my instincts warn me to proceed with caution. Red lights are blinking, yellow pauses, and then red is back again. Within I feel confused because Zaelyn is a good man with a solid foundation. When he speaks it is as if he consoles my whole body. I have never experienced that before, having a man treat me like I am a delicate flower, protecting me from any harm that may weaken me.

"Avery, here I am taking all of the floor space. Tell me about you?" Zaelyn leans back in his chair, sips his wine, and waits for me to start spilling my guts.

His eyes open wide as he gives me his undivided attention. I give him my brief life story and we laugh and talk for the rest of the evening. Dinner is out of this world. We feed each other dessert and wash it down with wine. After our wonderful dinner we go to the Laugh Factory for some entertainment. After the comedy show Zaelyn and I leave holding hands and laugh out loud as we walk to his parked car. On the way home we talk and talk like we have known each other for years. He parks in front of my building, exits the car, and walks around to the passenger side to let me out. As I stand our eyes meet and our lips connect. My body is sizzling.

"Thank you for a wonderful, wonderful evening," I say.

"You're very welcome, Avery. I'll call you tomorrow."

I kiss two of my fingers and place them against Zaelyn's lips.

"Okay, Good night Zaelyn."

"Good night."

Zaelyn drives off and I feel like skipping to my door. As I enter my apartment, I strip down to my undergarments, lie down on my bed and fall asleep like a baby.

Police sirens run through the block as if they are chasing a man on foot. It startles me out of my sleep. In a way it is good because I cannot oversleep for my interview today with Careen Walker. This interview is more of a formality on the process and procedures of the company. I anticipate a lot of paperwork to be filled out. I refresh my memory with some of the history on Red Alert just in case Ms. Walker asks me some questions. I go to the kitchen to make some breakfast. The last thing I want is to have my stomach growling while trying to speak intelligently. I place some waffles in the toaster and put some turkey sausage in a small black skillet. I keep yawning. That is what I get for not getting to bed until about four in the morning. But I have no regrets. My eyes have bags sagging under them and time is not on my side. I don't want to reschedule so I eat, clean up my mess, and search through my closet for an outfit to wear.

I get into the bathtub and close my eyes and Zaelyn's face appears. He enchants me. What a tangled web I have walked into. Diligence will define a resolution. Ultimately the outcome can be unpleasant or not. I want to get to know Zaelyn, but I am afraid. Opening up could result in peeling away harden scabs. I don't want to feel anguish, shed any more tears, or fall head over heels for someone who may eventually leave without an explanation. I can't take the outburst, silence, or the perspiration under my armpits when I am being truthful.

I place my hands upon my head as the water drips from my elbows. How am I going to handle his reaction? I stand in the bathtub and step out.

Ring-ring, Ring-ring, Ring.

"Hello."

"Hello Sweetie."

"Hi."

"Avery, I just called to see if you have any plans later on this evening?"

"No, I don't."

"Well, I would love to take you out for a bite to eat."

"Sure, Zaelyn, I would love to go out with you this evening."

"Great, I'll call you once I leave work."

"Okay, I'll be here."

"Talk to you later this evening, Avery."

"Okay."

Excitement swims through my body and I cannot wait until the evening to see him. I return to the bedroom to get dressed. I get dressed in ten minutes, fix my hair, slip on my shoes, and reach for my briefcase. Valley Road on Hamburg Turnpike in Wayne is less than ten minutes away.

After I park I greet the receptionist. She asks me to have a seat as she calls Ms. Walker. Speaking to Zaelyn this morning makes me feel on top of my game. I'm exuding confidence. Five minutes later a Caucasian woman enters. She is tall, thin, with noticeably big feet. She looks sort of awkward because her breasts are well-endowed, but her backside is as flat as a pancake. Her hair has streaks of blonde and her skin is pale—ghostly pale. She greets me with a smile that is discolored, possibly from smoking or drinking too much coffee. I stand in her presence.

"Good morning, Ms. Love, I'm Careen Walker."

"It's a pleasure to meet you, Ms. Walker."

"Oh, call me Careen."

We walk into a little office. There is a folder already on the desk and Careen explains all the paperwork first. She takes out copies of the needed documents as I fill out the forms. She goes on to explaining how the hotline service operates.

"Ms. Love, this is a very emotional service center. Many of the calls that we receive are from people who have AIDS or HIV. They can be abrupt, belligerent, frustrated, suicidal, and depressed about their lives. They call in with pen names and we greet them with pen names. Here is a list of names for you to choose from."

I go through the list and chose Sapphire because I like the color.

"Sapphire is the name that will appear on your computer. These are the shifts we have available 9 a.m.-6 p.m. and 12 a.m.-9 a.m., with an hour for lunch.

Which would you prefer?"

"I would prefer 12 a.m.-9 a.m."

"I must take a picture of you for your identification badge. This badge will enable you to enter and exit the building. We will schedule your training based on your shift. This helps you get a routine going. After training I'll meet with you to decide when to put you on the phones alone. Now the only dilemma is that we are trying to schedule everyone around the same time frame as far as their start dates. Currently, we are still interviewing to fill all the slots and that may delay your training schedule for a couple of days up 'til a week. Will that cause any problems for you?"

"No, that won't be a problem at all."

That may work out perfectly because it will give me time to work on the business.

"What I will do Ms. Love is call you as soon as I know that everything is set to go. I anticipate a couple of days, but you never know. You probably will hear from me possibly the first week of September. Do you have any questions?"

"Yes. I was wondering if you could provide me with a letter as proof of employment with my annually salary enclosed? I need it for my bank."

"Sure. I'll have the secretary type it up for you. You should receive it within a day or two. Is there anything else?

"No. I appreciate your help."

"Well, if anything comes to mind, please feel free to call me."

"Okay."

"Ms. Love, it has been a pleasure meeting with you."

"Careen, you have a nice day."

She walks me to the door. Now I have the rest of the day free until later this evening. I drive over to Bloomfield Ave. in Montclair to take another look at the building. Something tells me to call Mrs. Jenkins-Rollin so I do just to see if there are any other bids on the building.

"Good Afternoon, Tribe Realtors, Mrs. Jenkins-Rollin speaking, how may I help you?"

"Hi, Mrs. Jenkins-Rollin this is Avery Love. I don't know if you remember me. I'm the woman who was interested in possibly buying or leasing the building on Bloomfield Ave. in Montclair."

"Oh yes, Ms. Love, I remember. I've spoken to your lawyer Mr. Clausen about the building. I actually have a meeting with him tomorrow. What can I do for you?"

"Well, I am just curious to know if anyone else has taken an interest in the building."

"Unfortunately, no one has inquired about the building other than you."

"Thank you for your time, Mrs. Jenkins-Rollin."

"You're very welcome."

I sit there for a few minutes after I hang up and admire the building. Suddenly this young attractive man stands in front of my car getting ready to cross the street. We lock eyes with intensity and a look of pain is written all over his face, especially in his eyes. It's Travar. He distracts my thinking and I look away because I cannot face him. He stands in front of me for a couple of minutes and every particle of me is paralyzed. He doesn't turn away so I hold my head low because that is exactly how I feel. He eventually crosses the street and walks into Linkford Electronics store. My high diminishes down to the lowest of low. I drive off with pain in my heart.

Once I arrive home I sit on the sofa in a fog. The look in Travar's eyes has an impact on me mentally, physically, and spiritually. It hits me deep and tears slowly roll down my face. I know I did the right thing by telling him the truth. Maybe one day he can find it within himself to forgive me.

I don't want to harbor on something that I cannot change, so I transform my thoughts to the man who puts a smile on my face. My high rises and the tears dry.

Productivity consumes me and I find things to preoccupy my time. I decide to pamper myself from head-to-toe. I expected Zaelyn to call maybe around six o'clock, so I lounge around until five. Time is slow making the day seem so long. I eyeball the clock hoping the time will advance, but it is as slow as molasses. Anticipation is getting the best of me so I indulge in the moment with a good book. I am not able to concentrate. Zaelyn has a way of making me lose concentration and he isn't even present. Zaelyn's charm liquefies me down into a puddle and I am a damsel in distress who needs to be wooed. I am thinking about him constantly, missing him dreadfully, and can't wait for the phone to ring so I can hear his voice. Zaelyn makes me feel so attractive. His slow pace and sweet demeanor makes him even more appealing. The fire in his belly to succeed is the biggest turn on for me. I've been so afraid to step out of bounds, but for some unknown reason, I'm ready to lay my burdens down hoping that he doesn't turn a deaf ear.

The casual look that I was contemplating before just changed into a stunning look that hopefully will put me in the spotlight for the whole evening. I need to put a lot of effort into creating this seductive woman and it needs to be done with simplicity. I want to accentuate my assets with a sexy bronze halter dress, three-inch stilettos and a gold rope choker. I massage my hair with a dab of Carol's Daughter Tui Oil, and glaze my skin with a shimmer of gold tones. I insert a flower in my hair to accentuate my look. After all the preparations I look like I belong on the cover of *Fiend*, if there is such a magazine.

Buzz, buzz.

"Hello."

"Sweetie, it's me Zaelyn."

I buzz Zaelyn in and stand in front of the door until he rings my bell. I open the door slowly to surprise him. Zaelyn has a look of lust on his face. He wets his lips several times and runs his eyes up and down my body in slow motion until he connects with my eyes. His lips protrude as he speaks in a seductive Barry White type voice,

"Ooh baby, all of this for me?"

I raise my eyebrows as if to say yes.

Zaelyn steps inside the door and places his blue-black hands around my waist and pulls me close. He can be so aggressive. I like that. He massages my back with his strong hands and my body grows hotter than the sun. His caress upon my downy skin makes me drool for him. I nurture his left hand and the scent of sandalwood is like an aphrodisiac to my nostrils. I am drawn in. He kisses my luscious lips passionately. His multi-talented tongue stimulates my whole body. Our kissing becomes intense. The intensity increases until we gain back control.

We go to dinner and then afterwards we go dancing. We dirty dance, our bodies glued in rhythmic tune, slow, steamy, sensually luring us in as our fingers interlock as one. We sit sipping on wine, saturating in each other's eyes. Zaelyn leans in and gives me a red rose and a kiss. He feeds me chocolate swirl cheesecake with his fingers and I lick it off seductively. I wipe the glaze of moisture from his brow. Sex is on the brain, in our eyes, but we don't react. We taunt and tease each other throughout the night, lusting for more than just dancing.

Zaelyn is one of a kind and within the depth of my soul I want him to be my man. I want to love him unconditionally. I know without a doubt that he will shower me with love. He opens me up deeper than any flesh wound. I'm hypnotized.

I tell Zaelyn that this evening is an evening that I will truly remember. He looks at me and smiles. We leave the club at 3:00 a.m. Zaelyn parks across the street from my apartment building and walks me to the door. He looks deep into my eyes and moves in closer and closer until we bump heads. He sniffs my neck as I maneuver my neck wanting him to do it again. He lays his head right in the crease of my cleavage. I hold him tight not wanting to let go. Pulses rise. We make out in front of the building; bodies hot with moisture. His third arm against my thigh increases in size. I want him badly. I want him to take control of the situation and pick me up and carry me to my apartment and rip off my clothes. I want him to become a snake and slither his tongue all over my body. And in the morning he will lay beside me and we will awake together as the sunrises. A car zooms by and the sound of the screeching tires makes us flinch as our flames burn out. We stop immediately, both breathing heavily. That car just saved us from a night full of passion into a morning full of regret. I need to tell Zaelyn about myself, but every time I look into his eyes I picture him walking completely out of my life. We regain our dignity and kiss each other good night. I watch Zaelyn enter his car and drive off. Damn, it's late! Mr. Clausen comes to mind. I have a meeting with him at ten o'clock in the morning. All play and no work makes me a horny heifer.

T WENTY

THURSDAY is a challenge for me. Between the sleep deprivation, the hangover, and queasiness, my body is drained. Baby steps are taken to the bathroom and each one reminds me of the evening I shared with Zaelyn. The short journey seems so long and every step makes my head throb. I feel a pounding sensation that is like someone hitting me over the head with a hammer. *Oh, Lord, I won't do it again, just please take it away*? My reflection in the bathroom mirror scares me to death. I look a hot mess. Damn. I have to meet with Mr. Clausen today. I rub my eyes trying to figure out what I am going to do. Should I reschedule or take my chances and keep the appointment? I take two steps backwards still staring in the mirror and ask, "What would Johnnie do?" There could be a damn blizzard and if Johnnie had a business engagement he would be there with bells on. I splash cold water on my face over and over again. In between each splash, I debate whether I should go or not, but then it hits me that opportunities like this only come once in a while. I want to make a good impression. I don't want to give off the wrong signals. Zaelyn climbs into my brain and I am swimming with thoughts of him.

In the kitchen, I force down a slice of potato bread and drink a glass of water. I take a long hot shower to wake up my body. All the attention from Zaelyn is wearing me down. It takes an hour or two just to get back to normal. Looking refined from head-to-toe and shaking with a slight hangover off, I am ninety percent myself. The other ten-percent is pleading for mercy. *I'll never do it again.* Boy, I must be sprung for this man because I am doing things that are not in my character. If Johnnie were here he would probably say, "Gurl, do you." I certainly am, but it is a lot of work. I stand still for a moment and then slowly walk out the door.

The crisp September air feels pleasant and the sun is beaming high. Its brightness makes me squint. In my car I pull down my sun visor, and open the sunroof to catch the breeze. In spite of how I'm feeling physically, spiritually I am on all highs.

When I reach Mr. Clausen's office, I notice Mrs. Jenkins-Rollin and a couple of other folks sitting and reading magazines, and talking on their cell phones. I greet Tia, his secretary, and take a seat saying good morning to everyone. A few minutes later, Tia calls all of us in, escorting us to a large conference room. Mr. Clausen stands to greet us. There is a table with a buffet spread full of danishes, bagels, muffins, coffee, tea, orange and apple juice. It's surrounded by rich Italian leather chairs. A flat screen TV is mounted on the green stripe wallpaper. And a telephone sits in the center of the table. We all help ourselves to the food and wait for him to start the meeting.

"Good morning. I asked you all to come today so we can try and finalize this business opportunity for Ms. Love. I thought it would be a lot easier if we all met at one time in order to discuss how we can make her dream a reality. The idea Ms. Love has is to create a gallery of arts for unknown artists. The contractors went through the building to make sure all the codes are in good standing. And they appear to be. The inspectors made sure the smoke detectors, sprinklers, fire alarms, exit signs all are in working condition. And they are. They checked the flooring, boilers, pipes, ceiling, and the roof. There is no major damage. There won't be any alcohol served, so we don't have to concern ourselves with a liquor license. Ms. Love does want to serve beverages, appetizers, and pastries. There is a kitchen in the back area that does have a baker's oven, a conventional oven, a three-part sink, a refrigerator and a deep freezer. Now, the asking price for the whole building as Mrs. Jenkins-Rollin discussed is three hundred eighty-nine thousand dollars, which includes four vacant apartments on the top floors. If

Ms. Love decides to lease the commercial space it will be three thousand per month. Of course, she will need to decide which would be more feasible for her. I've looked into some grants, loans, and Ms. Love's personal assets and have come up with a scenario that may be quite profitable for her, depending upon the stability of the business. Here is my outline."

Mr. Clausen passes out his business plan, the blueprint of the building, and a copy of all inspections that were done on the premises. Everyone is looking at the business plan following along with Mr. Clausen as he explains the details. He has made my idea sound promising. I am even sold on the idea after listening to him. After he discusses everything in full detail the outcome is that I need to come up with fifty percent because the remainder is being provided through grants that he has already applied for on my behalf. I'm hoping that the business loan comes through and if I have to add to that then so be it.

"I've provided some slides of the building for us to review." Mr. Clausen says.

He goes through each room and I imagine how I want each room to look. *If I have to use every dime Johnnie gave me to make this happen, then that is what I will do.* I want it that bad. This is the first time I have ever wanted anything this badly. I've worked hard for everything in my life and I know that this is meant for me. God is speaking and I am listening with all ears.

Twenty-One

ZAELYN'S BUSINESS is not doing so great. He's overloading himself with his financial burdens and struggling to keep his business afloat. Foreclosure is a strong possibility. He's working extremely hard to make sure that doesn't happen. So he has had to make some cut backs of staff, and supply costs. He is under several different contracts with commercial businesses as well as residences and he can't seem to meet deadlines. There are threats of him being sued for not completing certain jobs. Complaints have been filed. He tells me he is stressing to the point where his chest tightens up on a regular basis.

As I'm washing dishes, I receive a call from one of Zaelyn's colleagues stating that he collapsed at one of the job sites. One of the members of his crew has called the ambulance and he has been rushed to Jaysen Medical Center in Hackensack. I drop everything and rush to the hospital with a lead foot, and park in a restricted zone. I run into the emergency lobby, fidgeting while I wait for the Triage nurse to acknowledge me. I tell her that I'm here to see Mr. Zaelyn Homes and she advises me that they have already taken him to the Intensive Care Unit on the sixth floor. I follow the signs leading to the nearest elevator. It seems the damn elevator is taking forever. As I head for the stairway I hear "*ding*" and I run onto the elevator and go to the sixth floor. I'm nervous when I approach the nurse's station. I see a thinly framed copper-colored woman with short hair, big eyes, pudgy nose, and full thick lips.

"May I help you?"

"Yes, I'm here to see Mr. Zaelyn Homes."

"Are you immediate family, Ma'am?"

"I'm...I'm...I'm his girlfriend."

"Ma'am, we had to sedate Mr. Homes, but you

may go in."

"Thank you."

Zaelyn is hooked up to all these machines to monitor his heart, and they feed him intravenously. His eyes are closed as if he is in a peaceful sleep. Approximately twenty minutes later a chestnut-brown colored woman enters the room. She looks to be in her late twenties with a flair for fashion. She has a very polished look about her. But her rotund face is full of dismay. I must have been invisible because she doesn't see me standing on the other side of his bed. She caresses his forehead and outlines the right side of his face. The woman finally looks up and is startled by my presence. I'm sure she almost wet her pants.

"Are you okay, Ma'am?" I ask.

She is breathing heavily.

"How long were you standing there?"

"I've been standing here ever since you walked in the room."

She looks at me as if to say, "for real."

"Ma'am, you had others things on your mind when you walked in here. I completely understand because I was the same way. One of Zaelyn's colleagues called me at home and I rushed over here like a bat out of hell. I probably have a ticket for my car because I could have sworn I parked in a restricted zone."

"Yeah, I know what you mean because Ashley, the receptionist, called me at the gallery and I dropped everything and rushed up the street."

"Oh, you work at a gallery?"

"Actually, I own it. It's on Main Ave. I'm an Artist."

"Where are my manners, we are here just chit-chatting away. My name is Avery Love. I am a friend of Zaelyn's."

"I'm Danell Owen. Zaelyn is my uncle."

"Nice to meet you, Danell."

"Likewise."

We both sit by Zaelyn's side stroking his hands and praying in silence. We keep each other company because he is heavily sedated. He doesn't move at all. Danell and I talk all night. We take turns running to the cafeteria to get coffee, and to the vending machines. We want to be there just in case he opens his eyes.

Danell looks around twenty-seven years old. She is average looking, nothing to run home and brag to your mama about. She has a wide nose, Angie Stone lips, and a natural short cut. Her eyes are her best asset. She is sexy with small breasts, wide hips and a plump apple rump. She owns a building on Main Ave where she lives and runs her gallery "Virtue" on the first two floors. She says she adores capturing beauty in people. There is an uplifting aura about her that makes me feel as if we have met before. Of course, I know this isn't the case. Her persona seems genuine.

Zaelyn ends up being in the hospital for two weeks. He is grouchy almost everyday stating that he has to get back to work or he is going to lose his company. I try and reassure him that everything is going to be fine even though I am not sure. The main thing is to try to keep him calm. Danell and I alternate days at the hospital so that he won't be alone. Zaelyn definitely shows a different side to him when he is non-productive. I understand completely because he is the kind of man who has worked extremely hard to build a company and a name for himself. Unfortunately, everything seems to be unraveling right before his eyes and he can't do a damn thing about it. His staff is dwindling by the day, so he doesn't have enough manpower to meet deadlines. His clients are furious. His personality is changing as a result. I'm trying to understand, but then he starts to lash out at me. Sometimes I just get up and walk out in order to bite my tongue. Non-confrontational is the way I like it, and the way he always claimed to be. Danell on the other hand, will tell him to shut the fuck up without hesitation. She has the utmost respect for him, but when he starts talking crazy her tolerance level is short. I laugh to myself because he never seems to have a comeback. He'll stare in space acting like he doesn't hear a thing.

Visiting Zaelyn gives me more of an opportunity to really get to know Danell. If we don't see each other at the hospital we talk over the phone. Danell is rare. She has a strong presentation and her personality puts one in a relaxed mode. She revealed to me that she's a lesbian. She has been with her significant other for almost five years. *Damn she is doing better than I am. I can't even keep a man for five days.* For some reason I find myself mentioning Zaelyn a lot. Maybe I think that it will indicate that my preference is for men instead of coming out and just saying it. Danell catches on quickly and says, "She gets it." I felt like a jackass, but at least she understands. She is cool about it and we never discuss it again.

Danell and I connect like sisters. I'm comfortable around her and enjoy her company. We start to spend a lot of time together. Zaelyn is busy trying to establish himself since he has finally been discharged from the hospital. For weeks we don't see each other. We talk on the phone almost every other night. That leaves more room for Danell and me to hang out. Soon it starts to cause friction in her relationship. Her other half, JaVonna is not feeling it. She has expressed it in public, behind closed doors, and anytime she feels the need to vent. I consider her to be a "drama queen". I don't see the connection between them because they seem like night and day. Maybe that is where the attraction lies? When I first meet JaVonna I consider her to be a "ghetto chick".

"I'm JaVonna Banks," she says as she forges a smile.
I keep my hands to my sides and say, "Hi." I don't even want to tell her my name.

Danell scratches her throat and then says, "Baby, this is Avery."

JaVonna looks me over from head-to-toe and twists her lips, while sucking her teeth. *That is so damn annoying constantly hearing someone suck their damn teeth and they haven't even eaten yet.* I want to shout, "WOULD YOU PLEASE STOP!" But I think about Danell and keep my mouth shut. JaVonna makes it known that she is twenty-five and an Airline Stewardess at Penn Airport in Newark, New Jersey. She mentions that she also models for many fashion catalogs.

"Avery, I was featured in Bluff, Hype, and Jazzy as a swimwear model."

"That's nice," I say.

I want to puke.

I am hoping that she can see that I am not intrigued at all. The expression on my face does not discourage her from yapping. She continues on and on until I have no choice, but to put her on mute. And I do this by getting up and walking away. Yes, it's rude, but I don't care. I have had enough.

Don't get me wrong, JaVonna is extremely gorgeous. Her exotic eyes accentuate her caramel-glazed skin. Long silky tresses complement her features. Her Coke bottle figure and size two frame could make a fat chick stress, "bitch." Either JaVonna has had breast implants or the Lord has truly blessed her. Her legs are long and shapely toned. She could probably have any man that walks by, but that is not her preference. She is nose wide for Danell. Danell could have her eating out of her palm, but that doesn't seem like her. I personally feel like JaVonna has a devious streak in her. I can sense it a mile away. We have all tried to hang out together, but it just caused controversy. She kept fussing about other women checking Danell out. Insecure is the first thing that comes to my mind. And she isn't trying to hide it.

Their relationship will reach the five year mark in two weeks. I don't think they are going to make it another week to even celebrate their anniversary. Danell even mentions that they might be getting engaged, but with her attitude that isn't happening any time soon. I just can't see it. JaVonna has a bad habit of constantly accusing Danell of having me as her second lover. Me! Avery Love, a lesbian. I beg to differ. Danell gets tired of being questioned about her whereabouts, and is constantly being called on her cell phone and text messaging her every half hour. It's ridiculous.

She has even accused Danell of sleeping with me. Girlfriend has no class. I mean, I'm sitting right in their living room watching them bicker. And JaVonna doesn't even care.

"Boo, you tell that slut she betta' not let me catch her alone. She ain't got nothin'on me. Huh, you gonna be missing this here," pointing at her crotch saying, "This is the shit. You ain't never in your life had shit as good as mine. Five years of pleasuring your ass. Five years of licking yo' coochie. Putting up with yo' bullshit. And this is the thanks I get? Danell, you tell that skank she betta' watch her back."

My eyes droop and darken. *Watch my back. Dyke, you best watch your back.*

Her mouth runs amuck, until Danell gets so fed up and says, "Shut the hell up. We haven't been together five years, yet. Get the hell out!"

"Oh, no you didn't," JaVonna says with her hands on her slender waist. She points her finger in Danell's face nearly touching it as she spews spit splattering her nose, upper lip, and chin.

"Danell, I ain't goin' nowhere. I pay half the rent here." Ooh, her blood seems to be boiling as she stomps her foot and erupts into a 'mad black woman' rendition by slapping Danell crossed the face. *Oh, no she didn't!* My eyes are glued. They start to wrestle each other, and then it turns into a catfight with both swinging and touching nothing but air. And then Danell eyes set. I lean forward on the sofa. She exhales deeply and balls her right fist and socks JaVonna right in her cheekbone, nearly cracking it. *Ooh, I know that hurt!* All that is heard is a screech from her pain-stricken mouth. But JaVonna has not had enough and keeps coming back for more so she punches her so hard, her hair flies in the air and all that is heard is a loud crash as she hits the hardwood floor. I flinch wondering if anyone hears them on the second floor. It looks like Danell has knocked her unconscious, but she hasn't. She leaves her stretched out on the floor. *Damn!* JaVonna is on the floor panting, crying hysterically, but Danell doesn't care.

In a crackling voice with her arms raised, Danell says, "Look JaVonna, I can't do this anymore. When are you gonna get some sense in that pretty little head of yours? I can't take this anymore!"

Tears are flowing down both of their faces.

I am not sure what to do.

"We used to be happy at one point and time, but now it is misery. Violence is not something that I want in my life or in my relationship with anyone. There are times when I dread coming home because of your insecurities, JaVonna. Constantly, I'm being falsely accused of things that I am not doing. I hear you complaining in my head before I even walk through the door. You are skeptical about women at the gallery. I'm not looking for anyone else. You were all I needed. Baby, I can't do this anymore." Danell's eyes pierce into JaVonna's.

Tears flow like a waterfall down Danell's face. JaVonna is still on the floor weeping with snot running down her nose and her eyes are puffy and red. She cuts her eyes at me.

"JaVonna, Baby listen, I will pay for you to get another apartment because I can't live another day like this."

Danell throws her hands up in the air, takes a deep breath as she sits down at the kitchen table.

JaVonna's face turns fiery red. She rises to her feet and spits out, "What the fuck do you mean you'll get me another apartment? Why the hell can't you move?!" Her rebellious tone is like fire blazing out of her mouth.

Danell stares at her. "JaVonna, you must've lost your damn mind if you think that I'm gonna move. I was living here first. You moved in with me, remember?" She balls up her fist and bangs it on the kitchen table.

JaVonna has a tantrum and shouts at the top of her lungs.

"So!"

Danell shows no concern. She remains seated at the kitchen table and says, "Look, JaVonna, I am not going to sit here and try to pacify your ass. You have to move, point blank! I can't take being stressed everyday. Hoping that one day when I come home the woman that I fell in love with will reappear." She sighs with exhaustion.

JaVonna's voice tries to mimic a little girl's voice. "Boo, I can be that woman." She walks towards the kitchen table to move closer to Danell hoping to soften things up a bit, but Danell pulls away.

"No, no you can't! You haven't been that woman for the last two years. JaVonna, I love you dearly, but it is more important for me to be happy at this point in my life. And you deserve the same. I don't think that we should even remain friends. Let's just go our separate ways." She stands, walks to the refrigerator, opens it, and pulls out a bottle of spring water and starts drinking it down like she is dehydrated.

"NO!!! Danell, you don't mean that. Listen Baby, we need to get away and take a vacation together. Some quality time will be good for the both of us." She then walks into the kitchen and gets on her knees begging Danell to reconsider. Danell's eyes slant downward. She puts her water bottle on the counter, and pulls apart JaVonna's arms from her knees and walks into the living room and sits next to me on the sofa.

"JaVonna, quality time we have every single day! But you have to act all "ghetto" and ruin the time that we should be enjoying! I don't know what is wrong with you!"

I feel sucked in the middle of an awkward moment and I don't know exactly what to do to stop them from bickering, so I remain quiet.

"Danell, don't do this, please?!" she says weeping hysterically. She crosses her arms consoling herself as if a close relative has died.

"JaVonna, I didn't do it. You did it! I can't go back and forth with the bullshit. I have a business to maintain and I don't need unnecessary stress in my life. Baby, you have to go!" Danell eyes look hard and dark.

JaVonna stands to her feet, walks into the living room, cuts her eyes at me again and grabs her keys. She speaks in a hoarse voice, "Danell, I'm gonna give you time to calm down and think rationally. If you still feel the same way tomorrow, I'll leave."

"I don't need to think about it. This is what I want. You gotta go!" Her eyes darken even more.

JaVonna's eyes narrow. If looks could kill Danell would have been dead. She walks back in the living room face-to-face with Danell and scrolls her eyes from her toe-to-head.

"Fine hoe!" Then she ignites in rage, face candy apple red. "Avery, you best watch yo' back."

She fast paces it to the door and slams it with all of her might. Danell stands numb, but relieved. She is obviously not concerned with where her ex-girlfriend will be staying for the night. I sigh, and then ask Danell if she's okay. She nods her head.

The next day Danell calls me and tells me about the letter JaVonna left. She reads it to me over the phone.

Dear Danell,
It's your loss. Tell that bitch, your new girlfriend that I will fuck her up when I see her.
The better cunt,
JaVonna.

Danell and I keep in touch, but I don't want to escalate the situation so I hang low. Two weeks have passed since her breakup with JaVonna. I think loneliness is within her because she is distant at times. I'm sure it is not easy letting go of someone you've grown to love. I can only wonder what that feels like, but by the look on her face it must be the worst feeling in the world.

One Saturday evening at my apartment while Danell and I are sitting on the sofa watching TV she looks at me in this peculiar way. I turn away and continue to watch TV, but she continues to stare at me making me feel uncomfortable. We lock eyes for a second and then out of nowhere, Danell kisses me on the cheek. A peck on the cheek turns into a peck on my lips. And then a passionate kiss that makes my body flutter. I look Danell in her eyes piercingly; pull her face close to me, swapping saliva. *What has come over me?* I stop and wipe the moisture from the creases of my mouth. And we sit quietly and stare into space.

"Avery, please say something?"

I can't. I am at a loss for words. Hardened clay describes my whole body. I can't even look in her direction.

I stare at the wall and say, "Danell, I really have no words right now."

"Would you prefer that I leave?"

"It would probably be best."

I can feel the heat from Danell but I keep my mouth shut. It is difficult for me to swallow and my body is a rock. Danell stands, and slowly heads for the door. The door closes with a squeak.

Weirdness runs through my body. *I just kissed a woman. Me. Avery Love just kissed another woman.* I lean my head back against the sofa and shut my eyes tight. I am in total disbelief. *I just kissed a woman.* Why did I allow this to happen? Why did I let myself indulge in it further? But I did enjoy the kiss. And this is of great concern. I liked the warmth of Danell's body against mine. We connected in a way that I can never imagine with a woman. My head is spinning. I feel like I want to drown in a bottle of red wine, but it won't help erase the thoughts. Confusion overwhelms me and my biggest concern is questioning if I am an undercover lesbian hiding from the truth. But women just don't appeal to me in a sexual way. The thought has never crossed my mind. I sit with my arms folded and stare at the television. I can't think clearly. I want a friendship with a woman, but not on the level of intimacy. Danell completes the search for a companion, but I don't know if we can continue this friendship knowing that she is possibly interested. Interested in me! *Maybe she is just caught off guard on the rebound because of her breakup with JaVonna.* Loneliness can sometimes make one react towards a situation without thinking clearly. I just want to put this aside and hang with no strings attached. If Danell disagrees than I guess I'll be hanging solo. I need to lie down and try to ease this headache that is intensifying and making my eyes heavy. My temples are throbbing as I walk towards the bedroom and snuggle under my blanket. I doze off quickly and images appear as if I am watching a movie in the theater.

Steam surrounds me as the door cracks open in the bathroom. The water is streaming down my body rinsing my tension away. Danell has a key to my apartment. She says that she has called out my name, but I do not answer. She hears the water running in the bathroom and invites herself in. I feel someone in the bathroom with me. I slide the glass door and there she stands. I'm lathered from my feet working my way up. The scent of my body wash 'Intimacy' is invigorating. The feel of the hot water is comforting. Warmth comes over me. Danell undresses. She steps in the shower, wetting her body. She looks sexy. Her body gives off a seductive scent that reels me in. She touches my hand and slowly strokes my arm. I stand under the showerhead and allow the water to fall down my body. I lean my head back as the water drenches my hair. Danell touches my shoulder, leans in closer and begins to suck on my breasts in a circular motion, pulling my nipples with her teeth. My mouth opens because she is taunting, easing her fingers down to my clitoris. She strokes back and forth until secretion forms. I began to kiss her on her neck, cheek, and lips, teasing her with my tongue. She moans. I moan. We enjoy every moment. She squeezes

*my breasts hard. Sucking my nipples with intensity
she bites the tips to arouse me. Danell places my hand
on her vagina and directs my fingers. She knows her
soft spot, and desperately wants me to nurture it.
Vigorously, I continue to stroke it until her eyes roll to
the back of her head. She moans again.*

I am startled out of my sleep and in a panic I fall
off the bed. My nightshirt clings to my wet skin. I'm
petrified, because I am not certain if the *act* actually
occurred, but soon I realize it was only a dream.
Hoping. Realizing. Totally confused.

I am wide-awake now with no intention of
returning to sleep for fear that the nightmare will
reoccur. I go to the walk-in closet and start to empty
my shoes out of the shoeboxes and place them on the
shoe rack, just to preoccupy myself. By mistake I kick
an old Jimmy Choo shoebox, nearly tripping over a box
filled with papers. It is so full that it won't close. I
rummage around and find some important papers
along with some old junk mail. I sift through them until
I come across some handwritten letters. The
penmanship looks weird like the writer had a nervous
condition. There are numerous misspelled words. It's
obvious that this writer has not been well educated. As
I read, I realize that the letters are in fact poems from a
male. I applaud his efforts and admire his humbleness.
I envy him because with the little knowledge he has, he
expresses it with feeling. *How wonderful is it to feel
rich within when you are poor.* I sit for a moment
before I realize that the individual who wrote these
poems is indeed Poppa. He beautifully paints a picture
of unconditional love. Poppa with his hardened shell
has the words that pour from his soul. He is a southern
man who has a heart that is as soft as the feel of pure
cotton. A hardworking man filled with pride of
supporting his family. Based on his writing I assume
the man he is writing about to be in his mid-fifties with
only one child. His spouse is his strength. In his
younger days he has hopes and dreams, but has to put
his aspirations on hold to provide the necessities: food,

shelter, and clothing. He sacrifices unselfishly, penny pinching each month. Regretful he is not. He is appreciative for he feels richness within, paving a way for his child to pursue a better life. The poem touches my insides. I don't recall how I got the letters and poems. The only thing that makes sense to me is that possibly Ma'am had them and as I cleaned out her belongings I must've put them in the boxes and brought them home. I take the letters and put them in a box and leave one poem out and put it in an old frame, and hang it on the wall in my bedroom. It reads:

> Delicate as a summery breeze,
> Her skin thin and easy torn,
> She is my first, my only,
> Conquering a world in heels,
> Spinning of wheels, as I'd imagine.

> Will her legs withstand?
> Will she maintain, instead of relinquish?
> Will she comprehend one grand released from
> man's hands?

> Paving a sense of direction?
> Pain buried as I turned away closing the door,
> Throwing her to the world to flourish and not
> be bitten,
> Devouring my flesh confliction of choice.

> Delicate as a summery breeze,
> Her skin thin and easy torn,
> She is my first, my only,
> Conquering a world in heels,
> Spinning of wheels, as I'd imagine,
> Her feet planted as that of a Maple tree.

After reading his poem I realize the grudge that I held on for dear life has helped me to make a decision. I need to let go of the past because it's hindering me. And as soon as I have this thought, proudness pours into my soul. It has taken this long to see and feel the burdens that I inflict by harboring bitterness. It's all starting to make sense. Poppa pushed me out into the world because he felt I had something to offer. He wanted me to be strong and independent. I must admit at the time it really didn't feel that way. I never realized how he was trying to prepare me for the real world in his abrupt sort of way. All these years my heart was closed for the man who had a part in giving me life. It has taken twenty-two years of wasted energy using the same reason to despise him.

Muddy waters overflow numerous times nearly drowning my soul. If I only had the chance to look him in his eyes now, I would probably grit and grind my teeth, hold my head high and say, "thank you." Thank you for your struggles, assertiveness, rules and regulations within the household, instilling positive reinforcement that I am a diamond, not a cubic zircon, and most importantly for loving me so much to let me go. But I still question, why? Why did it have to be so harsh? Why couldn't he have given me time to prepare instead of pushing me so uncaringly? The question, why, fills my stomach, but I thank God that I'm surviving. And I know that He is slowly healing me inside and out. But it is not going to be easy to let go of the pain and suffering and anger. It is not going to be simple to say all right what's done is done because I still hurt from it all. I can't just wipe the window sparkling clean with vinegar and water. It is still real to me. Poppa hurt me in the worse way and I never saw it coming. I have wanted men the opposite of him because of him. And I ate many portions throughout my lifetime. I always resented Poppa. And the more I think of him the more I have to find men who can take the pain away. But unfortunately, they never take it away. They only shade it until I am alone and the feelings tear me in two. It never leaves me. Most of the time my relationship with him has haunt me. But God has awakened me to realize in order to learn you have to listen to His word. He will talk to me, cry with me, and scream with me, just so that I won't be alone. He speaks to Poppa and he listens. Poppa listens with an attentive ear knowing that I can withstand all obstacles. Poppa sees something in me just as God sees something in him and it sure is not weakness. Burdens did weaken me, not allowing me to feel, and breathe with a sense of accomplishment. I bled internally because Poppa stripped my thin skin. It has taken me twenty-two years for my heart to open up again for him. The resentment is crumbling. As I sit on the floor I pray like I have never prayed before for forgiveness.

T WENTY-TWO

THE MORE and more I sit the more I contemplate that kiss and dream with Danell. Seeping through is Zaelyn and he confuses things a bit because he entrances me. He stimulates a tingling sensation that escalates throughout my body. I fantasize about him—us. Like a sex addict I want to feel the stroke of his third arm, but I also crave Danell's tender touch. Her moistened lips caressed me with sensitivity that no man has ever delivered before. My thoughts are scrambled because I want what I want. Selfishly, I weigh my options. There is a commitment on Zaelyn's behalf, blood connects between him and Danell and that alone can evoke disaster. Confrontations may arise once the words are uttered to both of their ears privately. And I'm not certain if my skin has thickened yet, to test the waters.

The men I've dated have had conflicting reactions to my status. One shouted. The other cried in silence, suppressing his true feelings. That was torture. But I wonder what the reactions would be from a woman's perspective. In my mind, I picture Danell being compassionate—a stand-by her woman kind of gal. This leaves me caught in a web of frustration. Instinctively, I realize that Zaelyn may not want to accept the truth. Listening to my inner voice whispering, *Just 'cause he says he will be understanding, doesn't mean that he will.* And what will happen once I allow the words to escape from bondage, *I'm HIV-positive.* I truly wonder if he may run for the hills, damn near tripping over his feet, trying to get away from me.

I haven't spoken to Danell since the kiss and a part of me wants to call. The other part wants to go over to her apartment and hold her. She just reacted to an impulse and did not know what the outcome would represent. I totally abandoned her, leaving her in a desolate state of mind. I didn't do it to provoke conflict. Danell caught me off guard. She leaves an open window for me to close, closing on a world that is unfamiliar to me.

Tonight will be the night—nightfall of hot passion, tongues twirling, eyes locking, hands exploring—lovemaking. At least that is what I see in my mind. *How will I tell him? Where should I begin? Should I remain standing, sitting, or pace the floor? Do I look him in his eyes? Do I kneel down while he's seated and gaze at him with a distressful look upon my face? Should I cry? Should I laugh and then cry? How will I react if he abandons me? Should I say nothing?* My head hurts.

Danell crisscrosses my mind distracting my thoughts. The image of her puts me in a fog. I want to vomit. Nothing seems to want to come up but still my mouth waters. This nauseating sensation in my gut is gnawing at me to leave well enough alone, but I can't. I must tell Zaelyn because I am already way too deep into things. Emotionally, I want him as mine. Physically, I want our bodies to unite. Spiritually, I want our connection to be strong and endearing. And then with Danell, I want all of thee above, plus I want to experience something totally out of my realm. But then the final outcome could be that I end up standing on the platform alone wishin' I hadn't said a word. I feel like I'm damned if I do, damned if I don't.

I call Zaelyn for a date, then I prepare him a home cooked meal which includes his favorite barbeque ribs, potato salad, collard greens, cornbread, and for dessert German chocolate cake with pecan-caramel frosting. Candles are lit all throughout the apartment. Music plays low. He's more of a beer drinker so I pick up some Corona's, Heinekens, Budweiser, and a bottle of Sangria for me that I chill in the ice bucket. And then my mind shifts to Danell and the bolder part of me, yes, Avona, picks up the phone and calls her.

"Hello."

"Danell, it's me, Avery. Listen. Um, I think we need to talk. Can we possibly meet tomorrow?"

"Sure."

"I'll call you with a place and time."

"Okay."

After Danell and I hang up the inner walls of my stomach feel queasy. Butterflies flutter like I have a school crush. She makes me nervous. Her confidence is uplifting. The determination she has of being single to fulfill her aspirations is a turn on for me. She accepts me for me, but actually she doesn't even know me. Not the true me. And at times the pretend person wants to surrender and take on her punishment like a woman, but I don't have that type of backbone to stand my ground without feeling like I will crumble. I'm stranded with thought. Wanting both people doesn't mean that I will have both. And then I question who will be more beneficial? I want Zaelyn to rock my world. Possibly I just want him for that sole purpose? Having his massive hands imprint my skin, and stroking me with a thrust of motion that tears down the blocked barricade. Taking the friction of latex inflaming my delicate skin because I've been longing—damn near starving for his animal-like passion. Lubricating me with KY jelly making me slippery wet. Just the thought makes me shiver.

Dinner is to be served at 8:00 p.m. The table setting is complete with rust and gold napkins with black china, ivory candles and flames dancing to "Ribbon in the Sky." It is already 7:15 and I am just getting dressed. Zaelyn's arrival will no doubt trigger me to expose the other side of me. The side that's confident, spontaneous, and bold that used to get me what I wanted in the past. I picture him as the aggressor. He seems to like to be in charge from the way he speaks. So why should I deprive him or myself since we have both been anticipating it. There will be high volumes of, "Who's your daddy! Who's your daddy?" Smacking my ass with the pitter-patter, pitter-patter, and pitter-PAT! As his Pina Colada smoothie gushes out of him inside of my hot pocket, calming me down with his easygoing strokes. I clap with a standing ovation. Just the thought of it makes my lips below quiver. I picture him being a citrus lollipop that I get to lick down as it dissolves into my mouth; leaving nothing but a naked, long, stick.

Zaelyn arrives on time and we sit enjoying our meal. Dessert is waiting to be served on a silver platter. Looking into Zaelyn's eyes and holding his hands makes me feel like I am sinking in quicksand. It's not a romantic scene. I'm afraid. I don't want to lose him. I am sure he can feel the throbbing of my pulse. I scratch my throat, taking deep prolonged breaths. Zaelyn has the biggest deer eyes I've ever seen. He blinks. In slow motion I wait until his eyelids open fully and without pause the words come.

"Zaelyn, I really enjoy your company and I would like to have the opportunity of getting to know you even more." I fake a cough. "I have thoughts about us being intimate."

Zaelyn's hand caresses me gently.

"But unfortunately there is something that needs to be said first. Zaelyn. Zaelyn...I'm...I'm...HIV-positive." I shut my eyes not wanting to see the grimace on his face. I pull back my hand, but he gently pulls it back and massages it ever so gently. Then I open my eyes. I feel relief from within. He doesn't react in the slightest way and that frightens me.

"Avery, I've also been thinking about us connecting. Lord knows it's been difficult smelling your lovely scent and admiring your beauty. It has been traveling through my mind since our last date. I am feelin' you like no other woman."

I close my eyes feeling his words. He swallows me with his affection.

"Avery, the chemistry is here and by you being honest with me it only assures me that this is fate. I want to be inside you, floating my juices around with yours, as we make love 'til dusk turns to dawn. I don't have an issue about using precautions. I just want to indulge in you like a bowl of chocolate pudding." He moistens his lips.

I smile. Zaelyn has wooed me right off of my feet.

The truth has been told and Zaelyn still stands before me with open arms. He starts undressing me with his eyes as he unbuttons his burgundy suede dress shirt and holds his arms down as it slips off his skin showing off his biceps of steel. They look plump and juicy. And then he unzips his black trousers and they rush to his feet. *He has some meaty thighs.* He steps out of his burgundy suede shoes, and pulls off his socks, showing me clear toenails. *I just hope the soles of his feet are not scaly, rough, and I hope there is no fungus.* He lifts up one leg at a time, standing before me in his silk boxers that show off a huge bulge. He wraps his arms around me breathing his Altoids breath on my already burning hot skin and unzips my dress as it caresses my body and falls to my feet. We are face-to-face as my breasts protrude and my sexy black thong makes him drool. *I am ready to be fed!* Zaelyn takes my hand and I lead him to the bathroom. He turns on the shower, drops his boxers and pulls off his wife beater. I step out of my thong. He stands close, cuddling me as he touches my breasts, squeezing, and pushing both of them together as he kisses them. The water is steaming up the bathroom making our bodies aroused. Zaelyn places one foot in the shower as he helps me in; the water beads against our bodies. He runs his fingers through my hair. He whispers in my ear, "You are so beautiful." I touch his back and spiral down to his third arm massaging as its size increases enormously. His blood flows quickly. He strokes my clitoris building secretion making me sloppy moist. I moan. He moans. The intensity grows and his third arm is as hard as a rock. He becomes aggressive in his burning desire to be within me. We make animal music. We lather each other allowing our hands to explore. I kiss his neck and lick his nipples, as the tension in me creates a friction that ignites. I am on fire. He teases me by gently biting my nipples and palming my ass. Foreplay makes us two horny dogs. Zaelyn turns off the water, picks me up and carries me to the bedroom. And all I hear at this moment is Etta James singing, "At Last." Our bodies are dripping wet. He lays me on the bed, spreading my legs apart, and sitting in between. Cuffing my wrists like a crab with claws, he teases me with the touch of his penis up and down my thigh. The feeling makes my mouth open, his tongue meets my lips and I moisten them. *Its finally gonna happen.* I point to my nightstand indicating for him to get a Magnum condom. He reaches over in and pulls one out, tears it open with his teeth, and rolls the lubricated latex condom on. *I want him badly.* Zaelyn lies on top of me and slowly tries to enter my walls, while kissing my neck, breasts, and navel, but the entrance feels cemented. I squint because the pressure is not pleasurable. I feel as if I am a virgin. I inhale with anxiety as he tries to enter for the second time and my eyes close as the walls partially open. I exhale. He is larger than I thought. Then he tries a third time and he strokes once, twice, until the rhythm moves my body along. He palms my shoulders giving him more of grip and spreads my legs with his legs allowing him to have his way. Suddenly, I am in the driver's seat positioning on top riding him forward, backwards, sideways, and in a circular motion. His arms extend on both sides of the bed and he pulls on the comforter for support. Sweat is dripping from my face, down my breasts and onto his stomach. He sits up and I continue to giddy-up horsy on his long, hard, stiff penis. Zaelyn flips me on my stomach and I am taking it doggy style. My head bobs as he thrusts with forcefulness. I moan loudly. That triggers him to go faster, harder, faster, and harder.

"Who's my baby! Who's my baby?" he stares at me with sweat dripping from his chin onto my back.

"Ooh baby, I am! I am," I mumble loud enough for him to hear while grinding my teeth into the goose down pillow. Zaelyn flips me on my back and places my legs on his shoulders getting a full workout; inward, outward, inward, outward until hip-hop beats formulate, pop, pop, pop! The wetness makes my vagina make beautiful music. My eyes roll back. He stands up and puts me on his hip as he pumps, and grabs my ass imprinting it with his fingerprints, as I palm his back and place one arm around his neck. His stamina is incredible! A loud howl cries out of him as he shuts his eyes tightly almost biting his lip. He is trembling out of control. I'm out of breath. But he is full of energy as if he has taken Viagra beforehand. I grit and grind my teeth some more, eyes fluttering and I wet my lips because my mouth's dry.

"I'm – c-c-c-, cu-, ccccuuummmiiinnn'!" I clamp both arms around his neck, tears scream down my face, at that second he releases while our bodies are sticky with our tropical juices. We both lean back wanting a smoke, but settle for a glass of water. Frantically we both realize that the condom has come off. I reach inside of myself and pull it out. Some of his thick semen resides in the tip, but the remainder is left inside of me. I rush to the bathroom to douche, hoping it will leak out. Zaelyn remains still until I return from the bathroom. I'm cautious not to say the wrong thing. I discreetly look towards him but he remains silent. He sits up and palms his face with his left hand, and shakes his head. I massage my face and began to pray silently. A moment of absolute pleasure may have turned into a life of regret or weeks of agony because the last thing I want is to become a single mother. Zaelyn stands up and walks into the living room for his clothes. I follow him. He gets dressed and stares at the rug as he buttons his shirt, never looking me directly in the eyes. I swear he makes me feel like he just paid for sex. Like, I'm some trick. Delicate walls start building up inside of me, but I don't let it show on the surface. Zaelyn states that he's getting ready to go, and this is when he looks me in my face and gives me a counterfeit smile. I see right through it. I nod in acknowledgment and lead him to the door. I give him a kiss on his cheek, say good night and slowly close the door. Zaelyn seems too calm, which throws up red flags. *I may never see him again.*

After Zaelyn leaves my apartment I become very concerned. Later I pick up the phone to call him.

"Hello," he says in a faded whisper.

"Hi, Zaelyn, it's Avery."

He remains silent.

"Zaelyn, listen, I just want to say that I feel terrible about what happened. I don't regret us making love because it was something I truly wanted and needed. I called out of concern. I am here if you need or want me to be."

"Avery, I appreciate you being concerned, but can we talk about this tomorrow?"

"Sure."

After I hang up with Zaelyn my feelings are cross. I want him to lean on me, but he is not receptive. I can't beat myself up about this and I won't. I'll wait for him to come around when he is ready to talk. The last thing that I wanted was for something like this to happen. I don't know how the condom came off. We shared an exhilarating night that could have possibly become much more. It is not just about sexual fulfillment. I want the whole package, the man, the house with the white picket fence, and the dog.

Johnnie comes to mind and I hear his voice; "Gurl, you can only give so much of yourself until your well is drained dry. Honey, sometimes you have to let go and allow the individual to come to you." Oh, how I understand this concept, but embedded in me is hollowness. I sincerely care about Zaelyn and want to be by his side during this difficult time. But he wants to be left alone and I have no choice but to respect his wishes. My heart hurts.

I can't sleep well because I can't stop thinking about Zaelyn. Then I start thinking about me already infected with HIV that I can be infected again with the virus. I know Zaelyn but not as well as I should. I didn't even ask him if he was ever tested. Actually, it did cross my mind, but the words didn't find their way out. I didn't wanna jinx my moment of pleasure. Who's to say when I may have another? I know...I know. I let my hot flesh get the best of me possibly putting myself at risk. Dwelling on it is not going to change the situation and I have to keep reminding myself of that over and over. At 9:30 a.m. I am compelled to call Danell at the gallery. Many days have passed since we last saw each other and I personally think that gives us ample time to allow the kiss to sink in. Danell makes a sistah feel shielded; shielded like a cloud of genuineness surrounding your whole body. I pick up the phone and call.

"Good morning, Virtue, Danell speaking, how may I help you?"

"Good morning, Danell, its Avery."

"Hi."

Danell sounds thrilled to hear from me. It's like nothing ever took place between us.

"Danell, do you have any free time this afternoon?"

"What did you have in mind?"

"I want us to meet so we can talk."

"Okay, what about one o'clock?"

"One o'clock will be fine."

"Is it okay if we meet over this way, Avery?"

"Sure."

"There is a Deli across the street from the store."

"Sounds like a plan. I'll see you at one o'clock."

I hope today is a glorious day. The temperature is in the high nineties. Dr. Fulmore comes to my mind and I call his office because I haven't heard a word from him about my results. My hands lightly shake as I call, but I get a grip once I hear Violet's voice.

"Dr. Fulmore office, Violet speaking, how may I help you?"

"Good morning Violet, its Avery."

"Good morning."

"Violet, do you know if Dr. Fulmore received my results back?"

"Yes, he did. He has been running around here like a chicken with his head chopped off all week. He probably forgot to ask me to call you. Do you want to come in today to speak with him?"

"Yes."

"I'll let him know that you will be stopping by. It should only take a few minutes."

"Okay, I'll see you soon."

That damn kiss enters my mind, again. A re-enactment floats around in my head. Airy is the word that comes to mind as I reminisce about the kiss. Danell has a strong affect on me.

I throw on some jeans and a T-shirt to go to Dr. Fulmore's office. As I enter my car my cell phone rings, but when I answer it there is no one there. The phone rings again and on the other end I hear a man weeping. It sounds like he's heavily intoxicated. His words slur together, but I manage to pick up on the voice.

"Zaelyn, is that you?"

The man pauses and then hangs up.

I call Danell's number for Zaelyn's address.

"Hello Virtue, Danell speaking, how may I help you?"

"Danell, I need Zaelyn's home address!"

"Avery, is there something wrong?"

"No, no, I just need to see him for something."

"Okay."

"It's 777 Ross Avenue, in Totowa. It's a large blue house."

"Okay, thanks."

I quickly rush to Zaelyn's home. I fling my car door open and run up three sets of stairs. I ring the bell patiently waiting for him to answer. He doesn't answer and I grow panicky. I start to pound on the door with full force. I ring the bell again and pound on the door over and over again. Zaelyn comes to the door and peeks out of the curtains.

"Zaelyn, please open the door?"

He stands with tears running down his face and a bottle of vodka in his hand.

"Zaelyn, please open the door?"

He turns the lock and I push the door open. He staggers backwards and leans against the hallway wall reeking of booze. I take him in my arms and just hold him. I hold him tight, letting him know that I am there for him. We stand in his hallway for a few minutes and then I manage to get him inside. He looks terrible. He has on the same clothes from yesterday and he has probably been drinking all night. His bachelor pad is neatly organized. This is the first time I have ever been to his house. Its two-levels. I hold him up with all of my might and then lay him on the sleigh bed. I search through the dresser to find some clean underclothes. I notice his computer is printing out information on AIDS and HIV. I also notice a confirmation print out of an order for a FDA- approved home testing kit.

Zaelyn seems to have drowned in his sorrows all night. He soothed himself with a bottle of vodka, but I think deep down inside he wants to be rescued. Why else would he have called? I undress Zaelyn's layers of funk and throw his clothes on the floor. I stand him up barely being able to hold him because he is heavy like lead, but somehow I manage. I struggle getting him to the bathroom, not certain where the bathroom is, as his feet slide across the wall-to-wall carpet. I take a deep sigh, and then huff as I finally reach the entrance of the nicely granite tiled bathroom. I sit him on the toilet seat while I turn the shower nozzle. As the water sprays out I get undressed so that I am able to get in the shower with him. I'm exhausted. Then I lean over and wrap my arm around Zaelyn's arm and lift him up with the little strength I have left. His body is heavy and my muscles are sore from holding him up. It's difficult trying to get him in the shower and I almost fall backwards. It takes three tries until I finally get him inside and stand him right underneath the showerhead letting the water drench his inebriated body. He is at his lowest and I feel responsible. Guilt spider webs over my body. I bathe him, rinsing him thoroughly as the water camouflages what looks like tears running down his face. His eyes are bloodshot and have pain written all over them. Gloominess grips his face. And it spikes my heart. I can't take seeing Zaelyn like this and I know that once he comes to he wouldn't want me to see him like this. There is a large lump in my throat, but I don't shed a tear because I need to be strong for him. I pull the towel from its rail and wrap it around his waist. I put his left hand on the rail and bend his leg to step him out of the bathtub. Then I step out still trying to hold him up. Now at least Zaelyn seems more awake. Awake enough to walk back towards the bedroom. He stands unsteady as I bend down to help him put on his boxers. Then I sit him on the bed. I help him with his V neck T-shirt, and lay him down.

I go into the modern kitchen to make him some coffee, and when I return he has already fallen asleep. I go back into the kitchen and turn the kettle off. Here I am walking around his house totally nude. I'm not even thinking about myself; Zaelyn is more important. I return to the bathroom and get dressed. *Dr. Fulmore.* Damn. I call Dr. Fulmore's office to cancel my meeting and ask Violet to have him call me with my results. *Danell.* I call her and cancel our meeting. Then Dr. Cristal pops in my head and I call to confirm my appointment. Gretchen tells me its today, so I cancel and reschedule. Exhaustion clings to me. I return to the bedroom and rest my head at the foot of the bed. Zaelyn's snoring is not easy to tune out, but eventually my eyes fold. When I awake Zaelyn is at the foot of the bed with me, his arm resting on my back and when I move his red eyes open. I speak softly because of his hangover.

"Zaelyn would you like a cup of coffee?"

He nods his head. I raise my listless body and head for the kitchen. When I come back he is sitting up against the headboard with his right leg overlapping his left. His hands are interlocked and rested on his lap. His droopy eyes have crust stuck in the corners and he just stares into space. His mouth is crusty around the edges and his lips are chapped. Grogginess is sketched on his blue-black face because of all the alcohol he has drunk. He looks at me strangely as if I am translucent. The expression on my face reads 'caution', and I feel uncomfortable. To break the ice I say,

"Zaelyn, are you okay?"

He gapes at me, but doesn't say a word. The uncomfortable feeling progresses into utter panic because I don't know his state of mind. At least if he's speaking I can tell where his mind is at or where it's headed. My tone is soft because I don't want him to erupt. Zaelyn seems in a fog. I walk to the foot of the bed and repeat,

"Zaelyn, are you okay?"

He continues to gape, but this time he finally answers in a faint whisper, "Yes."

I want to release a deep sigh, but I keep it in and slowly exhale in segments. I don't want Zaelyn to see the panic in my eyes. I need to try and change the subject. He just talks in riddles that don't make any sense. Then, out of the blue, he comes to, out of his comatose state. Strangely he transforms gradually into the Zaelyn that I know.

The kettle in the kitchen is whistling Dixie so I hurry to turn it off. I bring back a hot cup of coffee, sit on the bed, and hand it to him. He sips it making a slurping sound that annoys the hell out of me, but I do not allow him to see my facial expression. Three sips later and then Zaelyn looks at me.

"How?"

"How? What?" I ask.

"How did it happen, Avery?"

A puzzled look comes over my face, "Pardon?"

"Avery, how did it all begin? What did you do when you were told? And how are you really feeling about it now?" He rushes his sentences.

Zaelyn throws me for a loop and leaves me speechless. I know this is something he needs to understand so I swallow my pride and wait for the words to roll off my tongue.

I start pacing the floor as the memories replay

the pictures of that night scene by scene. Shutting my eyes and shaking my head, tears begin to fall.

"Zaelyn, it was back in January of 2000; I was at the law firm building in New York with a colleague. Back then, as I've told you I was a paralegal. I caught the subway and then a bus to Paterson because I had a late evening hair appointment with my stylist Aja who works in Montclair at this salon called, Villa of Locks. My normal routine was to always take the train and then walk to the parking lot to my car. It was nippy that evening. I got off the bus and I was a couple of blocks away from the parking lot walking in downtown Paterson. I passed this Electronics store that had a narrow alley that was pitch black. And out of nowhere someone grabbed me and dragged me in back of the Electronics store. He punched me with closed fists giving me two blackened eyes. He yanked my hair from its roots. I fought like my body was on fire. I screamed as if my skin was sizzling from my flesh. I screamed, puullllleeeeeaaaasssseee, puullllleeeaaasssseeee, don't! I'M PREGNANT! Think about my baby, my unborn baby, puuulllleeeeaaasssseeee! I was trying to think of anything that would make him stop. I just wanted him to stooooopppp. I was hoping...praying that he had a conscience. I continued to try, Pleeeeeaaaasssseee, my husband, my husband is dying! Please this is our first child...please, my family! It seemed useless. His eyes darkened as he spewed out in a voice of fury, You cheatin' on me?! I shook my head no, no. I tried to feed into his way of thinking. I tried. Zaelyn, I desperately tried to save my life. With a tight grip he strangled me with one hand while squeezing the back of my neck. I felt my airway closing and I tried to fight for freedom by swinging my one free arm. I clawed at his face like I was a cat fighting recklessly for my life. I pushed my thumb in his eye socket wanting to pull his eyeball out, but I couldn't get a good grasp because of the force with which he manhandled my body. He was distracted by footsteps and turned to look, loosening his hold on my hand. Once both of my hands were free I gasped for air like it was my last breath to take. I wasn't quick enough. He put all of his weight on my chest while using his legs to spread mine. The cement ground scratched my skin and I felt myself bleed. Oh God, please, I thought. I noticed a plastic bag on the ground. All I could think about was him trying to suffocate me and I felt myself panic. Tremors took over my body as he parted my legs with his hot, sweaty hands, scratching my inner thighs with his jagged nails. My breathing was erratic. He had the audacity to say that I needed to "loosen up" because I was as dry as a desert. THAT SICKO! So he intensified his motion by ripping my tender skin until it bled. His forcefulness made my delicate skin sting and burn around my vagina like he had poured acid on me. God, I screamed at the top of my lungs, helppppppppppppp! I tossed and turned my body trying to get away. Shut up bitch! He snapped. Followed by a backhand slap that nearly knocked my two front teeth out of my mouth. He hit me so hard I thought I was going blind. I felt helpless as he tortured me while breathing heavily in my ear. It left me feeling stagnant, and so full of fear. I shut my eyes because I did not want to see his face. I did not want it etched in my mind. Lord knows it's true. I did not want to see it! Repulsed by his odor, vomit that had been lodged in my throat regurgitated onto the ground.

The act seemed long and agonizing. His thrusts were more aggressive, whispering in my ear that he was *coming*. I grew bitter. I screamed for help! He tried to muffle my screams by forcing his smelly hand over my mouth, as he released his demonic semen in me, but I continued to scream, muffled and all. He panicked and ran off, leaving me. He left me traumatized, and shaking like a junky. I couldn't move my legs or my body for that matter, for what seemed like hours. I was in shock. I wiped the snot that was running from my nose with the tail of my torn blouse. My face was throbbing and blood stained from the blunt punches.

I literally wanted to die, Zaleyn. I wanted to slip into a deep coma with no desire to wake up, yet a powerful energy seemed to surround me and I managed to lift myself up on my two feet. I barely made my way to the front of the Electronics store. I looked up and down the street hoping to see someone, anyone. I tried to cross the street but as I moved toward the middle of the street my legs grew weak while a moving car was coming and I fell right in front. The person slammed on their brakes nearly running me over and came to my rescue. I heard a man's voice calling the police; I guessed he was using his cell phone. He asked me a couple of questions, but nothing was making sense to me. I couldn't comprehend or respond. After a few minutes I heard sirens and then I felt him leave my side. By the time the police arrived, he was long gone. I never got the chance to say thank you."

I grab some tissue from the dresser and continue to explain. Zaelyn looks attentive and remorseful by the look in his eyes, but he does not distract me. I pause, wipe the snot from my nose and continue.

"Zaelyn, he whispered things in my ear that were provocative as if I were enjoying the act. He stripped a part of me away forever!" Zaelyn's forehead has a wrinkle in it and his eyes droop with anger.

I lose all control and begin to cry hysterically. Zaelyn sits on the bed watching helplessly as I scream at the top of my lungs, WHYYYYYYYY MEEEEE! My eyes are swollen and red. I take in deep breaths swallowing hard. I hold my hand up to my mouth trying to get my words out. My voice is raspy with emotion. Zaelyn's eyes are glossy and a tear forms. Sniffling, as he stands to grab a tissue. He walks over to me and takes me in his arms and wraps me up in his warmth. He makes me feel well protected. He holds me as if he is holding an infant and his love fills me from within. I've never experienced that feeling before and for the very first time *a man* is actually able to break through the barriers and allow me to free myself from the pain. My rapist has dictated my life for so many years and I have tried to continue on with life, but it has tortured me because I have never talked about that day. Zaelyn is the first in many ways and it took every ounce of energy for me to tell him.

I look Zaelyn in his eyes and say,

"When Dr. Fulmore told me that I was HIV-positive I felt my heart skip. My airway was closing and I wanted to die. Thoughts of taking my own life ran through my mind, but I was never bold enough to act on it. I started hallucinating about that night. I was waking with night sweats thinking that my rapist was in my apartment with me coming to finish me off. I hibernated in the house for many months until my best friend Johnnie saved me from myself. He saved me from a life of misery." I look up at Zaelyn's ceiling and smirk.

We sit back on the bed and Zaelyn holds my hands. I lower my head. He lifts my chin and says in an emotional voice,

"Avery, you are strong, beautiful, intelligent, and vibrant. Don't allow this tragedy to consume you into a weed of despair. Flourish and rise to your destiny."

Zaelyn's eyes are red and weary, but sincere. His words inspire me. Maybe my prayers are, and will finally be answered since he has broken the barriers of distress. I want, need, and deserve a good man in my life and I am so glad that we are together. It is so important to have someone in my life who can take the time to try and understand me emotionally.

Twenty-Three

AS I AM getting ready to leave I ask Zaelyn if he wants me to start a pot of coffee. He nods his head. I am heading for the kitchen when I notice pictures on the mantle and one in particular catches my attention. My eyes have to be deceiving me. I freeze, as my eyes stare at a wedding picture so full of bliss. I lower my head, hold back my tears, and go into the kitchen to start the coffee, and afterwards I gather my things, kiss him on the forehead and leave.

The weekend goes so quickly that Monday seems like Sunday. I park right in front of my building and drag myself through the front door. I have skipped taking my medication from Friday to Sunday and my body is really feeling weird. I pull at the front door to the building and it's as heavy as steel. Scrambling for my mail key I open the box to find a letter from Wachovia Bank. Normally I would tear the envelope in two, but I don't have the energy so I wait until I get upstairs to my apartment.

In my apartment I see the red light blinking so I check my messages. Dr. Fulmore called Friday and said that everything is fine. He apologized for the false alarm, but he wanted to be sure that spot wasn't anything major. I smirk because that is one less thing I have to worry about. I throw my keys in the mail bin and sit on the sofa debating if I should open the letter now or later. I want to open it, but I don't want to get discouraged if they deny my loan. What the heck, I might as well open it and find out. I unfold the letter, and my eyes brighten. I have been approved for the business loan. I kick my feet up and start moving my arms in a circular motion while jerking my body with glory. Then slowly it all hits me. *Zaelyn.* My eyes break up into tiny puddles because I know in my heart that I have been played. The picture...the smiles...the vows...the family. I close my eyes and try to block it out but I can't so I go into my bedroom and sit at my desk. I turn on my CD player and listen to Rihanna, "Now I Know," and everything makes sense for the first time. I reach for a piece of my good writing paper and begin to write Zaelyn a letter.

> *Dear Zaelyn,*
> *I hope all is well when you receive this letter. I just want you to know that I appreciate all that you've given me, mostly your time. But I've come to realize that time is very precious and I don't have it to give at this point and time in my life. There are so many things that I want to accomplish and having the distractions of a man won't do anything but stifle me right now. So basically what I'm saying is "see you" and have a nice life.*
> *Avery*

I put the letter in an envelope and affix a stamp to it and walk downstairs to put it on my mailbox. Then I return upstairs.

I listen to the rest of the messages and Mr. Clausen and Mrs. Jenkins-Rollin have called. I call Mrs. Jenkins-Rollin back first.

"Tribe Realty, Mrs. Jenkins-Rollin speaking, how may I help you?"

"Hello, this is Ms. Love returning your call."

"Oh, yes, Ms. Love, I called to inform you that there is another potential buyer for the building that you are interested in. Normally I don't call to alert anyone, but you have been so persistent about that particular building. I called Mr. Clausen and also informed him. I just need to know if you are ready to finalize the deal."

"Yes, I am ready. I will call Mr. Clausen and let him know that we need to meet to finalize everything."

"Oh, how wonderful! I am so very excited for you."

"Thank you."

All that I can think about at the very moment is

God is soooo good.

I hang up with Mrs. Jenkins-Rollin and immediately call Mr. Clausen.

"Mr. Clausen's office, Tia speaking, how may I help you?"

"Hi, Tia, this is Avery Love calling for Mr. Clausen."

"Hi, Ms. Love. Unfortunately, Mr. Clausen is out with a client, but as soon as he returns I will let him know you called."

"Sure, let him know that I am ready to sign the papers on the dotted line."

"I sure will, Ms. Love."

"Thank you."

The building in Montclair is made for me. There is nothing holding me back and I am driven full force to pursue the only goal that has ever challenged me. All the pieces are coming together and the final outcome is me signing on the dotted line. My faith has been broadened over the last few months with God right by my side.

I hit the message button on my answering machine and I listen to a woman's squeaky voice leaving her name and telephone number for me to return the call. In bold letters RED ALERT appears on the caller ID. I call the number back and a woman answers,

"Thank you for calling Red Alert, Jayne Thompson speaking, how may I help you?"

"Hello, my name is Avery Love and I am returning your call."

"Oh, yes, Ms. Love, I was calling to inform you of our schedule for the training. You chose the shift from 12 a.m. to 9 a.m. I just wanted to know if you are available to start tonight? We have already arranged a phone buddy for you who works the same shift."

"Sure. That would be fine."

"Great, I will let Careen know that you will be there tonight. You will more than likely train for the three days and then the fourth you'll be on the phones by yourself. Of course, others will be available should you need assistance. Ms. Love we look forward to seeing you. You have a nice day."

"Thank you, Ms. Thompson."

Now my plans are coming together. Anonymous will soon be opening. This job will definitely help out as far as extra income. I wish my parents were here to see the progress that I've been making. I can see Poppa, proud, but too proud to say so. Ma'am would be hugging and kissing me to death. I really miss the both of them.

The phone rings again, and this time it's Mr. Clausen's office.

"Hello."

"Hello, this is Mr. Clausen; Tia explained to me that you are ready to sign on the dotted line."

"Yes, is there any way that you can have Mrs. Jenkins-Rollin fax you the forms just to get things started. You can then fax the forms to me and we can meet later today or tomorrow to sign the originals?"

"Normally Ms. Love, that is not how it is done, but you seem so anxious to get things moving. I'll see if I can convince her. What's your fax number?"

I wait for him to get back to me with Mrs. Jenkins-Rollin's response. Time is moving slowly. I nervously bite my nails. Twenty minutes pass and I am down to the cuticles. Forty-five minutes later the phone finally rings and I am hoping that it's Mr. Clausen at the other end.

"Hello."

"Hello, Ms. Love, I am faxing the paperwork to you now. It gives the amount of the cashier's check that you will need to finalize the deal. I asked Mrs. Jenkins-Rollin to meet us tomorrow morning at 9:30 to sign the original documents. Once you have completed the forms fax them back to me so that I can get things moving."

"Certainly, I will have the forms back as soon as possible, Mr. Clausen and thank you."

"Do you have a date set for your grand

opening?"

"Well, actually, yes. I want to do the grand opening for November 4th, which is on a Friday. I figure most of the necessities are already in the place, I just need to make some final touches and quickly distribute some flyers."

"You have clearly thought things out and I hope that everything works out in your favor."

"Thank you, Mr. Clausen that means a lot."

When I hang up I realize how much work I have to accomplish almost nine weeks time. I grab the phone book and start making calls. I need a business sign so I call around. I call Ink Marker for flyers and business cards. I also need to call Verizon to setup a business line. And then I call a place about purchasing a microphone and a stand. Lastly, I call a caterer because there is no way I am going to be able to make different varieties of food by myself. I write a list of things I need: table cloths, napkins, napkin holders, vases, silk flower displays, and candles with holders, liquid soap for the bathrooms, toilet paper and paper towels. I hear the fax coming through so I walk over and snatch it. I read over the fine print and the amount I need for the cashier's check. I decide to head out to Target, Pier 1 Imports, Wal-Mart, Crate and Barrel, West Elm, and Costco for some cleaning supplies. My last stop is Wachovia Bank to request a cashier's check in a large sum of money. I've never had to write a check like this before, but it's for my future.

Damn, it has just dawned on me that I have to start training tonight. It's not like I have any plans or anything, it will just throw me off a little because I am used to being in bed at that time. My day is so hectic. I kind of wish I had company through all of this. I feel lonely because Danell and I rarely speak now. A part of me wants to call her just to chat, but a part of me is saying, *leave well enough alone.* I miss her company, her friendship, even after the kiss I still think about her, but my preference hasn't changed. I still adore men.

Eleven-thirty is approaching so I put some pep in my step so that my first day I will not be embarrassed by arriving late. When I arrive at Red Alert I am calm. I'm hoping that I will not have to shake anyone's hand because they are clammy. I push the buzzer so that someone will come and open the door.

"May I help you?"

"Yes, my name is Avery Love and I am starting training tonight."

"Ms. Love, I'll be right down." The gentleman says.

Two minutes later the door opens and a young gentleman greets me. He introduces himself as Khalis.

"Nice to meet you, Khalis. I'm here to start training. Careen Walker is my manager."

Khalis looks at me and smiles because he must already know that information. I guess he can tell that I am nervous, but he doesn't throw it in my face. He seems mature, even though he looks like he's possibly nineteen or in his early twenties. He is easy going and seems very approachable. I'm hoping that he will be the one training me. We walk into this spacious room with cubicles all around. I glance at a couple of desks in passing and notice pictures of family, friends, and significant others. The atmosphere is comfortable. Careen greets me and introduces me to the overnight crew.

"Avery, this is Carole, Sly, Elsie, Rae, Kraig, Paula, Starlin, Horace, and you have already met Khalis." Everyone eyes melt me down, especially the women. I don't expect it to be any other way. There are a couple of young men who give me eye contact and look at me as if I am a piece of candy. I return a look of *not interested,* just in case.

Careen asks me to sit with Rae. Rae is short and chunky. She has wide hips, a double roll stomach, and quadruple junk in her trunk. She wears her hair in cornrows, which accentuates her face quite nicely. Her acne-prone complexion leaves scattered dark spots around her forehead, chin, and nose. Rae goes over the dos and don'ts of the company. I can tell that she's very friendly. She doesn't seem phony and uninterested in sharing her knowledge. She explains that when calls come in we are supposed to use our pen names and so does the caller. Everything is pretty much anonymous. Rae goes over each screen and how we document the calls on the callers account. "Avery, we feed our information on each call to the proper institution where the caller goes for treatment. This helps assist them in dealing with their illness because the psychologist, psychiatrist, and their primary doctors are all informed on their mental and physical conditions.

"Avery, sometimes I leave here crying. It can be very emotionally draining knowing that someone on the other end of the phone is coping with the possibility of dying. A lot of times I feel helpless, but something keeps pulling me back here to keep on trying to soothe their pain," Rae says as she notices a call coming through. She nudges me to put on my headset. She waits until I am settled and then takes the call. Her lips are glued together and then they part with enthusiasm.

"Thank you for calling Red Alert Hotline Service, my name is Ariel. How may I help you?"

"You said your name is Ariel? What the hell kinda name is that, Ariel? Who's your mama so that I can slap her silly?" The vulgar woman says.

"Excuse me, ma'am?"

"Ma'am, damn you make me sound old as shit. Dammit, this is Daisy. Ya' hear me? I am thirty-five-years old. I got three children that I can't find. Do you know where they are?" she asks defiantly.

"Daisy, unfortunately I don't, but I bet they are good children."

"Well, Ariel, if you should see 'em tell 'em they momma say she love 'em."

"I will Daisy."

Daisy yells out to someone named Jessie.

"Jessie! Jessie, where are you going with my beer? You think you slick trying to sneak behind my back and drink all my fuckin' beer. I bought this beer with my damn money. Hand me a cigarette!"

"Ariel, are you there?" Daisy asks.

"Yes, I'm here, Daisy."

"Yeah, I'm gonna sleep good tonight. Ariel, you know my children?"

"Daisy, I'm sorry I haven't had the pleasure of meeting them."

"Yeah, someone came and took 'em because I was high. I left 'em in the house by 'emselves for a week. I was flying high smoking crack. I was chillin'. Damn babies were home hungry many times while I's out tricking. Gotten beaten pretty bad from some of my clients. And my pimp, huh, he almost killed me leaving me sprawled out on the ground in the back of the Rainbow Motel. Not once, but several times 'cause I didn't make 'nough money for his muthafucken pockets. Ain't that some shit? It was *my* pussy! Ariel, he whooped my ass 'cause I didn't have 'nough clients or 'cause he was in a bad mood and wanted to fuck with somebody. Sometimes I would only make $10.00, $15.00, or $20.00 dollars per dick. The lowest was $5.00 and I had to be pretty desperate to spread my legs for $5.00 bucks. But I did. Wha' the fuck. Ariel, hold on for a minute?"

"Jessie! Where the hell is the rest of my beer! Ariel, you know what I am so damn tired. Body wore the fuck out by being turned out by these worthless muthafuckers poking my shit all out of shape. I used to be pretty white bitch. I used to catch a man at a drop of a dime. I had legs to die for like Tina Turner. I had a good job and got mixed up with the wrong crowd. I started skipping work, staying out late on the weekdays when my children needed me the most, and got hooked on damn crack. I was messed up pretty bad, but after four or fives years of suffering I got into a Narcotics Anonymous-NA program, but after a few weeks I messed that up 'cause didn't let the program get me. I was too busy tryna get it. I got got. I relapsed. Uh-huh. I craved crack like it was dick. I was obsessed with it.

Damn near sprinting to 12th Ave, Alabama Projects, Governor Street, and 10th Ave. Fuck my children! Fuck me! That's what I said to myself as I was staggerin' from block to block. I said it so much that I believed it. Just sellin' my soul to the devil like it was nothin'. Shit. If I wanted to get high I got high. Next thing you know, I lost my job, been evicted a couple times, and I was living single after my funds ran low. Then I started working the corners of Broadway. My children used to look up to me. Now they probably won't even look at me, let alone recognize me. I'm not the same person I used to be and I am ashamed to even look at my own reflection. I'm paying the price living with AIDS. Ariel, I'm drying up like a damn prune, but Jessie doesn't seem to mind. He says that I am sexy in his eyes."

Rae and I look at each other because Daisy is no joke. She knows that she has messed up badly, but never in the conversation did she say that she was trying to get her life together to possibly get her children back. I don't feel empathy for Daisy, but I do admire the fact that she's honest about her lifestyle. She doesn't blame it on anyone else. I wonder how her children are doing, coping with the fact of having an addict for a mom. Let alone a mom who is infected with AIDS. It is heart wrenching, I'm sure.

"Ariel, are you there?" Daisy asks.

"Yes, Daisy."

"Yeah, you saw my children?"

"Unfortunately, Daisy I haven't."

"Well, if you should let 'em know that I'm sorry."

"Daisy, I will."

Daisy sounds so sincere and it makes me swallow and feel a slight lump in my throat. Rae's eyes become watery and she puts Daisy on mute. She grabs one of her tissues out of her box, dabs her eyes, and returns back to the phone. It is difficult for me listening to this one call. Daisy seems both ill mentally and physically, but through all that she has endured she still has not forgotten about her children. She is an

241

unfit mom, but she's still a mom who cares immensely for her children.

Rae completes the call with a perplexing look on her face. It's possible that after every call she analyzes the circumstance and it troubles her deeply. Women losing their children for a three minute high. Torturing their bodies allowing anyone to enter them. And when their job is finished, they clean themselves up, and go back out there to repeat the same thing for possibly twenty dollars or less. *Damn, is it worth it?* I wanted so badly to ask Daisy that one question, but I knew I couldn't. There are creases forming on my forehead because it's so disturbing. Obviously she feels regret, but she's a junky and that sickness won't allow her to stop. For some reason, I see Daisy as a motivational speaker. She's telling it like it is and she doesn't give a damn if you get it or not. She speaks her piece.

The volume of calls slows down and time is moving slowly. I can hardly keep my eyes open at this point. I get up on my break and pour a cup of tea. Sipping it, I return back to Rae's cubicle. She is about to print out a call sheet and then stops to show me how to do it.

"Normally at the end of our shift we are supposed to print this sheet out of all our incoming calls. The sheet has the private information of the caller and we keep a record and file it in a secured cabinet."

Rae and I talk for the remainder of the day and once our shift is over we drag ourselves out into the parking lot. She waves goodbye and so do I. When I arrive home I am so exhausted that I fall on the bed and quickly zone out.

When I awake its two o'clock in the afternoon. I have so much running around to do for the business. I get up and take a shower and head out. I go to Party City for other supplies. I stop at the carpet store for a welcome mat. A.C. Moore for some oil burners, and other decorative supplies. And then I met the telephone technician at Anonymous. While I am running all of my errands time flies by.

I start to prepare for work all over again. Dang, I feel like I just left that place. I watch a couple of DVD movies, take a nap, and cook dinner around 9:00 p.m. I arrive at work at 11:30, which allows me to lie back before I go on the floor to see who I will be sitting with. I get a little too comfortable because the next thing I know its time for me to get up and sit with my phone buddy.

"Avery, you can sit with Horace tonight," says Careen.

I notice Horace sitting at the far end of the room and I walk towards his cubical. I introduce myself again and he hands me a headset. I quietly sit down. Horace is preoccupied with himself. I am so bored that my eyes are drooping. I try hard not to fall asleep but it's so difficult. Horace is a pretty boy. Very attractive, but his self-indulgence sickens me. He's young and thinks that he's every young ladies dream. Don't get me wrong, he has a nice physique, natural locks, and a dentine smile. I am desperately hoping that we will get a call within the next ten seconds or I am going to die. Thank God, my prayers are answered.

"Thank you for calling Red Alert Hotline Service, my name is Josh. How can I help you?"

"Hi Josh, my name is Birdie and I really need to talk to someone."

"Birdie, I'm all ears," says Horace.

"Josh, I am an emotional wreck. I am consumed with booze. Finally...I admit it. That's my companion. My nurturer. I thought booze was my friend. My lover. You know how a friend is there for you through thick and thin. A true friend. Yeah...I miss my children and it is killing me inside. You know som'thin' every time I feel myself *feeling* I numb my pain with drinking. Why? 'Cause I don't want or didn't want to face reality. I have two children that I see only on the weekends because I am constantly in and out of the hospital. Why did I allow myself to become an alcoholic? Josh, this is the first time I've ever been truthful about who I am."

"Birdie, we as people make decisions in our

lives, some good and some bad. You sound like a devoted mom who loves her children."

"Josh, I love them so much that I would die for them. What am I talkin' 'bout, I'm already dying for them. Why did *he* do this to me? I feel like I am already dead. I loved booze so much. I trusted it hoping it would always make me feel nothing, and it did majority of the time. I would be knocked out cold. Booze and I had a ten-year history. Then I met a man. And I was winging myself off the booze gradually, but it didn't work. I was hooked, but it didn't stop me from getting to know this man. He was not my children's father, but he played the role. He seemed concern about their well-being and that alone opened me up to give him a chance. I tried to stop cold turkey with my drinking, but I needed support and I was too embarrassed to admit that I had a problem. I tried to keep it a secret, but I'm sure he knew. He accepted the alcoholic and all. And I fell in love. Oh, how wrong was I to even think that I had found my soul mate. He died last year and that is when I found out that I have AIDS. I wanted to kill myself, but when I looked into my babies' eyes I couldn't do it. I couldn't silence myself. I am angry, bitter, and envious of people who are able to have freedom with their children. I'm constantly sick and I prefer that they don't see me this way all the time. It hurts so much."

"Birdie, I can relate with this analogy. You see, it's like a pile of garbage in a landfill. Think of that landfill as your body. You are consuming all this junk, numbing it with booze, drugs, or whatever and thinking that you have gotten rid of it all. It is just sitting there, piling up...waiting. Yeah, it's waiting for you to decide when you are tired of faking the funk. Birdie, you're stronger than you think and I am sure that your children love you. They are full of joy to see you even if it is the weekends. They get to see, touch, and soak up your company. Always think about the good times with them. Tell me Birdie, are they always smiling when they are with you?"

Birdie is crying while listening to Horace. We hear her sniffling and when she speaks her voice is cracked.

"Josh, they are always smiling, kissing, and hugging me. They like to tell me stories about school and what they did throughout the week with their grandparents. I'll admit that I am jealous because I don't have the opportunity to interact as much with them. Josh, like you've said, as long as they are happy in my presence that should be enough to keep me going. I just miss them so much. I often think about the four...three of us together and maybe I was better off alone." She lets out a sigh.

"Birdie listen, you have no control over your heart. Once you fall head over heels for someone it is as if you are floating on thin air. You are wrapped up in the new experience. There is nothing wrong with that. We all go through it, but unfortunately we all don't experience what you are experiencing by loving someone who left you alone with AIDS. I wish that I could comfort you more than I am trying to right now, but this is all that I can give."

"Josh, you have given me more than you will ever know. Thank you."

My mind drifts off as Horace ends his call with Birdie. *What can I do to help these people?* It's affecting me sooner than I anticipated. I commend them for their inner strength and the more I think about things the more hypercritical I feel. Here I am living my life everyday and I can't find the courage from within to expose myself. What does that say about me? I am disgusted with myself and then I start thinking about when Rae showed me how to print out the sheet for the incoming calls. I discreetly look around to see if anyone is watching me. A feeling of paranoia consumes because I know that I am up to no good. Horace seems distant after his call with Birdie. I ask if he's okay. He just looks me in the eye and says, "No." I don't expect him to be honest. I thought he would pretend to be fine and act like everything is okay, but he doesn't. It makes me look at him differently. He documents the call, gets up to go into the break room, and that's when I make my move. I click print. Then I grab a piece of paper and a folder and go into the backroom where the printer and file cabinets hide in the dark. There's a file on top of the cabinet with a listing of anonymous names, addresses, and phones numbers. *Someone must be trying to set me up.* I become even more nervous as I keep watch on the door. I scan the folder and copy every sheet, then place it back on top of the cabinet. I put the copies I make into the folder. I'm shaking and my armpits are drenched. Something has compelled me to do it. I will suffer the consequences whatever they may be. My thoughts are to solicit each and everyone on these sheets and get them out of their homes and welcome them into mine, Anonymous.

When I return to Horace's cubicle I hurry up and delete the last print job in his queue. And then I put the folder in my bag. There's dampness underneath my clothing. I have broken the confidentiality rules of the company, but I have to do something. My motive is to help, not destroy so it seems to validate my actions. The only person who could be destroyed is me and I am willing to take that chance. It pains me to listen and do nothing.

Once Horace returns he says that he isn't feeling well and Careen has let him go home early. I end up sitting with Khalis from 2:30 a.m. until our shift ends. He receives a call as soon as I sit down.

"Thank you for calling Red Alert Hotline Service, my name is Ty. How can I help you?"

"What's up Ty? This is the one and only Storyteller."

"What's up, man?"

"Well Ty, things are certainly not up right now. My life is twirling within this tornado and I am trying so desperately to swirl out of the twirl. I'm constantly battling with boxing gloves that don't seem to fit. They say on the label inside, one size fits all, but man that ain't true. It is possible that one day they did fit, but I am dwindling down and my hands have lost some body fat. I am sixteen-years-old. Don't know who my momma is because I never really had one. She died while giving birth to me. Damn, the pain she must've felt. I keep seeing images in my head that don't make sense and it angers me."

"Storyteller, what is it that you are seeing?" Khalis asks.

"Man, I see a woman struggling, fighting, crying, and stuck in a zone of weariness. Ooh, she is alone and empty. Empty because she feels helpless, she has no one there to help her. She's reaching out her arms and folks walk pass her ignoring her. Whispering, cutting eyes at her as if to say, *Lady, get a job*. She is panhandling for a meal. She is pregnant. Oh, I keep saying, *someone, anyone help her*? But no one does. Why? Why won't they help her feed herself and her unborn child! Selfish muthafuckers! It angers me. Makes my AIDS infected blood boil."

"Storyteller, I can see why you are angry. Shoot! That would make me angry. Ask yourself this question, how do I plan on handling the anger that resides within? And then ask yourself, how are you going to release it? Do something positive before you explode and you do something negative. Regardless of you being ill or not, the PO-PO (police) ain't tryna hear it."

"Yo' man, you're right. They don't give a damn if I have AIDS or not. I'm just another low life piece of scum out here making trouble with nothing else better to do. They would be more than happy to put my ass away. Ty, you are the man. It's good to know that there are still some good people out in the world that actually take the time to listen and care. Peace, my brotha'."

When Khalis ends his call, I literally have my mouth hanging wide open. It is amazing how he handled Storyteller. It leaves me speechless. Storyteller sounds like he knows this woman spiritually. She comes to him in his dreams and it pierces his heart. Emotionally it affects him so profoundly that he needs to talk with someone.

It has opened my eyes to a new lesson in life. People go through stages whether they are ill or not. And through each stage there is always something that is needed, wanted, or desired. I believe Storyteller if given the opportunity to help the woman with child in his dreams, he would with no questions asked. And I also believe that he needs to speak with someone at Red Alert because there's an impulse of anger that can turn into a life of not only living with AIDS, but also dying in jail with it. Mr. Combs is such a blessing because even though the outcome of many who call in time seems to be running out, they know that there is always someone that they can reach 24/7.

Storyteller is the last for me, my mind is made up. Tomorrow I am going to solicit everyone on these lists. I excuse myself to go to the ladies room. When I get into the stall I pull out the sheets from my briefcase to see if Storyteller's name and address is on the list. And it is. My mind is moving fast. I need to set everything in motion, to fold, sponge wipe, and seal forty or more envelopes with the flyers that I have previously ordered. I have to buy some stamps at the post office and mail the flyers out. Everyone is pretty local; Passaic, Passaic Park, Clifton, Paterson, West Paterson, South Paterson, Montclair, Bloomfield, Newark, Teaneck, Englewood, Englewood Cliffs, East Rutherford, Rutherford, Jersey City, Irvington, East Orange, Orange, South Orange, and Hackensack. Some folks live farther away; Elizabeth, New Brunswick, Plainfield, North Plainfield, South Plainfield, Piscataway, Rahway, Trenton, and New York. Within my gut I know this is what I have to do, not for me, but for the many that are still hibernating in their homes ###their bodies. They are feeling alone, wanting to reach out, but are afraid that they will be abandoned once the truth is exposed. And in that instance, it can literally make one feel like they are in an invisible bubble. Everyone who once knew you doesn't know you enough to realize that you have practically vanished off the face the earth. That alone can break a spirit.

Twenty-four

NOVEMBER 4TH has arrived and it is a day of recognition of my birth for me as well as "Anonymous." The doors open at 7:00 p.m. To my amazement the turn out is better than I expected. Everyone is greeted at the door and given red gift bags with condoms, red ribbons, and pamphlets on AIDS and HIV. Folks are jam-packed. The music is upbeat, the artwork is phenomenal, and the photographer is unbelievably talented. Everyone is nibbling on appetizers and gulping down my secret citrus punch spiked with ginger ale. I can't believe all of this is happening; my dream is now a reality. Tears form like tiny drips from a faucet as each one splashes onto the hardwood floor. I am enthralled to see folks laughing, smiling, and mingling amongst the crowd of unknowns. A part of me wants to run outside and yell in the middle of the street, "I did it, Johnnie," but folks may think that I am inebriated or something worse. It's just a thought. I do step outside to have a moment to myself and to express to God how much I appreciate all that He has given me in this short time. I give a shout out to Johnnie letting him know that I will forever be grateful for all the motivation, inspiration, conversations, and mostly for the love and generosity he has given me. It's because of him that I have Anonymous, not just because of the monetary gift, but also because of the life lessons. It's such a joyous time for me as I cry, laugh, and smile. I feel a presence surround me and I know that Johnnie is with me. I return back to my guests, and everyone's feeding off of each other's energy. I can see it on their faces, smiles stretching, arms embracing, and the wonderful aura in the room itself. I go upstairs to check on things and everyone's sipping on punch while engaging in conversation. It's the first time that I have seen a bunch of folks under one roof all being so happy-go-lucky. I return back downstairs and I notice a young man walking through the door. He looks to be sixteen-years-old. He's beyond slender, almost anorexic. Our eyes connect as he slowly slides his feet across the hardwood floor as if he has raw bunions. His blotchy dry skin has sores that he has bandaged with an artistic X underneath his eye, about his neck, and on his right arm. His eyes are low, but his smile brightens his face with a glow. I look him over as he mingles with ease like he is just passing through on a whim. I hear someone yell out, "Storyteller," and I quickly turn in the direction of the voice. Storyteller acknowledges him and they pound fists to greet one another. *Is this the Storyteller?*

The night is young and I am a beam of light walking on stage to welcome everyone. I speak into the mike and the sudden volume makes everyone bite down on their teeth. Hands quickly cover ears. It takes a few minutes to turn the volume down.

"Welcome, welcome, to Anonymous. I am the owner Avery Love and I greet you today to say, thank you. Thank you for coming and exposing your many talents. I am truly blown away, and ecstatically thrilled to see a lot of young faces. As we all know Art is expression, whether it is verbal, non-verbal, emotional to the eyes, or soulful to the ears. I would like everyone to leave here this evening with a sense of fulfillment. Seeing all of you here fills my soul to its fullest capacity. Please, absorb the energy around you. Feed off of each other and allow your talents to explode. We have refreshments to your right; upstairs we have a photographer, lounge area, and restrooms. Down here to the left are our art exhibits, and more restrooms near the back. And where I stand is where profoundness is born. We are going to start with a young woman named Vission. She will be singing a song that she wrote in acappella. Let's give her a warm greeting."

Everyone's cheering, applauding, and whistling for Vission as she walks on stage. Her stage presence is captivating.

"Hello my sistah's and brotha's. I'd like to dedicate this song to my Nana who is sick in the hospital as we speak."

Vission has an angelic voice. Yeah, this sistah can sang, not sing. She has a soulful voice, like Nancy Wilson. She gives all of herself as the tears release down her face. The crowd gives her much praise. She's most definitely going places. After her performance she goes to a side booth and sells her demo called, I-Full. I walk on stage to introduce the next performer. My adrenaline's pumping. "How's everyone doing?!"

The roar of the crowd pumps me up more.

"Let's give it up for my man, Sax, on the saxophone. He will be performing a melody called, Evolution beyond Expectations.

Sax plays his saxophone like he is making love, passionately. There is depth in the piece that sounds of sorrow, endearment, confusion, comfort, and acceptance. It's powerful and emotional. I listen with my eyes, ears, heart, and soul. My eyes became teary. I feel so blessed to experience all of this talent. I can no longer hold back my tears so I just let them flow. After Sax the crowd goes crazy, whistling and shouting, and letting him know that they enjoyed his performance. When he leaves the stage he heads to the side also to promote his demo called, Inn the Moment.

"I see everyone is enjoying themselves," I say to the crowd.

They applaud loudly. And someone yells out, "YEAH, YEAH!"

I laugh.

"Everyone...please help yourself to more appetizers and beverages. We will take a thirty minute break to give you time to admire the artwork and take some pictures."

Offstage I go into the ladies room to use the bathroom and freshen up before I start the second segment. I hear two ladies standing by the mirror talking about how beautiful the place looks. One says that she has not been out in months and that she received a flyer in the mail and decided to check the place out. Her voice sounds a lot like Daisy. I guess I'd remember Daisy's voice just about anywhere. Daisy and the woman are still talking as I eagerly try to hurry out of the stall, but they are already drying their hands and heading for the door.

I walk towards the buffet table. All the food looks very appetizing. I stack a plate of Buffalo wings and celery sticks, and sit eating while watching the crowd. Everyone scatters all over like ants. No one is leaning against a wall bored to death. Demos are being sold; artwork is being looked at, and the photographer doesn't have a moment to catch his breath. I smile, lick my fingers and wipe them with a napkin. I get the photographer two glasses of punch because he looks parched. After I finish filling my stomach I glance at my watch and it's time to head back on stage to start the second segment.

"How's everyone feeling?"

The crowd yells, "GOOD!"

Everyone and their momma can tell that I am feeling good too because it's written all over my face.

"Well, I want to introduce our next performer doing an untitled piece, Storyteller."

Everyone gives a round of applause.

His movement is slow, but smooth. He looks as if he is in pain, but once he's in front of the microphone his facial expression change, like the stage is where he belongs. His eyes look like little crystal balls and I can literally see his history. I feel a connection with him like we are one and the same. I have never experienced such a strong connection that has hit me so deep from within. I am certainly intrigued by his presence, analyzing every detail of him. Swallowing; feeling emotional because he has touched me spiritually. He positions himself on stage and begins to speak.

"How is everyone doing? I just..."

He pauses for a moment and then continues.

"I just wanna say a few words before I start my flow. For starters, my name is Tyde Jobar Graham and

I am sixteen-years-old. I have AIDS."

It is him. I can tell by his voice.

The room is silent. It's as if someone has just died and we are burning candles in their memory.

Storyteller closes his eyes. He raises his arms spreading eagle and leans himself back symbolizing his body as a cross. Three seconds later he repositions himself and starts his untitled piece.

Everyone stays silent, hands covering their mouths, wiping their tears away with a swipe of their hands. I am in awe and blown away all at once. Tyde amazes me with his candidness. He inspires me in a way that I feel compelled to get on stage and announce what I haven't been able to divulge to the world. It's so different then dating because I feel so obligated to tell them the truth. There's a lot at stake. If these folks are not as receptive towards me as they were with Tyde, I'm screwed. I know divulging my secret could be fatal and the outcome is what scares me the most. Anonymous is a part of me and I don't want to have to close the doors on my dream. If Johnnie were here he probably would say, *"Look, honey, you've come a long way and I know it has not been easy. You have fought your demons. You dismissed yourself from past encounters. You have grown to feel compassion for others. You have leaped out on faith. Follow your instincts and it will not steer you wrong."* I walk on stage as nervous as can be. My eyes are like two twin rivers. I need an extra push so I look towards Tyde and say, "I admire you." He nods. We embrace with our eyes an everlasting hug and I begin sobbing right on stage. The room is so full of emotion and at that very moment something from Tyde transforms inside me giving me the strength to carry out my thoughts.

My voice cracks as I begin to speak. I pause to take a sip of spring water. I glance over at Tyde and I swear that I see Johnnie standing right beside him. I am startled at first, but then warmth comes over me with another push to get me going. My eyes are closed but then I open them, take a deep breath, exhale, and stare at everyone in the audience. I can feel little beads of perspiration rolling down my armpits. I see blind spots in front of my eyes from the vibrant lighting. I literally feel like I am about to faint. Holding my ground, I begin to speak again, but this time with confidence. Looking over the audience for the second time I begin to recite my history.

"Look at me and tell me what U see?
Yes, I am African-American,
Stand about five-feet-eleven inches tall,
My hair is natural,
My lips are full,
Nose is wide,
Eyes are brown,
But other than the obvious of me being a woman,
Look at me and tell me what U see?

I am not the woman I used to be,
I was fierce,
Men fiend for me,
Like I was displayed on a silver platter,
And every desire within my body was fulfilled,
No questions asked,
No time to have regrets,
I was in my prime,
Climbing the ladder to my success,
But with a blink of an eye,
My world crumbled,
I became a hermit in my own nest.

Why?
A stranger premeditated my death,
Wanting to pave a path of his remembrance,
Inflicting me with taint-taste of torment,
So, I ask that you look at me?
Use your eyes to magnify.

Why?
'Cause even with me sharing the truth with you,

You still can't see what resides within me.
I am absolutely,
Unequivocally,
HIV-positive.
Wake Up!"

   It's quiet. My voice cracks and I swallow and
speak with my head held high. That's when I noticed
Travar, Aja, Danell, Blu, Zaelyn, Mr. Clyde, Ms. Sweet,
Mr. Clausen, Mrs. Jenkins-Rollin and Mr. Xavier
Combs III standing in the crowd. I keep my head high
and speak from the heart.

   "The piece that I just recited is about how I
became HIV-positive. I was raped and 'til this very day
my rapist may still be on the loose. I almost allowed
him to destroy my life, but fortunately I had a best
friend who pulled me out of my hell. He later died from
AIDS, but during the time that he was here, he
influenced me enough to believe that I could
accomplish almost anything. He encouraged me to be
honest about being raped. I never told him that I was
HIV-positive, never was bold enough. He was my role
model and now I hope to be for others living the same
lifestyle. It's not easy and I still have a long ways to go,
but I am ahead of the game because I have both feet
inside instead of one in and one out the door. Tyde, you
have also inspired me tonight. You've opened up my
eyes to see true artistry. You my brotha' are an amazing
character of strength. And I feel blessed to be in your
presence. Everyone in this room has given me hope to
nurture my baby, Anonymous. Thank You."

   The audience applauds loudly, whistles, and
nods their heads in relevance.

   I have overcome my deepest fear and all the
bricks that were overlapping me have fallen to the
floor. I have love from my extended family and my life
has changed forever. It is difficult to sum it up as to
how my life has changed in words, but I am no longer
the reflection of what I used to be. I am reborn into a
shell living with HIV, but I am living my life to the

fullest. Filling my circle with positive folks with caring hearts that has helped mold me into the woman I am today. I have been fed plenty from total strangers. Gratitude and appreciation is just a small fraction of what I feel. To sum it up, I am truly blessed!

THE END

TESTIMONIES

"What I like about this book "*Anonymous*" is the fact that it's about things that go on in real life. I like when Avery writes in her journal she named Sis because it keeps her strong. After finding out that she is HIV-positive, she still decides to go on with her daily activity so she won't contract full-blown AIDS. I like that because when my cousin found out that she have HIV she gave up, not taking her medication, and now she has full-blown AIDS and a death wish."
—Paterson, New Jersey, age 15

"Back in 1995, I was in a drug program when I found out that I was HIV-positive. I was not pleased at all. In fact, I contemplated ending my life. Soon after I went through therapy and learned a new way of life. Yes, you can learn a way of coping with the virus.

Today, I'm living healthy with no type of sickness, and I am undetected. It is important to remember living healthy means for me to stay positive—mind, body, and soul and to take my medication "cocktails" everyday. "*Anonymous*" is a must needed read for those who live in hibernation."
—Newark, New Jersey, age 53

ACKNOWLEDGMENTS

First and foremost, I like to thank God for everything He has blessed me with. I thank Him for the good and bad experiences because it has molded me into a woman of greater strength.

I have to give praise to my oldest son, Craig; you never stopped believing in my capabilities. You always told me that you were proud of me for stepping out of my boundaries. It matters that you admire me and appreciate me as your mother. I did the best that I could to raise you as a single-mother. And I know it has not been easy riding this roller coaster life, but I promise it will get easier as time goes on. We may not have had all the luxuries that life has to offer, but we always have each other. We have struggled, but our perseverance has kept us glued even from a distance. Our struggles only give me more to write about and you tools to learn from. It allows me to reflect on where we used to be and where we are going. God is sooooo good.

I feel compelled to give thanks to someone who is not a family member. Someone who inspired me in a way that made me challenge me, Mr. Lydell McNeil. You see Lydell and I were old school chums here in P-town. I saw Lydell in the barbershop, *ScissorWorks*, and he read a couple of my two page poems and had boldly expressed, "Karla, won't you write a novel." I recall giving him a look that spoke without words. I let the thought ponder for a minute and then I said, "I don't wanna write a novel. I don't even know how. Where would I start?" I went home that evening and his voice was stuck in my head. Every single day I heard his voice just nagging the hell outta me. I mean it irked my last nerve. But...something transpired. My spirit was speaking so loudly. Man, it fascinated me. And I began to write like I was obsessed with it. I mean it didn't seem like work. It felt like love. I had a strong, passionate love for it. All I can say now is that I have no regrets. I disciplined myself and it was worth every tiresome day. I did it! I wrote my first novel and I say with all sincerity, "Thank you, Lydell."

To my editor, Miriam Tager, I'd like to thank you because this book wouldn't be what it is today without your guidance. Thanks a million.

To my Internet friend, Chael Needle (A & U Magazine aumag.org), I thank you for the many conversations we've had through e-mail and your guidance with my writing. I also thank you for writing an uplifting review on your website of "BackBone" (my first published works) Click on LifeStyles to view).

To my photographer/friend, Don Sherrill, I just want to say without your influential words my manuscript would have been collecting dust. You inspired me to continue on my journey and I thank you from the bottom of my heart. You captured my vision of what "Anonymous" stands for and I will always have a part of your God-gifted-talent to admire. Thank you.

Special thanks to my mother, Lucille Ward, when I needed someone to read my first rough draft, you volunteered without hesitation. I thank you for all the love and support you've given me throughout all of my trials and tribulations. I guess I get it honest 'cause you are a strong, black woman. I love you.

A special shout out to Kamau Khalfani- (The Learning Tree- Wednesday WBAI 9935 FM: 2:00am Cablevision Ch. 75: Thursdays 10 p.m.), you brotha' are as positive as they come. Your voice resonates of substance and truth. Profound. You have strength of character that leads leaders and I find it a pleasure to know you. God Bless.

I give thanks to my father, Jimmy L. Baker, I hope you

read this book with an open mind and embrace the messages that I've delivered. Peace, Love, and Freedom.

To my uncle, Robert Ward, I thank you for taking the time out of your busy schedule to read my first draft of "Anonymous." Thanks for believing in me and encouraging me to keep moving forward.

My dearest friend, Jerry Mouzone, I thank you especially for your love and moral support. I thank you for your guidance and spirituality through my ups and downs of writing this book. I thank you for your patience and realism. I love you, man!

To a brother with a passionate flair for art, Darryl Harris (Nu-Xpressions), where do I start with you? Well, I thank you for motivating me to strive to the finish line of fulfilling my destiny. You saw my vision with clear eyes. Thanks for the many, many dramatic sermons.

To a brother with sweet melodies, Andre Hunter (Record City), I thank you for your thoughtfulness during my times of battling with my personal life issues. You always reached out with a CD that took the tension away and put me back on track.

To my barber LO, (Diamond Cuts), not only are you precise with my fabulous cut, you are precise with the words that you speak. I feel so blessed to have crossed paths with you. Keep your eye on the prize and run with your dream. I got your back.

To the proprietor of (Diamond Cuts), Mike, I thank you for having a respectful place that I can come to. It is truly a pleasure to have met you.

To Edward Alexander, all I can say is that I did it! With all the setbacks, headaches, and even with my hard drive crashing on me, I made it happen. With all the tears I've shed because I didn't think I would be able to complete what I started, I made it happen. With all the revising, editing, and reading, I made it happen. And of course, with your help, *we* made it happen. I hope you're proud of me.

To Mrs. Polly Alexander, I sincerely thank you from the bottom of my heart for opening your door and welcoming me into your home when I was in need of a place to rest my head. I really appreciate your kindness. I'll never forget what you've done for me and I will someday relay the favor to someone else in need. God Bless.

To my friend/personal motivational speaker, Anthony Hines, you always seemed to be right on point with your phone calls. There were times when I was feeling bluer than blue brother and your voice would uplift my doubts. Our general conversations would distract my distress and by the time I would hang up with you I would feel full again. I truly appreciate you for being you. Kisses. Luv yah.

To M.W., I thank you for listening to me babble on and on about this book. I thank you for your input and understanding of why this subject matter was so important, and I appreciate your honesty and humor during and after I completed this manuscript. I know you haven't met a woman like me with so much anguish and so much love. Peace out.

To Teresa McCutchen, to a woman I met at the Paterson Free Public Library. I wish you all the blessings for 2008/2009 and I hope to see your life story in the hands of many women of today titled, "I Stood Alone" as a testament of sacrifice, struggles, and triumphs.

And lastly, Donneil Jackson, an aspiring new author

with her first novel, "Chante's Song". Ladies check it out! Girl, thanks for the many e-mails, suggestions, and phone conversations about 'us' making our first debut as Black Women Entrepreneurs. Girrrrrlllll, we have arrived!

To Red Cyber City, thanks for the encouragement, warmth, and true understanding of my passion. I really, really, really, appreciate it.

A special shout out goes to Ron Milord, man you came through for a sista when I was stuck between a rock. It is difficult finding good people to help you fulfill your dream, but you didn't hesitate and I really appreciate your help.

To my associates/friends/family:

Dawn Alston, Angela Mahaley, Aiesha Small, Hakeemah McCollum, Gail & Al Wilson, Melinda Frazer, Kim Lipscomb, Tamra Wilson, Tanisha Avant, John "Wes" Maple, Carolyn McFadden, Irene McKoy, Linda Miller, Derricka Thomas, Barbara Anthony-Gordon, Barbara Coates, Felicia Ward, Beth Gwathney, Yvonne Causbey, Samuel Johnson, Alex Alejandro, Joan Parker, Wallace Eckford III, Ricky Laguerre, Douglas Darby, Ashon Anderson, Richard White, Bennie Stevens Jr., Sam Joyner, William H. Crawley III, Hope McFadden, Deborah Mitchell, Lakisha McMillian, Melanie Troncone, Universe & Family, Sharon Caldwell, Michele Matamoros, Michele Taylor, Sherane Bunting, Carla Pinkney, Johnnie Mae Heriot, Nichelle D. Howe, Larry Howe, Gaye Glasspie, Wayne Elliott, Tiffany a.k.a Tiny, Davon Manley, Richard Walker, J. E. Baker, Kenny & Sheila Baker, Carlton Baker, C.B. Baker, Bill Baker, M.C. & wife, Jack Baker, Evelyn Fairley, Christine Baker, Matthew Johnson, Shirley Ward, Tedra, Kim, Tempestt, Lavar, Martha Baker, Estelle Ward, Rashaan & Lezly Ward, David & Maxine Ward, Elsie E. Baker-McKoy, Cynthia, Paula,

Linda, Cynthia, Mary, Venus Moore, Lamar Leftwich, Gerald Kinchen, Councilman Anthony E. Davis, HiFred Simms, Gerald Simons, Tillman Simms, Shirley P. Repass, Maxine Roberson, Michael Bailey, Dr. David Nunez, Lakisha F., Ashlee C. Carter, Peter James Bracke, Santa Susana Sanchez, SuQuan McDonald, DJ Willie Will, Randall Lassiter, Stephanie Ward, Stephanie Fletcher, Tyrone Robinson, Yadira J. Santana, Ronda Nicole Freeman, Jermaine Mickens, WaKenna T. Rosado, Starlin R. Polanco, Malachi Dominic Fairmon, Sharik Nakeem Davis, Melvin Charles Mitchell, Larry Dushawn Francies, Larry Donel Gales, JaVonne Lamar McKinney, Samuel Colon, Kashon Demon Williams, Janice Louise Buie, Jeanette Acevedo, Kamilah Bugg, Joyce A. Campbell, Alejandro Santi Naranjo, Michelle L. Witherspoon, Maria T. DePaula, Deatron Shiver, Shaba Makia York, Caroline Cleaves, Shequita K. Crocker, Ana Hernandez, Toccara L. Hinson, TaKea Cherie Brown, Pamela D. McQueen, Qwan Ramaine Wright, Camille G. Gaston, Alexis Generals, Charlene Renee Conover, Glenn Hutton, Derrick A. Cuavers, Ofelia Magaly Cacsire, Nyeshia Lawson, Robin Lynn Langford, Wanda I. Malique, DJ MAD T.O.F, Shaquan, Tamara Renee Watkins, Khadijal L. Bolds, Theresa Brower, Kenny, Rob, Danny, Marilyn Doreen Robinson, Lynnell McKay, Xavier Villcis, Robert McIntyre, Michael Johnson, Mark Champion, Brunilda Solano, Keisha Woodford, Paterson Free Pubic Library staff (Kevin, Rafael, and Edward), PatersonOnline.net, Sun Digital LLC and REPROMAN Productions.

To the many organizations:
Oasis-A Haven for Women and Children; Eva's Shelter for Women & Children; YouthBuild Organization; YouthCourt Adult Learning Center; Narcotics Anonymous; Alcoholics Anonymous; The Magic Johnson Foundation; Knowhivaids.org; Iris House; www.MACAIDSFUND.ORG; Paterson-Tas (People Take Action Save Lives); A & U: America's AIDS

Magazine, Keep A Child Alive, and Planned Parenthood.

WORDS FROM THE AUTHOR:

"JUS' DO IT"

HE'S GONE.

The innocent part of life that breathed inside of my womb for nearly nine months. The little boy who weighed seven pounds and two ounces. The one who had that bright smile so full of joy. Yes, he's gone.

For those of you who don't know, his name was Anthony—my youngest son. When I think back it seems like I was just cradling him in my arms and wiping drool from the corners of his mouth. Time spun so quickly and reality set in that he was only six years old when he was diagnosed with a form of cancer called Glioblastoma (malignant brain tumor) back in 1995. I tell y'all I *thought* my soul and spirit had died. Actually I thought my life was going to end on that day, November 2. His emaciated seven-year-old body lay lifeless in my bedroom. Witnessing him was enough to break me down to the point of no return. I kid you not. And I think in some ways it did.

Many questions sped through my head. What was the purpose of moving forward? I didn't know. But I knew that I had another son to care for. And deep down I wondered if I could care for him in the same way. So much had been stripped from me. So much had taken place and I didn't think that I would fully recover. I just didn't know.

You know, sometimes you are not thinking about whom, what, or when. Sometimes you are thinking about why. Constantly asking yourself why did this have to happen to me—to him—to us. I had no answers—just many questions that had gone unanswered. My life had changed. My son had changed. Our lives had drastically changed and I questioned, if for the better. What were *we* going to do? Our bond grew stronger, but weakened, as he got older. *I loved my children more than I loved myself.* I devoted my life to them. And when Ant died I was lost within. No one could help me. I had to help myself. And truthfully, I hadn't a clue as to how I was going to do that. I just knew that I had to find a way. I felt so alone.

Writing reentered my life. It became a way for me to cry with words, to vent, scream, and yell at the top of my lungs. Whatever I needed to do it allowed me to get the hurt out. I released my inner woes with *poetry* and it helped me. But still it didn't seem like enough. I was hurting like a mutha—. I kept reverting back to that day and wallowing in so much pain that I wanted to just die. Obviously, it wasn't my time to go. I realized my destiny awaited me. It was already planned. It was just up to me to make it happen. Anthony knew of what I was feeling without me speaking it. He felt it, I suppose. He had a strong spirit. He knew that I would someday challenge myself. And he was right. But it wasn't done alone. You see, people read my poetry. Some wanted to use it for their wedding vows. Some wanted me to write to their lovers expressing their apologies. Some suggested that I write a book, but I lacked confidence in myself. I never went to school for writing, had no mentor, no instructor to guide me along the path and it made me feel like I had no business trying to do something so over the top. I had no faith. But it took Anthony's illness and him constantly praising me that I began to believe. I began to feel. But my world was torn. My son was dying. And I began to break. I was falling fast, but I *never* picked up drugs. I tried to smoke once and nearly gagged myself to death. I started sipping on 22.ounce Heinekens trying to pass out. I was afraid at night because it was so quiet in the house. My mind stayed awake. But then I found myself getting hooked on the beer because it put me in a daze. That was the only way I could sleep in *that* room. I started hearing noises. I started hearing laughter. Footsteps. The doorbell would ring at 7 a.m. every morning and I would crawl out of bed to answer it and no one was there. Gradually the ringing stopped. Things started happening at the house that I couldn't explain. And it was *not* a figment of my imagination. I saw things. I felt things. Let's just say I *thought* I was losing my damn mind. I quit drinking for a few years. There were so many things I could've done and I am sure I had many drastic thoughts, even suicide. But what saved me was *hope*. I had hope that things would turn around. I had been through so many setbacks in my life and if I managed to get through them I could get through the pain. I had my angel, Anthony watching over me.

What can I share about Anthony? Man, he was magnificent, smart, and witty with a strong over-abundance of love for people and life. I truly miss him. His last *words of appreciation* to me were during the wee hours of the morning. He was lying in his hospital bed in my bedroom with so many things to be angry about (cancer, paralysis, stroke, going into a coma, having a blood transfusion, going blind, and just the stench of *death* lingering—just waiting with diligence to take a big part of me away. In that moment release from him so fearlessly, "Ma, you'a sleep? Ma, you'a awake?" Anthony proceeded with his thoughts. "Ma, stop talkin' about things you wanna do. Ma, jus' do it. Ma, be happy." How? I questioned. How can I be happy when a part of my joy is being taken away from me? HOW? I didn't know. But I learned, *how*. Oh, How and I became good friends. I considered How my mentor. How taught me a different way to survive during my darkest moments. How taught me how to listen, observe my surroundings, and write down my thoughts candidly. How taught me how to nurture my passion. And I began to see growth within myself. How opened me up and I took my son's strength, his courage, his wisdom, his love, his advice, and I internalized who I was based on my life's struggles. I put pen to paper as I had when I was a ten-year-old child, during a time when my life was bleak. I vocalized silently—my woes, frustrations, and tears into words. And it saved me because I was able to release it. Yes, get it out. I wasn't looking for anyone, but a pen and a piece of paper to soothe me for sanity and survival.

I'm glad I followed my son's advice because even though I didn't realize it at the time, he knew all along that my purpose was deeper than I'd ever imagine. I have fulfilled my dream of becoming an inspiration, just as he was to me. I had never been given such influential advice from anyone in my entire life. Who would have known that it woulda been from my dying son. I have a lot to be thankful for, even in the midst of my troubles I am still here pushing forward to encourage others to never give up on what your heart desires. Never let anyone persuade you that your dream is farfetched and cannot be attainable because they are wrong. Follow your instincts and let God guide you. This is the only advice I can give.

—Karla Denise Baker

COMING SOON....

SPITTIN' 'EM OUT LIKE BABIES"

ISBN: 13-978-0-9815668-1-8

&

A SEQUEL TO ANONYMOUS

SLEEPIN' WIT' THE VIRUS

ISBN: 13:978-0-9815668-2-5